ARDIS CONTEMPORARY RUSSIAN PROSE

Vassily Aksyonov

The DESTRUCTION of POMPEII

& OTHER STORIES

ARDIS, ANN ARBOR

Ardis Publishers
2901 Heatherway
Ann Arbor, Michigan 48104

Library of Congress Cataloging-in-Publication Data

Aksenov, Vasilii Pavlovich, 1932-
[Selections. English. 1991]
The destruction of Pompeii / Vassily Aksyonov.
p.   cm.
Translated from the Russian.
Contents: The destruction of Pompeii — The steel bird —
Quest for an island — Super-deluxe — Rendezvous — Victory.
ISBN 0-679-73441-4
1. Aksenov, Vasilii Pavlovich, 1932-   —Translations, English.
I. Title.
PG3478.K7A27   1991
891.73'44—dc20   90-28781
CIP

Distributed by Vintage Books,
a division of Random House, Inc.

CONTENTS

INTRODUCTION

Vassily Aksyonov, one of Russia's most popular authors, was born in 1932 in the city of Kazan, to a family of successful Communist intellectuals. In 1937, however, his parents were arrested and sent to the camps. Aksyonov's formative influences were unusual: he went to high school in the concentration camp zone of Magadan where his mother, Evgenia Ginzburg, was exiled. (His mother has left her account of prison in *Into the Whirlwind*). After graduating he went to medical school at Kazan University where he encountered persecution as the son of "enemies of the people." He ultimately got his degree from a medical school in Leningrad and moved to Moscow after his marriage to a Muscovite.

The young doctor did not stay in practice very long: after four years and publication in the wildly popular magazine *Youth*, he left medicine for literature. Given his background, one might have expected him to lack the very thing which marked all of his early work–a strong sense of humor. His novel *Colleagues* came out in 1960, quickly followed by *A Ticket to the Stars* (1961) and *Halfway to the Moon* (1962). These last two novellas were translated all over the world and were a sensation with the Russian reading public–especially the young.

With the works of Aksyonov the real language of young people walked in the door of Soviet literature. Readers were struck, (just as they were in America when John Dos Passos published *Manhattan Transfer*) and readers told each other in amazement that at last someone had recorded *the way people of our generation really speak.*

What came to be called "the prose of blue jeans" had finally come to Russian literature on the pages of the magazine *Youth*, and along with it the concept of teenage alienation (something hard to find earlier). Whether it was connected to the translations of Western writers such as Salinger or whether it was simply that the culture was finally stable enough to afford teenagers who had the possibility of acting irresponsible is hard to say. In Aksyonov more than anyone else, this generation found its writer, and he had a musician's ear for the exuberant, ironical twists this sub-culture was putting on the Stalinist Russian of the previous generation. But it was not just this jarring use of slang that bothered the critics: Aksyonov's heroes had an ironic attitude to the world. He became simultaneously famous and notorious, because even if he tacked on a conventional moralistic ending to many of his early works, one thing was clear and disturbing: these characters were having *fun* and were not apologetic about it. He stood for Westernizing influences, a love of technology and jazz, and a belief that the submerged voices of the questioning young should be heard.

Aksyonov became one of the editors of *Youth*, and it appeared that the liberal trend in Russia was safe. But then came Khrushchev's attack on modern art; in addition to a possible ban on future publication, the "young prose" group was threatened with the one thing which mattered most to them–the loss of travel privileges. Like so many others, Aksyonov bowed to this pressure and publicly recanted. Privately, however, this experience seems to have led to the writing of *The Steel Bird* in 1965, his most openly political work up to that time. This novella about the nature of tyranny treats the Bulgakovian theme of the artist in conflict with the tyrant, a subject that came to occupy an increasingly prominent place in Aksyonov's work as time went on. Although the novella was not published in the Soviet Union until the era of glasnost, it was immediately recognized as a major departure by those who were able to read it in manuscript or Western publication. This brilliant work is a distillation of Aksyonov's mature style and themes, and is especially remarkable when one considers the period that produced it.

This same year, 1965, is also the year of one of Aksyonov's best stories, "Victory," included in this collection. In this dizzying, concentrated story of a chess match, Aksyonov expresses a political point of view that was unacceptable to virtually everyone, namely that the intelligentsia would bow to the proletariat (and the current political order) even when it should not. The idea that in many ways the intelligentsia itself had let the genie out of the bottle during the Revolution is one which will permeate Aksyonov's major novels as well.

When the Russian tanks invaded Czechoslovakia in 1968, the normal development of Aksyonov's generation received a jolt. The end result for Aksyonov would be the novel *The Burn*. If early in his career the young writer had implicitly accepted socialist ideals, and had then gradually begun to question the reality he observed and the ways those ideals were translated into action, this Aksyonov declared that all dogmas were open to question, and that questioning itself was the way to freedom, artistic and otherwise.

Written in 1968, the novella *Rendezvous* (included here) needs little explanation against the background of these political events. Published only in 1971, the story caused a small sensation even in a heavily censored version, as Aksyonov parodied the poet Blok's concept of the beautiful lady, turning it into a symbol for regime which stifled creativity, namely, "the stinking lady."

By this time Aksyonov's curiosity about the world had gotten him into a great deal of trouble. To some critics it seemed that he thought everything Western superior to anything Russian; to others it appeared that he was against materialism wherever it might be, and that many of his heroes were on a quest for spiritual peace rather than a new pair of jeans. The works themselves indicate something more complex. It is true that in his major novels, as well as in stories like "The Destruction of Pompeii" and "Quest for an Island," and most of the works in this collection, it appears that imagination itself and the spiritual experience of life are opposed to philistine absorption in the world of objects, Western or Soviet. However, that would be to take Aksyonov at his word, a dangerous thing to do with any writer. What his work also shows consistently is a fascination with the joy of the good life, the creativity involved in making all the objects which often hypnotize his characters. These characters may be mistaken in thinking that a thing or money may bring them happiness, but there is no mistaking that the creator of these characters makes poetry out of the brand names that stand for a free world: Marlboros, Coca-Cola, Johnny Walker, Topanga Canyon.

Aksyonov worked on his most important novel, *The Burn*, from 1968 until 1975, almost as if he knew it would mark the end of his career as a Soviet writer. This work may be seen as Aksyonov's ultimate statement on the fate of creativity in a totalitarian society, as well as his most autobiographical work. After so many years of focussing on the outer world, he came back to himself. The Magadan sections of the novel, about his own boyhood in the camp zone, function like the Pilate chapters in Bulgakov's *The Master and Margarita*, and contain all the horror of one who is bearing witness to the fact that his entire country has been forced to live a lie for generations. Fragments of this novel were published as stories in the Soviet Union, but it was impossible to get it through the censorship as a whole, so it was first published in the West by Ardis.

A trip to the United States in 1975 (arranged with great difficulty, despite Aksyonov's fame), was to prove crucial. His account of the trip, published in a journal in 1976 to great acclaim and some criticism, was something quite new for Soviet readers–the West without moralizing.

(The moralizing would come later, when he wrote a much less enthusiastic account of his impressions of life in America in the non-fiction *In Search of Melancholy Baby*.)

The last story published by Aksyonov while he was a Soviet citizen was "Super-Deluxe." He was then virtually banned from publication, due to a worsening censorship and a frank interview published abroad. Defiant and angry, Aksyonov began the project which was to cost him both his Soviet career and citizenship: the almanac *Metropole*. The many editors of this almanac gathered together diverse works by diverse authors–some famous, some unknown–works which had one thing in common: they had been rejected by the censorship, not for political reasons, but on *artistic* grounds. The anthology was rejected by the Soviet publishing establishment and was then published in the United States. The price was very high for most of the authors, who suffered bans and financial hardships as a result. All of Aksyonov's books were taken out of Soviet libraries, no small task given his popularity, and his current projects were halted. He was strongly encouraged to leave the country, which he did in 1980, stopping in Paris on the way to America, where he quickly found a career in academia. In 1981 he, like many other prominent figures before him, was stripped of citizenship.

Now a professor at George Mason University, Aksyonov continues to write, and most recently completed a novel written in English, *The Yolk of the Egg*.

At first all of Aksyonov's major works were published in the United States, but then as glasnost changed the publishing climate in the Soviet Union, requests came in from all over to reprint his works in his native land. He visited Russia several times during the last few years, and each visit, each interview was an event: his generation had not forgotten its writer.

Lena Karpov, 1991

The DESTRUCTION of POMPEII

POMPEII

& OTHER STORIES

THE DESTRUCTION OF POMPEII

(A STORY FOR BELLA)

Every time you approach Pompeii you think: "Now here's a little corner of paradise." The platitude is inescapable, for prior to plunging down into Pompeii from a high point on the road above the city, you catch sight of the marvelously chiselled shoreline and white houses rising from the bay in terraces interspersed with the eternally verdant flora. The eye is captivated: greenery swirls above the city with abandon and climbs the steep gray-white wall of the mountain range that shelters the town and the shore from the north winds. And each time "all these things" (as modern idiom would have it) loom before you, you sense a powerful uplifting of the soul, some half-forgotten moment of ecstasy, and the expediency of your own presence here. And inside the car, in the space between the windshield and your own forehead that little platitude flashes by: "now here's a little corner of paradise."

In early spring that year I set out for Pompeii with the most serious of intentions. I had made detailed preparations to spend no less than a month here, far from the frantic noise and dirty slush of Rome, in the hope of bringing a three-year project to completion, that of polishing off a major opus in my specialty. I had meticulously selected books and manuscripts and loaded them into the trunk, which also contained the clothes necessary for the "sundry occasions in Pompeiian social life." Now with respect to these "sundry occasions in Pompeiian social life," well, I must confess that I was jerking my own knee a bit there, for as I packed the suitcase, I kept saying to myself sternly—now none of those "social occasions in Pompeii." Only a jog in the mornings, work in the afternoons, a walk in the evenings and a bit of listening to the radio before going to sleep. Track shoes with thick soles, a typewriter, and the transistor. Oh, the times I'd become entangled in the so-called romance of that seaside resort! The number of totally scandalous escapades had been so huge that I tossed into the suitcase most of my classy threads (the distinctive hallmark of our circle) for the "sundry occasions in Pompeiian social life."

In our circle the thing to do in those years was to be taken for a foreigner at first glance, but absolutely not at second glance. You were supposed to be slightly scornful of both your own (those long since recognized not to be foreigners) and of foreigners (those who were obviously not your own).

So, as I was tossing various kinds of silk shirts and sweaters from London into the suitcase, I was tacitly allowing the idea that Pompeii nonetheless would "suck me in" to slip through the net of all my strictures about serious intentions. However, since I was tossing all the stuff in haphazardly without sorting it out, I was more or less telling myself that if I should get sucked in it wouldn't be for long and that it would just be for a momentary diversion from my righteous labor.

I booked a room in the old Intourist hotel Oreanda[1] which faced onto a row of palm trees. In among the palms, almost obscured from the view along Shoreline Road, stood a plaster of paris statue of Historic Titan[2] painted bronze. By some strange fluke he had been dragged here to the inner courtyard of the hotel, where the masses could take no pleasure in contemplating him. To tell the truth, even if you could detach yourself from thoughts of what he represented, the figure itself still looked rather strange: a fake bronze patrician in a thick coat who stood under the shade of palms, in the midst of magnolia leaves and the purple flowers of a Judas tree; he held his right hand outstretched, palm upwards, as if he were weighing a small watermelon or bolstering up some dairy maid's tit.

It's funny that I was in no way annoyed by having it for a neighbor! Quite the contrary, this figure hidden from everyone except me and several other patrons of the Oreanda suddenly struck me as being a rather likable and, to a certain extent, even congenial fellow. I made a distinction between this Historic Titan of mine and all his other millions of replicas, and I pretended that he was a hypothetical consultant, adversary, and evaluator for my righteous labor.

The Oreanda is situated on Shoreline Road, directly above the sea. Having stashed my suitcase in the room, off I went to acclimatize myself in the way creative types have traditionally "acclimatized themselves" in Pompeii: you sit on the pebbles three meters from the Mediterranean Sea with a manuscript of your cherished opus in hand, gaze at a page on which something has been inscribed, like "one can also reach this conclusion, based on the theory of disturbances, from yet another point of view once focus has been centered upon the collapse of the system which takes place under the influence of certain disturbances, when the system's energy level is expressed as Eo and there is a total disregard of any possibility of the system's collapse." You repeat these expressive, carefully coined lines and, at the same time, attune yourself to your primeval and primordial homeland as you listen to the waves reshuffling the pebbles, and deeply inhale the smells of boundless courage and joy.

Try to steer clear of Shoreline Road with its idle crowd of vacationing barbarians, the facade of the hotel covered with a scaffolding where devil-may-care painters are idling about. Don't be tempted to drop in at the café, either, where that familiar company of Romans convenes by the window on the second floor.

It goes without saying that there were two or three Georgians in this company, too, who oversaw and paid for everyone, proposing toast after toast to Arabella.

"Ara-bella!" one Georgian would say, holding his wineglass high above the table.

And everyone gazed at the glass as if it were a fortune-teller's hypnotic crystal ball and repeated: "Ara-bella!"

It's funny that in the Georgian tongue "ara" is a negative particle and that Georgians, in toasting our famous Arabella, almost seemed to be consecrating their drinks to a sort of mysterious Non-Bella.

Arabella rose up from one of the small café tables and extended her glass of wine to me. She and I had been slightly acquainted, so she was holding this beverage out to me, the one luxury which she possessed, in a kind of mute gesture of welcome. Her hand had stretched through the glass, and, exposed to the wrist, was now offering me something pleasant.

Should any speculative talk arise as a consequence of this, I will certainly explain that at that moment it was simply impossible for me to have had either Arabella or, what's more, the wineglass in my line of sight due to the obstructions in my plane of vision caused by my position.

Meanwhile, a painter had calmly climbed down the scaffolding to the café window, taken the glass from her hand and bowed spryly to thank her. He had just about positioned his little pinkie on the glass stem so that he could partake nobly of this noble beverage when he suddenly interrupted his enchanting ritual and hollered at someone in a powerful voice: "Nikolai! Lie the brick down! I order you, lie the brick down! Lie the brick back or I'll shoot!"[3]

There was absolutely nothing around from which he could have fired a shot. In discussions later, this fact was echoed far and wide along Shoreline Road. Why would he shout "I'll shoot" when there wasn't a weapon to fire?! He bellowed "I'll shoot," you understand, but what did he have to shoot with?! These people are really something: they shout "I'll shoot," with no firearm at hand, but what can you do about it, they're such braggarts?!

Passersby looked to see whom this painter was shouting at so loudly and they all spotted another painter in splotchy overalls who was standing on the scaffolding and painting a third-floor balcony. He was painting away to his heart's content, sluggishly and sloppily; he blew his nose on his sleeve, not suspecting a thing. Above him, a second painter; there likewise stood on the balcony a third painter, who had a brick in his hand aimed at the crown of his co-worker's head.

A long, drawn-out second:
1) The first painter was still holding the glass of fine wine. The second painter was holding a brick aimed at the third one's head. The third painter was holding his brush with a shaky, drunken hand.
2) The second painter smashed the brick against the third painter's head. The third fell from the scaffolding onto the asphalt, where he lay sprawled out. The first painter drank down the glass of wine.
3) The painter with the empty glass in his hand dashed off somewhere—either to save the victim or nab the criminal. The second painter, his face bathed in a dazzling smile, finished off the third painter with a second brick. And the third one, with a violent twitch, flopped onto his back and once more sprawled out, spread-eagled and motionless.
A dark puddle began to collect.

Shoreline Road burst into a babble of shouts: "He did it for his broad, his broad, his own wife."
Some brave individuals tore through the door leading to the balcony. The murderer, still bathed in a dazzling smile, scrambled across the railing, and his body flew head over heels, struck against the second-floor balcony, and plummeted like a sack down to the asphalt right beside the first victim; immediately a second dark puddle began to collect.
As in Bizet's opera, over a woman, a whore—the hairdresser Svetka—and out of jealousy, two skilled workmen perished in broad daylight.[4]

They hadn't even had a lot to drink.

From the crowd of vacationers under the surveillance of the voluntary militia came a steady hum of voices. The appropriate vehicle drove up and individuals designated for such tasks removed the corpses. Slowly, the vehicle moved away.

The person responsible for what had happened dashed out of the hairdressing salon on Shoreline Road. The dazzling bright polyester-clad body under her white work-smock, now flung wide open, glistened with the delightful chimera of unruly flesh.

It's been reported that they had even had two kids, and some people used the past tense in reference to them because they assumed that Svetka's kids vanished together with their fathers.

The hairdresser lunged at the ambulance car with her hands; shocks of tufted red hair seemed to bounce across the roof of the vehicle. Her hands left black marks. And it's with hands like this that they shave us!

Later, I had the impression that the destruction of Pompeii began precisely from this moment. It was as if that fatal incident initiated the collapse of the resort town and all its sanatoriums, restaurants, and monuments to workers and to Historic Titan. As if the painter with the brick had given a signal to the volcano. As if only then the whiffs of smoke had begun to appear above the rocky spur suspended in the golden sky. In actual fact, however, if there was any link between the two occurrences, it was more likely to have been the other way around: puffs of smoke began to appear much earlier. No one noticed it for a long time because, strange though it seems, the residents and tourists in Pompeii were not in the habit of observing nature closely. Generally, they observed only one another, for it was exclusively in the collection of individuals that they saw the source of their pleasures or, as it's fashionable to say now, *kaif,* their version of *la dolce vita.*[5]

To be precise, the puffs of smoke were noticed only when they had turned into really thick smoke. However, the vacationers supposed that it was just a local tourist attraction and the natives thought it was just a case of some experiments or other being conducted in the mountains which had to do with nothing more or less, putting it as simply and bluntly as possible, than our armed forces. The military strength of our republic was such that the possibility of any natural disaster occurring could just be dismissed.

The thought didn't even enter anybody's head, of course, to search for a link between the pink smoke in the mountains and the wave of strange acts which, like a deluge, rushed ashore. The sudden flare-up of passion in the painters' guild was just one of the many ensuing episodes.

Stories like these began to circulate:

Early one morning a highway patrol inspector was supposedly seen at one of the major intersections. He was shaving, sitting on the roof of a patrol car in front of a huge round mirror installed there to facilitate traffic safety, but certainly not for the convenience of shavers.

Rumor has it that in the Carthage Bar one evening black marketeering voluntary militia men sort of beat up a Dutch tourist. They were listening, you see, to some old songs and he, you understand, was disturbing them—either by trying to peddle some piece of merchandise or by asking them to fix him up with a girl. Yet, if one takes into account the special relationship between the Dutch and the People's Voluntary Militia of Pompeii,[6] this is probably the least credible detail in all of the many strange events which were reported.

And something else, too. One couple at a dance held in the club at the Woodworking Plant shed all their clothes and gave a public exhibition of the act of coitus. What's more, they not only escaped being beaten up, but even enjoyed the loud applause of the other dancing youths. And, in addition, the club's director appeared before the City Council with a bouquet of wild poppies[7] when he was summoned to undergo disciplinary criticism. What's amazing is that they accepted the bouquet.

The director of a film crew from Rome placed a call to the very same City Council and proposed, in conjunction with the film he was shooting in Pompeii about life abroad, that the whole town be converted into a film studio, that is, to restore capitalism, for all practical purposes, in Pompeii.

Also, some criminal types bashed a zinc bucket over the head of the pensioner Karandashkin[8] who, as a free service to his country, was selling state lottery tickets on Shoreline Road. Of the hundred thousand tickets which the muggers took from him not one was a winning number. Subsequently, Karandashkin sent an open letter addressed to all honest people of the planet, only to have the letter published in the newspaper *The Furnace of Health*.[9] This led to a very absurd polemic which came to a halt only after the Ideological Commission issued a direct order.

Yet, the record for mindless cruelty in those days turned out to be the attack on the circus tigers by some deadbeat tramps. They chased

the beasts, frightened to death, out of their cages with fire extinguish-
ers. These tigers had performed as circus entertainers for ten generations, so they now jumped through hoops simply because of genetic
traits, not in response to any training. Once they had scattered
through the town and come into contact with the strange lifestyle of
the resort's inhabitants and tourists, they quite naturally ran wild
again. The thunderous roars of these ill-fated creatures could be heard
in Pompeii right up to the last day of its existence.

However, there were also occurrences of some questionably perspic-
uous acts of virtue. Once, late at night, a threesome grabbed Matvei
Tryapkin,[10] the chef at the sanatorium Homeland, by his coat lapels
and demanded: "You have 50 rubles?" Now where would a drunken
cook get a hold of such a sum of money? The robbers frisked the poor
fellow and, once they'd convinced themselves that he wasn't lying, gave
him a gift of a 50-ruble note.

What is the link between people's behavior and the action of fiery
lava from the underworld—one of cause and effect or the opposite, a
direct or indirect connection? No one knows, so everyone remains
confused. The pink cap on top of the volcano grew larger with each
passing day.

But, oh how successfully my work progressed at the time! In the
morning I would leave the hotel in my springy track shoes and begin to
run up the asphalt-covered grade which led from the lower to upper
level of the park. During the minutes just before dawn, when the dark-
blue crest of the horizon in the East charts its domain with special clarity because the sun is about to burst out from behind it at any moment,
my brains were teeming with all sorts of good ideas. I saw page after
page of my opus, *Repercussions at the Quasi-Discrete Level,* dance before
my eyes.[11] And my whole steam engine all warmed up quickly, skillfully
and synchronically—the lactic acid in my muscles oxidized and broke
down, oxygenated hemoglobin stretched my fallen alveolae, and my
aesthetic gland, not to be caught napping in this burst of energy, gladly
awoke and took in everything ecstatically: the tea-rose bushes, which
secretly and lovingly beckoned from under the stone walls where they
had cornered a bit of light, the secret and slightly wanton swaying of
the billowing Persian lilac, and the naively euphoric smell of the dew-
drenched wistaria. What lines I managed to write then, what marvelous
lines! "The system inclined towards collapse does not possess, strictly

speaking, a discrete spectrum of energy. Particles which fly off during its collapse travel into infinity!" What lines!

I took breakfast right at my work table; I would eat a couple of cold, boiled eggs prepared in advance, drink some instant coffee, and read my new sentences through the window to Historic Titan. He would usually screw up his tiny barbaric eyes (a strange mixture of genes from a steppe nomad and a Swiss clerk)[12] and stare at me in a thoroughly indecisive manner. Nonetheless, it was my impression that he condescendingly approved: write, I say, write on. What is there, huh, to keep you from writing with your swanky gold Mont Blanc pen[13] on the pristine page? Write, but don't forget about the people who compensated for their passion to write with prison bread and water.

The countless replicas of Historic Titan can be divided into two basic types: majestic images and lifelike images. Yet that Historic Titan of mine, secreted among Pompeii's blooming flora, was neither one nor the other. Some nameless sculptor had captured him in this emigre pose, it seems, while he was strolling casually and mindlessly. He'd probably had his quota of such empty days when he was making history: times when the movement falters and splits into stupid factions, the greengrocer's and butcher's bills pile up, but a ray of light, however slim, still glimmers in the kingdom of darkness—the Knopf publishers have promised an advance and in Rome the colonel of the centurions has been shot and wounded.[14] A small matter, but all the same good news. At any rate, he could enjoy a quiet stroll with his neighbor, the tooth-extractor Gruber,[15] and say, illustrating with his characteristically Volga palm turned upwards: well, well, Herr Gruber, you won't believe it, but it's a perfect archetypically round breast, such a compact and solid little watermelon... This HT of mine was really no titan at all, just a slightly perplexed and unhealthy patrician who bathed infrequently and talked a lot. A neighbor like any other neighbor, a regular *citoyen.*

I recited to him: "—... as a result of the effects of relativity the level represented by the variables L and S splits up into a series of levels represented by the new quantity J...."[16]

He heard me out with no particular show of enthusiasm, but also with no strong reaction—as if he were making use of the pause to get a word in about his little watermelon.

On one paradisic morning (judge this epithet by what was said earlier), I noticed a thin crystal glass containing good wine on the palm of my Historic Titan. On the pedestal below, curled up like a pretzel, slept Arabella, her head on the historic shoes. My gaze woke her up.

"Good morning!" she said, "do you know that Pompeii is threatened with destruction?"

"When?" I asked.

"Will three days from now suit you?" she inquired.

I thought a bit and replied, "Three days? That's a long time."

"Maybe it'll be less. Make haste."

"How did you happen to turn up here, Arabella?"

"I stumbled onto his lordship here in the bushes quite by chance. He startled me, this poor abandoned child of history. He spent a long time telling me about Astrakhan watermelons and, as always, was grossly exaggerating. However, I listened to him the whole night through. After all, he's been unfortunate and isn't understood by anyone except his poor wife. If you trace the lineage of Polovtsian aristocrats,[17] he and I even turn out to be distant relatives. It's sad that the European branch of our ancestors split off so long, long ago. Their bough withered, but ours has borne fruit right up to the present. And who's to blame for that? I offered him all that I possess. The glass in his palm, you see? He's noble, you see, 'cause he hasn't touched it. He left it for me to have this morning. How sweet of him! No, no doubt about it—his private life was definitely misunderstood."

She stood up and stretched. Her white slacks and blouse were covered with bronze colored dust. The Titan was beginning to flake here and there.

O Rome's darling, mythical Arabella! Every time you encounter her you think it's just some trick of television photography or that newly invented holography. She scampered up the statue of Historic Titan like a monkey, securing her bare feet cleverly in the sculpture's defective spots, and took the glass.

"Good morning!"

Head tossed back. Large gulps. A huge neck muscle was adeptly pumping down the moisture which had stood out overnight under the starry fermenting sky.

"What's that? Something transmitted via enemy radio stations?" I asked.

"Oh, no! I myself put it in his palm," the pretender Arabella reacted in fright, "this is my wine, I swear."

"I'm not talking about wine."

"What about, then?"

"The news. Pompeii's destruction."

"Oh, that!" she remarked, dangling her legs gaily as she hung from

HT's arms. "Yes, yes. It's either the song of an angel or blatant lies
from the radio."

I began to put on my track shoes.

"How's the writing coming?" Arabella asked. "Read me a few lines
from *Repercussions.*"

I obliged.

"Bravo!" she exclaimed.

"And how's your singing doing?" I inquired.

"I'm fed up with it," she said with a laugh. "You've got it easy—you
sit there like a lump and write. Performing songs on TV is desperately
boring."

"But your fans..." I started to say.

"I know, I know," she said, dismissing the comment with a wave of
her hand. "I'm trying to find a different way to get them to prop up
their existence. Are you actually getting ready to jog? Take me with
you."

We started off running together—evenly and rhythmically, with the
intoxicating smell of wine from her puffs of breath. But when I later
glanced to my side, I no longer found her next to me. I turned completely around and, in the distance which was growing more blurry
with each step, caught sight of a truck vending beer. Painters and film
people had gathered around it. Arabella, with her palms extended outwards, was encouraging our dopey citizens to prop up their existence.[18]

That evening ash began to fall on Pompeii. A lackluster moon lit up
the crest of the mountain range, above which there floated a rose-pink
luminescence. Here and there, serpentines of fire crept along the
wooded slopes.

Foreign radio stations were reporting Pompeii's destruction loud
and clear. Our capital calmly but forcefully denied the rumors as slander.

That night I finished work on my monograph and set off for the
hairdressing salon. For some reason I had a sudden urge to alter my
appearance radically: maybe, to have them trim a bit off the temples or
give my moustache a new twirl. In short, willy-nilly, my legs carried me
off to the hairdresser's.

Picture me that evening: an enormous strapping redhead with a
glint in his eyes! Good intentions forgotten. Forgotten, too, and thoroughly ventilated from my mind—the well-turned phrases in
Repercussions. Clearly realizing that Pompeii had "sucked me in" this
time, I moved cheerfully towards the vortex of the "suction"—the hair-

dresser's.[19] Flakes of ash flittered gracefully, swooped towards the lamplights of early evening and fell on the crowd of barbarians who, as always, were yearning for *kaif.*

A Greek liner had docked hard along Shoreline Road. Music drifted from that direction. They were playing the new hit record "Love Machine" over and over again. A teeming crowd milled around at dockside. Everyone except the most arrant lazybones was trafficking on the black market: young pioneers, pensioners, musicians, and even centurions in uniform. And just between us, there were even centurions in civilian clothes. It even seemed that the ultimate purpose of black marketeering had already been lost sight of; the primary goal of making money had been forgotten. Now it was merely a chaotic and greedy exchange: a hunt for clothes, drinks, various types of Japanese baubles, and tobacco.

Here I am at the hairdresser's: over the entry prerevolutionary naiads hold aloft a wreath; on the left side of the door is a memorial plaque honoring the underground meetings of the Pompeii cell of our beehive; on the right a memorial plaque honoring the visit of the "great chronicler of the twilight era when public consciousness began to fade."[20] There remains some question as to whether he spent a long time here and what he did during his visit, whether he ever had his moustache curled or the hair on his temples trimmed.

However, it seems that during the twilight epoch there wasn't a hairdressing salon on this site, but rather a sanitary house of ill repute. Of course, perhaps this, too, was nonsense—just a city legend told with a faint jeer. Uncouth boors usually spread only spiteful and bawdy stories about the chroniclers and it's impossible now to reconstruct the truth—archives have been destroyed and the historical record has been completely distorted through propaganda.

Anyway, I walk into the reception room and right away I see my reflection in two dozen mirrors. Quite an imposing sight: the arrival at the hairdresser's of a whole crowd of enormous, redheaded gargantuans. Two dozen armchairs and an equal number of hairdressers, too—pudgy, skinny, busty, tushy ones, in creased and soiled smocks, and all of them in the same state of intoxication. A full load of customers. One is cackling insanely, twitching in the armchair with his arms and legs; another has bent his flabby body over and is moving his hands idly back and forth above the floor as if in search of underwater treasures; a third, having grabbed the chief hairdresser by the buttocks, is swirling around on his armchair and serenading her with the waltz song "He's shy—not bold." The rest are shaving, more or less.

What's the first impulse of the redheaded giant who's just entered? Why, he'd like to drive all this rubbish out of the broadway barber's temple with a whip and at one fell swoop plop down on all twenty-four chairs, because for some reason he is insanely pleased with all two dozen of the women. A most shameful impulse, of course.

Cut-down-to-size, I notice: here, it turns out, even the waiting line— five to seven other musclemen—has to hang around idling; in what way am I better than them?

There's nothing that can be done about that. This is the drunken rubbish you have to live with: a community of people stuttering and slurring words and poisoned by cheap disgusting port wines, that one-ruble swill with a slimy chemical sediment, the so-called "Mumbo Jumbo."[21] With rubbish like us, not only Pompeii but, in a year or two, even Rome will topple. But we somehow have to live together with them, that is, with ourselves, and to face destruction with them. Emigration? No, that's just smoldering embers, both inside and out.[22]

The line rocked back and forth, drunken and pot-bellied, with mind-lessly smiling eyes and faces smeared with volcanic soot. No one in the present company suspected that a short distance away, on the far shore of the dark, oil-slicked sea in the "lands of Capital," hundreds of hair-dressers spend their time in charitable quietude with the reserved as-surance that they can expect only upstanding customers. On the other hand, I said to myself as I joined my comrades on line, in a certain sense there is the same—if not worse—rotten smell everywhere.

"The same—if not worse—rotten smell is everywhere," I said out loud to boost the courage of my comrades.

"It's worse in our metallurgical district," said one smiling fellow.

"Why are you looking?" a second smiling fellow asked.

"'Cause. I'm just looking," said a third smiling fellow.

"He waunts to look," uttered a fourth smiling fellow.

"Lat'm look," the fifth smiling fellow said.

"Look, if you waunt," the sixth smiling fellow said.

"Look, does no difference to me," said the seventh smiling fellow.

The redheaded giant looked at the group of port winos, not without a certain sense of horror. One of the smiling degenerates stood out from the others and made a definite impression on him: the powerful mold of a foolish old face—a retired colonel of the Legion of Honor. At least all these heirs of Caesarism have preserved something in their features, I thought, it may be the stability of an ungifted but majestic epoch. Should I stick with them, the last piers of society?

A peal of thunder slowly rolled over Pompeii. For a second the stormy sea was lit up. The floor of the hairdressing salon heaved violently. The prerevolutionary Dutch tile cracked and shattered.[23]

Perhaps all that's left is to join ranks with Caesarism, the redheaded giant thought. Theirs may be the only pillars which haven't begun to rot from the inside. He offered the colonel a Marlboro cigarette.

"On television they're saying the overseas lands are putrifying," the colonel said, inhaling the pale blue smoke. "But actually, we've got the cesspool here and they've got the economic achievements. And what's the reason?"

"What?" the redhead asked.

"Ain't no decent organization," the colonel explained willingly. "They criticized Marshal Tarakankin[24] and that criticism was right, I agree. However, they forgot that the Marshal had a brain. The kind of orders he gave? Why, to delay demobilization of all personnel with demerits for the same number of days as they had black marks on their record."

"Why is there no latrine here?" one smiling fellow asked in surprise. "The comrade here's pissing without the presence of a latrine."

"Every pencil wants to piss, but they hold their lead in silence," said another smiling fellow.

"Marshal Tarakankin arrived at our trireme," the colonel continued, "in time for demobilization. They saw the personnel off with an orchestra, but detained seaman Pushinkin[25] for 105 days because in his three years of service he had chalked up 105 days in the brig. Everyone else returned to their productive civilian jobs, but Pushinkin roamed aimlessly through all compartments of the trireme and became disgustingly louse-ridden."

"Pardon me, but what link is there between this situation and the economics lag?" the redheaded giant asked.

"They've forgotten how to organize things right," the colonel explained. "Moreover, the campaigners fighting against cosmopolitanism seriously damaged the quality of our science. Just look around—no self-respecting tomcat will eat today's sausages."

"You've got sour aspic for brains," the redheaded giant mumbled as he moved away from under the pseudo life-jacket colonnades of Caesarism, not without some dismay.

Then, yet another blow. In one terrific burst, a gust of hot wind blew down all the palms on Shoreline Road. One of the prerevolutionary naiads toppled off the frieze and cracked into pieces. The glass

door to the hairdresser's shattered with a loud bang. Flakes of ash and
the vile trash of this public resort flew into the salon itself. Filthy
smocks clung to the extremely enticing bodies of the twenty-four
frightful tarts.

A second or two later and there was only the barren waste of catas-
trophe before our eyes: crimson flashes of sheet lightning, palms
bowed over by the wind's iron broom, a bloated sea with our naval
fleet clumsily sliding down into its gluttonous mouth—had that poor
fellow Pushinkin not served on one of those triremes?—and the torso
of the naiad flung onto the street. Remember at least this, if all else is
forgotten, remember at least this!

A group of youths walked past, guffawing and singing the song
"Love Machine." In the process of stepping over the naiad, one of
them propped his leg on her in order to lace his shoes. All's normal;
life flows past, empty of memories; the organizations responsible cope
with the ravages of natural disasters; the prognosis is good; Rome
stands firm, unshaken.

Suddenly, all at once seven closely shaven and neatly cut citizens
came out of the beauty salon.

"Next!" boomed the voice of the chief hairdresser on the loud-
speaker. The PA system, it turned out, was still working there.

The redheaded giant fell onto a chair, right into a woman's eager
hands. How can they condone such filth when their guild's service is
public beauty? Fingers with broken nails and chipped polish darted
nimbly across the redheaded client's chest, belly, and groin. A gigantic
and eager mouth, smeared with lipstick, laughed above him. Tits were
falling out of the unbridled polyester blouse. The wet hem of a skirt
stuck to the protruding lower abdomen, and everything below brought
to mind that deep-water Agave known for its passion for lurking, sucking in, and swallowing innocent fish.[26] So, that's who's got the redheaded giant: Svetka, the disgrace of the city, the widow of the two
painters.

"So, that's who's got me!" the obscene mouth laughed. "The red-
headed one, red one, saucy one, shameless one! Let's get out of here,
Red, let's get the hell out of here! I'll give you a shave on the beach!
Take all this stuff! I'll do it to you 'deluxe' style on the beach!"

"Excuse me, but it seems to me that's against all the rules," babbled
the redheaded giant. Nevertheless, he stuffed his pockets with boxes of
powder, creams, and a rubber atomizer containing Shipr cologne, and
helped Svetka to take down from the wall an ancient mirror with a special golden frame.[27]

"Tomorrow, Senkina, you will be fired for laying the customers," said the chief hairdresser.

"Watch out or you'll be sacked yourself, Shmyrkina," Svetka shouted back. "It's not a private operation we've got here, it's a guild. You yourself fuck behind the partition and the customers aren't satisfied."

A bushy crack opened up in the ceiling. A volcanic wind whirled through the salon, lifting up a tornado of cut hair. Face to face, the two women rapidly snarled at one another something completely offensive and incomprehensible.

The redheaded giant began dragging the mirror to the beach. Behind him Svetka was dragging spotted bed sheets.

"Oh, momma dear! What a customer I've hooked, oh-ah-oh," moaned Svetka.

The redheaded giant gripped her thighs in his hands, but turned his head so as not to see her terrible face.

Waves of gray pebbles lay on the beach and in all their troughs there was grunting and squealing. Sin was being committed everywhere, and ashes fell onto all this carnal bestiality.

In our case the sin was aggravated by the stupid mirror—it stood at the heads of the copulating pair, and every time the red-headed giant raised his head he could see his strangely undisturbed face.

Behind him, in the mirror, the crimson sea was becoming more and more luminous, the volcano was burning brighter and brighter over Pompeii.

Then two chicks in hip-hugging jeans appeared in the mirror. They stood with their horsey faces downcast, swaying back and forth. One of them held her hand on her friend's pubis, while the other squeezed her friend's breast.

"Here, Galka! Look how the pros work!" one of them said, sort of hiccuping in our direction. "But we are still trying to find our *kaif.*"

Right then and there they tumbled down into some pit, where they expressed their ecstasy in real bawdy language: oh, I got banged sweet, ah, I'm all wet, oh, Galka, oh, Tomka, look how starry the sky is, look a star is falling a star is falling....

What they took for stars were falling volcanic bombs. The tortuous and jolting eruption began reducing the carnal bestiality's bellowing to an exhausted lowing.

"I tell you, Client, you made me rustle," Svetka uttered. "I haven't had a feast like that since Nikolai and Tolya killed each other."

The soot was smeared all over her face; her eyes shone thankfully.

I looked at myself in the mirror. Where had the redheaded giant gone? My balding head was melting away like a candle, my body was swelling up like yeasty-beasty, sourdough.

A scorching stone crashed onto the beach, cast up a fountain of pebbles, spun like a top, and rolled into the sea, where, with a hiss, it sank in a cloud of steam.

I got up and walked away, hardly moving my elephantine feet. Buttons on my shirt popped off and my hairy black stomach hung down, suddenly unbelievably swollen.

Roofs of the houses along Shoreline Road cracked under the pounding of boulders. Broken windows were raining down. Neon letters which survived here and there spelled out abracadabra. A powerful flame was raging inside a little store with the coquettish name of Sweet Tooth. However, next to it, people who had gathered in the morning were quietly standing in line at the neighboring grocery store. They were waiting for the delivery of some fantastic boiled salt pork, although there could be no chance of a delivery since all the passes above Pompeii were enveloped with smoke and covered in flames.

Orchestras were playing everywhere. "Love Machine" thundered from basements, from under the canopies of open-air restaurants. People of all ages danced in a frenzy. It was freedom of movement unthinkable in the times of Caesarism: eyes bulging and mouths lusting; the eerie Pompeiian shimmy.[28] Socialism which imitates capitalism is socialistic to the point of tears.

Of all the people who had it good in the burning Pompeii, the gloomy fat guy with dirty dark locks hanging down on both sides of his balding forehead had it worst of all. The arrogant elephantine fat guy was meandering feebly and mindlessly through the crowd until he saw a telephone booth for long distance calls. From that booth he could immediately plug into the capital's telephone system, but, strangely enough, it was empty: apparently, nobody had any need at all to call Rome. The fat guy stepped into the booth.

"Do you know that we are burning?" he asked his colleague at the institute, the first person whom he managed to reach by phone.

"Old man, it's too late for philosophical questions!" playfully laughed his colleague—in principle, an okay fellow, who, as a matter of fact, was no different than me: the same kind of crafty slave of the communal system which swallowed us all up.

"No, not in the philosophical sense at all," said the fat guy. "Pompeii is perishing. The volcano has gone mad."

"Well, that's no topic for a telephone conversation," his colleague uttered angrily.

Everything is clear. Now they will put me down as a provocateur. I hung up the receiver and through the glass I saw Arabella who, dancing and waving her hands, headed up a very merry company. A calm herbivorous snake was lying softly coiled around Arabella's shoulders.

"Hey, come out of there!" Arabella shouted to me. "Why are you swelling up over there in the telephone booth? Look, gentlemen, how this character has swollen up!"

A couple of merry Georgians pulled the fat guy out of the telephone booth and offered him a bottle of wonderful wine.

"Where do you get such wine?" I was surprised. "And where, in general, do you find all these nice things?" I asked simpleheartedly. "How is it that you Georgians manage to live rather sumptuously in the midst of all this wretchedness?"

"No problem," the Georgians answered merrily.

A scorching piece of rock hit the telephone booth and instantly wiped it off the face of the earth. The face of the earth, in turn, slid apart under our feet and formed a crack half a meter wide. We jumped over the crack and walked along Shoreline Road passing lines of people craving *kaif* and those having a good time inside of burning cafés.

A small clever boy, a "young naturalist," was following on Arabella's heels and whining: "Lady, give me back my yellow-belly. I took it on loan from the zoological lab for some research."

"Child!" Arabella clasped her hands. "Do you really mean to separate us? Can't you see how your yellow-belly likes hanging around my neck? Child, the snake and I love each other!" She took the head of the yellow-belly in her palms and kissed it on the mouth. "Child, I confess that I myself am quite a yellow-belly and if you are truly a young naturalist, you must study both of us."

Something like a ball of lightning flew over Shoreline Road and hung over the main square of Pompeii, over the City Council building and over the most powerful and majestic sculpture of Historic Titan.

"We are all yellow-bellies!" enthusiastically shouted our entire company: Oh, that magnetic Arabella!

What was hanging in the distance over the square did not hang for long. It struck and scattered in a zillion sparks. Then, for a second, a phosphorescent light appeared and illuminated the main square. One could see the statues of various epochs falling: a border guard, a woman tractor driver, a tank driver, an astronaut...—and now the principal, most powerful statue began to fall down. It became frozen in my memory just like that—in the state of leaning and falling because the phosphorous disappeared and the crash of the statue's fall was muffled by the swelling uproar in Pompeii: orchestras, shouts, laughter, and the crackling of fires. A thought flashed through my mind—and how is mine, my personal HT doing there, what has happened to him?

"No victims!" exclaimed one of Arabella's retinue.

"An extraordinary phenomenon of nature, comrades! A volcanic eruption with no loss of life. It is the counterpart to the neutron bomb: material goods are destroyed, people remain whole. That's precisely what I reported to Rome on the hot line: no losses of human life; courage is making a stand against the elements!"

By his entire appearance, this man, dressed in an official two-piece suit, with our beehive pin in his buttonhole, was supposed to personify the stability of our all-embracing administration, but a small muscle was twitching in his face, and a bottle of cognac was sticking out of his jacket pocket.

Arabella encouraged him with her soft palm, caressing his neatly combed hair from one side of his head to another.

"Poor child, deserted in the midst of the fiery elements! This morning you were still reigning in your City Council office, and now you are all alone! We won't leave you! Take heart!"

"I am taking heart," the secretary looked trustingly at Arabella. "That's exactly what I reported, I managed to say on the hot line: courage is making a stand against the elements...."

"Lady, give me back my yellow-belly!" begged the young naturalist. "It's time for it to eat."

Someone who appeared to have once had and lost some secret power approached, holding in his hands a bottle of Pepsi-Cola and a glass.

"Your reptile, does it drink Pepsi-Cola?" he asked the young naturalist, looking at him with his still penetrating eyes.

"It hasn't tried it yet," the young naturalist mumbled, "but I... I, personally, Comrade Colonel, drink Pepsi-Cola with pleasure."

The colonel in civilian clothes, chief of the local Department of Centurions in Civilian Clothes, began to pour the bubbling Pepsi-Cola into a glass and to treat the young naturalist and his snake to it. The boy swallowed the foreign drink greedily, while the yellow-belly hanging down from Arabella's shoulders only delicately sipped the brown moisture.

Our company was growing. It had turned into a crowd. The men and women and the young and old were walking; children and dogs were jumping up and down; cats were scurrying back and forth; and tigers from the local circus dragged along like sheep. The whole crowd was following the darling of all our people, the metropolitan area, and the barbaric regions: the television mirage, Arabella.

She once sang in an expressive voice in the attics and basements of Rome and was famous only among the attic-basement elite. Then, suddenly, this strange creature with the hypnotic voice appeared on TV among all the mug-ugly peddlers, and all of our preposterously savage people, tired of hearing about their achievements, did not boo her; they fell in love with her. What miracle brought her into the telecommunication system? Wasn't it the first symptom of the present seismological storm?

Where were we going? For some reason, uphill—closer to the fire. Along the steep narrow streets of Pompeii, past the burning houses and closer to the scorching heat, we were ascending the Hill of Glory. In the houses, homemade vodka-distilling machinery was exploding, television tubes were bursting, and mirrors were melting, but the inhabitants for some reason didn't seem to take notice of the destruction of their property. Everybody was in a rush to get whatever *kaif* there was left and to join up with us.

"You've become younger again, pal," Arabella told me. "Where's your hairy belly? Where's your muddled look?"

Indeed, I felt a kind of strange youthful lightness. More and more easily, happier and happier, I was jumping over the streams of scorching lava which spread over the cobblestone road. Once, among dozens of other faces in a piece of broken glass, my reflection flashed out at me—this, it seems, is how I looked about twenty-five years ago, in my student days.

Strange transformations in age kept occurring during our entire procession: the young naturalist in his shorts, for example, now resembled a very boring senior lecturer, and the chief of the secret service—a masturbating schoolboy, one of those who always hang about in school restrooms.

"Stop!" the secretary of the City Council suddenly shouted. "Here's the special supplies warehouse!"

In front of us were the smoldering ruins of quite an ordinary house. A black Tiber[29] limousine was ablaze next to it.

"Five minutes before the destruction of the City Council building I gave an order to Ananaskin[30] to do a complete inventory," the secretary of the City Council explained worriedly. "Oh, no, Arabella, I assure you, I, personally, don't need anything: I'm just curious what the results were."

The gas tank in the Tiber exploded: a pastorale for the fire storm in the background. The door to the special supplies warehouse fell off and Ananaskin appeared on the porch, hunched over from the weight of a huge smoked sturgeon that he was carrying on his back.

"Here's all I managed to save," he wheezed.

"Dear Ananaskin!" exclaimed Arabella. "Humble secret supplier! Gentle distributor with respect to labor! Are you shaking, Ananaskin? Take heart! Kiss the yellow-belly and join us."

Moaning, Ananaskin put his mouth to the snake's lips. Someone immediately came to his assistance, then a second and a third; they put their shoulders voluntarily under the beam of sturgeon, its weighty hulk.

We were drawing near to the top of the Hill of Glory where, among the destroyed bas reliefs, there flickered a little ribbon of the Eternal Fire. So touching, in the raging of that Non-Eternal Fire!

"It wasn't for us that this fish swam, and it wasn't for us that they smoked it, either," Ananaskin groaned. "They were expecting an important person. But now there's no point in keeping their secret—it was the proconsul himself! Fortunately, he did not arrive...."

"What do you mean didn't arrive?" asked a man standing behind Ananaskin's back. "Who do you think is volunteering his help with transporting this beam of sturgeon?"

The little guy turned out to be the one who the entire Pompeiian administration had been expecting with great trepidation for two weeks already—the proconsul from Rome. It turned out that his plane landed right in a puddle of lava and stuck there like a fly. No car was provided and the guards ran off in different directions to the barber shops. Now the proconsul was walking among the people, trying to be inconspicuous.

Behind him, under the beam, the pensioner Karandashkin was walking with a zinc pail on his head. The procession of the four volunteers was brought up in the rear by my plaster-with-pitiful-remnants-of-gilt Historic Titan from the Oreanda.

"Are you up to our sturgeon, comrades?" questioned Ananaskin.

"It's precisely labor like this that liberates peoples from those forms of exploitation which have become standard for them," Historic Titan spoke out.

"Just where is it we're going?" Karandashkin asked from under his pail. "Where will we eat this fish?"

"Don't you understand?" a Georgian dancer expressed his surprise. "Ara-bella will now sing to us from on top of the hill!"

"What a blast!" the pensioner shouted loudly.

"What a blast!" echoed the entire procession.[31]

"How could I abandon them, these dear scarecrows?" Arabella thought with a quiet smile. "How could I deprive them of myself? What would they have without me? Sappho, George Sand?"

At the top of the Hill we all took our places. All around dry grass was burning, alabaster was melting, and the bas reliefs of heroic deeds were tumbling down. Down below, to the thunder of its own jazz, Pompeii was collapsing.

> Flaring up higher, growing more crude,
> The feast is raging, the talk is rude...
> My dear little girl, oh, Pompeii,
> Child of Caesarina and of slave...[32]

Arabella sang out and then cleared her throat a bit.

"I haven't sung for a long time, but now I will sing everything for you—from the beginning to the end, or from the end to the beginning, or from the middle in both directions."

The volcano was roaring like all the radio jammers of Caesarist times and of our days put together, but the feeble voice of the singer was heard all the same.

"Whazz she singing?" asked Karandashkin, knocked off his rocker by the sturgeon, which he had never before seen or eaten in his entire life.

"She's singing her own stuff, not ours," explained the proconsul sluggishly, giving rare fish its customary tribute.

"It's amazing music, not human," croaked the Historic Titan pensively, quoting his own thoughts on classical music (*Collected Works,* Volume XII).[33]

Flowing around the Hill of Glory, the streams of lava poured down onto Pompeii. From the top it seemed that everything was finished, but more new crowds of people still kept ascending the Hill.

There came our workers and vacationers, the crowd fishing for contemporary *kaif,* the advocates of maximum satisfaction of their own constantly growing needs. Everybody was sure that it was a live broadcast of Arabella's performance, so therefore nobody thought of the destruction of Pompeii. Television and the government know what they are doing; in this world there are no miracles.

Thus, with this faith in faithlessness, we all fell asleep on the Hill of Glory. Each of us was forgetting everything blissfully and irrevocably. For example, as my brain began to go to sleep, it was forgetting stanzas from *Repercussions,* my proud work designed to win the minds of humankind, and a thought about the vanity of vanities flashed through my head, but was immediately forgotten.

Nobody woke up, even when it started to rain. Streams of water descended from the merciful heavens on high and pacified the volcano. We were sleeping in clouds of hot steam, and then under the constantly increasing gushes of a pure north wind. The wind blew away the steam and cooled off the settling lava, but we were still sleeping.

When we woke up, a cool and bright new day had arrived. Thousands of light, clean creatures were sitting on the Hill of Glory and didn't remember anything. A quiet and unfamiliar landscape stretched all around us. We were all looking at each other—author of *Repercussions,* tamed tigers, cats, dogs, painters, film people, musicians, Arabella, Georgians, Svetka the hairdresser, the chief hairdresser, the retired colonel, the colonel of the secret police, the young naturalist, the secretary of the City Council, Karandashkin, Ananaskin, the proconsul, the lesbians, Historic Titan, and all of yesterday's troglodytes of materialism. We were all looking at one another, not recognizing anybody, but loving everyone. Thousands of eyes were looking around with the hope of grasping the purpose of our awakening.

Finally, we saw a small tongue of fire at the top of the Hill and next to it there was a hot loaf of bread, a wheel of cheese and a pitcher of water. That was our breakfast. Then we saw a narrow path which ducked in between the cliffs and rose towards a pass in the mountains. That was our way. A second later and on the steep spur of the volcano appeared a snow-white, long-haired goat. She was our guide.

That's what happened in Pompeii that year at the beginning of spring. Later on during the excavations, scientists were surprised that no traces of human bodies were found in the destroyed buildings. In only one building, something resembling a school, they found a slithering emptiness in the lava which pointed to the fact that, probably, some time ago it was filled with the body of a small harmless snake. This allowed archeologists to make the suggestion that the inhabitants of Pompeii kept in their houses tame herbivorous snakes called "yel-low-bellies."

June-July 1979

    Written in the notebook which was Bella's gift in the spring of the Metropole year.[34]

Translated by Joel Wilkinson and Slava Yastremski

QUEST FOR AN ISLAND

dedicated to all Proffers

"Returning once again to Ajaccio." On each successive arrival this literary phrase rang in the mind of Leopold Bar—"the most important essayist alive in Europe today," according to the periodicals. In earlier years he had exerted some effort, trying to formulate a variant title. During the intervals between his trips (meaning the major part of his life) the name of the island's capital didn't cross his lips in any form because he never thought about it. However, he remembered from his childhood a geography textbook which featured "Ajaccio" rendered in Cyrillic letters, creating an odd concoction like eggnog with pepper. The native Corsicans—a substantial number of whom are favorably disposed toward the separatist movement—use the "j" and "c's" in writing "Ajaccio," but they pronounce the name of their capital more along the lines which the Cyrillic invites, saying something between "Aye-cho" and "Eh-cho"—subtleties which would never be learned in the schools he had attended. But the French (and Corsica does belong, after all, to France) turn "Ajaccio" into a pleasing mouthful of consonant clusters of the sort so characteristic of Russian but much less typical of the language of Molière. LB lent his support to the mother country, spurning the fashionable separatist cause, the way he spurned all fashions, because he had never been one to tag along with the crowd. Besides, just think about it: if all the islands in the world gained independence, a traveler would require a whole stack of additional visas.

"Irony charts a path to capitulation," LB had once told his readers. The gravity of blocks of limestone weathered by the wind. The doleful but mighty contours of citadels resisting the wind. Stand here in the rain with your weathered limestone face, as though you had not made half a million surrenders. A life lived gravely in a grave world can lay the sole basis of art—so I'm thinking at the given moment. The given moment. A moment given to me...

The rest of the arrival proceeded as usual. A bizarre-looking taxi with no meter—just the driver, who calculated the fare from Campo dell'Oro airport to the Fesch Hotel merely by staring at the rainy skies to reach a figure specified down to the centime. Then in the hotel lobby the same synthetic skins, striving for the cozy atmosphere of a hunting lodge. The same porter glued to the television, which was now storming with all the passion of local soccer: Bastia was beating Toulon. And the same Negro lying on a sofa in a dark corner, sleeping soundly and muttering indistinctly with one hand thrust inside his pants. Who was he, this black man who had been fast asleep in that same corner a year ago? As on the previous occasion, LB took no interest and walked past with his suitcase in hand, going straight to the elevator.

How enormous and simple the world is. LB granted no validity to fantastical projections, even though he had been enthralled by them often enough in the past. The problem of overpopulation, or some question about distributing population evenly across the globe, skirted the plain essence of things: the world is elemental, uncomplicated and tragic. As the norm of everyday existence, tragedy stamps the myriad signs of life—bread, a bar of soap, sperm, getting dressed, undressing, checking into a hotel... but no, don't smile. Don't yield any ground. The world is simple, and humor is the immoral, sly subterfuge of literati grown overly literary. LB does not belong to their ranks.

Here was last year's room, where nothing really crucial had occurred at the time, except for the fundamentals—breathing, sweating, urination, defecation, sleep, awakening, thinking and some sneezing as well, it seems (he had caught a touch of the flu). White walls and dark heavy furniture, decorated with carving, no less—all in the Mediterranean style. A balcony overlooking the rooftops of Ajaccio. On the balcony—a bubble-dotted puddle, left by several days of rain. In the puddle lies a garden hose, coiled in sheer mortification. Reliance on metaphor produces a lot of nonsense, but a bad metaphor is preferable to a good one. Shun metaphors, even though some crafty devil tries to slip them into your phrases at every turn. A garden hose is lying in the puddle. LB started undressing in front of the mirror. "How did I get to look like this? Is the reflection faithful? Taking off my cap reveals a big broad forehead sprinkled with reddish-brown freckles. A mangy disarray of thinning hair, worn long. The edematous chin—a constant source of unseemly bitterness. Some people find me handsome perhaps or at least significant-looking. To take a different standpoint, I make a pretty ridiculous sight. Such watery eyes. Bubbles, puddles, melted snow amidst the buildings of a housing project. Off come the jacket, the sweater, the shirt. Over the trousers on each side hangs a game bag, half-full—flab bags, lard left on the shelf too long... What meaning resides in the leisurely contemplation of one's person in various mirrors in dozens of three-star hotels throughout the world? Who am I? Is the reflection faithful? Am I handsome or ridiculous? Is my body a junk heap or a vessel, the form of my soul?"

Posing one question after another and gazing at himself with mounting intensity and concentration as he removed his clothes, the Swayer of minds throughout Europe gradually began calming down. No more extremes, no more metaphors, no more fuss: he simply *was*, he was what he was, his shape was the shape of a particular individual, and Corsica would have to cope again with his presence for awhile.

The next morning Leo Bar was drinking coffee on his balcony. That night had brought to the western Mediterranean events of far greater consequence than his own arrival—so he told himself with a smile. The winds had changed. A strong southeasterly current had displaced a northwestern slush-bearing front and had even managed to dry the sidewalks, terraces and roofs. It had turned out to be a windy, grayish day with flashes of sunshine, a day much nicer than Bar would have predicted for Corsica in December. On days like this, dressed in gray trousers, black sweater and a cap from London, Leo Bar—viewed from the left at three-quarter face—had the look of a typical Englishman.

You could have the look of an *Englishman,* period—Bar smilingly proposed to himself that morning. It was impossible to have the look of a *typical* Englishman. Typicality already implied some measure of fixed character. It was possible to have the look of a typical poet by simply being a poet, but impossible to have the look of a typical Englishman without actually being English. That was the case, wasn't it? Bar's main aspiration, incidentally, was to produce no impression whatsoever. To get lost as an alien-in-the-midst, blending into the humdrum routine of Corsican life. Here in the off-season nobody would take the slightest notice of some visitor's exceptional nature. There would be no personal contacts, no pesky little plots. The hunt for plots was the scourge of literature, the scourge of life itself. The goal of this trip was the implementation of the right to solitude. Uhh! what smug triviality. "The right to solitude" smacked of today's false romanticism, it was the phrase of a super-phony. Even though he did actually feel like being alone. After the scenes from the theater of the absurd, played by his Paris editors, after gorging himself nightly at La Coupole, after several months of acting as both sniper and target, there came this urge to go slack, to fade into the background and live a vegetative life. "Live a vegetative life." Again, an intellectual's cliché. This was really the main goal of the trip: to escape the shackles of intellectual clichés. Yet another trite expression—"the shackles of intellectual clichés." And a third—"to escape the shackles." One, two, three... via the creaking cogs, pulleys and weights of the literati life. Was it truly impossible to break free? Don't pose difficulties for yourself, don't set tasks, or else the island—a phenomenon of nature—will turn into a phenomenon of literature. Just get going and keep your attention focused, don't interpret, don't overdevelop, don't exaggerate. Simply reflect. There was the key: give an unaffected reflection, like a puddle. "A stork is perched on a roof against tranquil skies—the storm has passed." Reads like a *haiku*. Ye gods, more literary clap-trap!

In this state of torment, superbly self-inflicted at the breakfast table, Leopold Bar went out for a walk on Rue Fesch. Overhead, all along the street, which was squeezed narrow by the shuttered Italian houses with peeling paint, ubiquitous laundry was flapping in the wind. A traffic jam clogged the street: some distance away, a blue van had stopped to make a delivery. By blocking the vista at one end of the street, the van created the illusion of a deep blue sea, out of harmony with the weather. LB turned to walk in the opposite direction and soon reached the Square of the First Consul. This was very likely his favorite spot in Ajaccio. Thin colored tiling on the sidewalks, enormous palm trees surrounding the dullish gray, well-weathered Consul, several stores, including a bookshop, radiating despair, and a Lancôme perfume outlet, the most inspiring of the lot; then the palm-lined avenue stretching to the port; and there, in the obscure distance, the market with its smells of humanity's cradle—pepper, garlic and seaweed. But now the Société Générale bank. Changing money comprises one of the morning rituals of all globetrotters, and Leopold Bar certainly qualified as a globetrotter, a multinational man on the move.

The pound was falling, the dollar was falling, the lira was falling, while the mark crawled upward like a spider on the slimy thread of speculation. Tear out that miserable tongue of yours! On the marble steps of the bank sat an enormous shaggy cowardly dog. The type abounds here on Corsica, more than anywhere else. An island of little brave men and big cowardly dogs. If this dog was guarding the public coffers, you might say that the service would be performed more effectively by a statue of Napoleon. Damn your phrase-mongering! Two absolutely marvelous old Italian ladies, dressed in weary black, well-scrubbed, with every hair in place, were changing their native currency into foreign money. Why does the lira fluctuate so much, when Italy is so stable and sound? The time has come to dispel the generally held misconception about the country's unreliability. These two Mediterranean signoras are five-hundred times more reliable and substantial than all Milan's scummy leftists and rightists, brandishing their portraits of Lavrenty Beria or Benito Mussolini. Leopold Bar, where are you drifting? Into politics? Put on the brakes! The teller was smiling for some reason as he counted the crisp French bills. Did his good mood depend on currency fluctuations? But here was the rule to stamp on your skull: no mingling, no personal contacts whatsoever. Plenty of contacts, ties, relationships, friendships, quarrels and reconciliations have already been established on the continental land masses, even if the island does provide chances to mingle. Fence yourself off!

"Things good?" asked the teller, trying his English.

"Merci," responded Bar as he stuck the money in his pocket.

"America?" persisted the teller, watching the customer's gesture.

Then he gave a wink directed slightly off-side. Leo Bar glanced out of the corner of his eye and realized that he personally had never been the object of the friendly looks. Over to the right stood the shaggy coward with a front paw on the ledge of the teller's window.

"That's Athos," said the teller.

"Is he a watchdog?" Leo Bar, the lilly-liver, was entering into contact, after all.

"Oh no, monsieur! Just a friend. He's..."

LB left the bank and caught sight of his reflection in the window of a sporting goods store across the street. "Terrific, just the same" flashed through his mind when he saw that slightly overweight fellow. Then he had a sudden recollection of himself holding forth about a Bertolucci film the day before yesterday at the Deux Magots. With a certain aplomb he had stripped away the external trappings, and in no time at all a whole circle of people had formed to listen to *the* Leo Bar... You've got to shake off this crap!... at least some of it, this nonsense, this scruffy celebrity-hood, the self-importance. What a ludicrous, laughable megalomaniac! "The cultural phenomenon of modern-day Europe" should try turning into a human being for a week. Become an islander!

The newly emerged seeker of islander mentality went walking along the narrow street, passing the Imperial Bakery, the Napoleon Barber Shop and some souvenir stores with window displays showing an endless array of items commemorating the islander who had proved so successful in his quest for continental mentality. The rebellious lieutenant, with saber drawn and hair ruffled by the wind, appeared on plates and kitchen calendars; the idol stood in his tricorn, set forever; his busts ran the gamut from matchbox dimensions to natural scale; and the faces of the brunettish couple were painted on ashtrays, stamped "Napoleon and Josephine." The street curved uphill, and the top of the slope around the bend brought a view of the sea with the ocean liner *Napoleon,* a gigantic casino on the shore and a square with an equestrian statue, ill-proportioned but quite magnificent, nonetheless. The breath of one man's fate... the hapless little schoolboy.... What a life of tumultuous upheaval: troop movements, fodder, powder, indemnities, diplomatic crossword puzzles, overthrowing a throne and founding a dynasty. Did you have enough time on St. Helena to grieve for your own independent organism? Here on the island the souvenir shops preserved an outline of human possibilities: birth on an island which promised a vegetative existence, but then a climb to fame, the mutilation of a nearby continent, and finally a quiet expiration, after vegetating on another, distant island. There was an entrancing model of human destiny!

Leo Bar halted in his tracks, struck by a thoroughly disgusting, disgraceful thought: wasn't he drawing a comparison between his own fate and Napoleon's? He'd been taken unawares by some contemptible thought-process encompassing laundry waving in the street, the nose of the *Napoleon* jutting into sight behind the casino, a slice of the equestrian statue, a part of a plate with Josephine's portrait.... What a goddamn disgrace.

At this point he felt that he was not walking alone in the realm of shame: he sensed the presence of someone behind him. When he turned around, he discovered Athos, who had been accompanying him the whole way and now stood frozen in his tracks with his left front paw raised.

"A real disgrace, pal," said Leo Bar to Athos.

The wind was making a fierce rustle along the quay, taking a romp through the palms in file formation. On a yellow wall fluttered a dark blue leaflet with a sole remaining corner stuck. Intermittently the wind would spread it flat, showing the picture of a child's face with the words, "Mama, speak to me in Corsican!" Sitting at an oval window, a lackadaisical fat man with a magnifying glass was studying the tiny figures of a stock-exchange report. "Location de Voitures sans Chauffeur" said a sign above the door. A car rental agency. Now that was a pretty simple idea: rent a car. A drive in somewhat unfamiliar territory airs out the mind, chasing away idiotic preoccupations with one's own person. The fat man stood up to meet him, giving him a big friendly smile. From the depths of the garage came running an intelligent creature with silky hair—a spaniel named Juliette. In a few minutes Bar had at his disposal a Renault-5, a highly popular model among the locals and one which he saw shaped like a pear. He got behind the wheel. The fat man with his highly clever eyes was standing in the doorway of his rent-a-car. There was something about his face.... "He's a Napoleon who didn't make it. He could have commanded vast armies," thought Leo Bar.

"If you don't have a destination in mind, monsieur, I'd recommend Vivario," said the fat man. "It's right in the center of the island. The road zigzags quite a bit, but after you've made the trip, you can tell your friends that you know Corsica like the back of your hand."

He was smiling politely but with a trace of condescension—a real psychologist. What friends? Just what friends might hear Leo Bar boasting that he knew Corsica like the back of his hand? You, psychologist, are thinking in clichés. Instead of responding to the man, LB reached down to pat Juliette. She instantly began snarling and jumped away from his hand. Not a pleasant feeling: why was the dog so hostile?

"She's afraid that you'll take her with you," laughed the fat man.

"She's so happy here with you, is she?" Unable to resist, Leopold Bar had released some venom.

"This is her home. She's never known another one," said the fat man, as he handed him the necessary papers and a map. "You must agree that people get that way, too."

"Even entire nations do," said Leo Bar.

The fat man broke into a hearty laugh. This conclusion of their exchange had obviously given him tremendous pleasure: he'd made contact with an intellectual's world.

LB drove along the quay, furious with himself. Once again he had failed to stand firm behind his barricade, once again some idiotic, routine little plot had tried to swing into motion.

Driving an unfamiliar automobile actually did prove to be a rather pleasant, diverting activity, and the Renault-Cinq was indeed a sensible car. A heavy-bottomed pear wouldn't be bad at all as its symbol. That somewhat heavy little rear on these pint-sized vehicles gives them an apparent, if not real, solidity, and you step on the gas with more confidence than you might have in some bigger, more expensive cars. The steeply ascending road, the rapid changes from one weather zone to the next, Corsica's stone villages hanging over precipices like medieval fortifications, the intensifying blueness of the sky, and the topographical patterns of the landscape left far below—all filled Leo Bar with a feeling of communion with the island, the Mediterranean and Nature itself. The wind, growing fresher all the time and even acquiring the smell of light snow, was carousing inside the Renault and blowing Leo Bar's problems out the window. Then came the sudden realization that he had driven beyond the 2000-meter mark, bottomless ravines yawned beside him, he had a perpendicular wall of rock to his right, and a patchy cloud was drifting by at a lower level. He started thinking about the unmatched dangers of icy roads on slopes like these, he thought about the tread on his tires, and then he was imagining himself losing control of the car, unable to brake, sliding over the cliff, which did not even have a guardrail at this stretch of the road—despite the high altitude and hairpin turns! Bastards! Adrenalin made his blood churn, and he naturally began to lose control of the car, skidding toward the left edge of the road... but then a Citroën-DS darted around the bend ahead, and next, three cars passed LB and sped out of sight in rapid succession—a Volkswagen, a Simca-Matra and a more confident fellow Renault-5. All in a few seconds... some amazed-looking, wildly laughing faces flashing past him... A man ashen with terror took the curve... he saw a forest glade, fir trees and people playing in the light snowfall....

Leopold Bar in his somersaulting automobile had not yet hit the bottom of the abyss, when his trembling double stopped at a pass to catch his breath. They'd go on playing in the snow, just like that. Nobody would even notice the demise of "the most important essayist alive today." The funny thing was that he would automatically lose his title, right on the spot, because he'd be leaving the ranks of those "alive today," while a standing among all those who weren't alive today would involve a whole new count. An ordinary human body is not discovered quickly, it would eventually be identified, a belated shudder would pass through the thinking world, the tremor would last awhile—until the next edition of the news, as in the case of Camus: existentialism in action. Oh, rosy people so full of life, playing there in the snow!—have you no pity for Leo Bar? "Didn't know the man," atheists would say. "Every human being has our pity," Christians would say. "Must have lost it on the down-shift," sportsmen would shrug. "Ahh, Leopold Bar! What a terrible shame," some pretty, lone intellectual would say. "Thank goodness he left us a fairly sizable cultural legacy."

Beside the sign for Vivario stood a large Corsican donkey, eating the sparse grass. "Vivario! Vivario!" exclaimed Leopold Bar, in extraordinarily high spirits for his own funeral feast. He hopped out of the car and kissed the donkey on the tip of the nose. My friend, when the Almighty summons you and me to his olive groves, let's stick together, let's share a bower of straw in paradise, and don't take my proposition as magnanimity or condescension, we're truly equals, you and I, and Athos too, and Juliette and Shakespeare and Camus and that little bird flying past—a sparrow, isn't it? maybe a wagtail?... sorry, I'm not too swift when it comes to amphibians, reptiles, mollusks, fish or the Sillonette school of criticism, but perhaps this divorce from the animal kingdom simply points up my narrowness—a narrowness determined by centuries of so-called culture, that whole pile of smelly rubbish! You might even be smarter than me, my Corsican donkey, because you have no prejudices.

Like so many other small Corsican towns, such as Vizzavona, Sartène and Cauro, Vivario was built into a cliff. A building apparently having two stories when viewed from one side would turn out to have six stories when viewed from the opposite vantage point. In the tiny square where Leo Bar parked his automobile, a modest bronze Artemis with a dog stood under a stream of water: "Paese di L'amore," read the name—"The Spring of Love." Vivario was the home of Corsican blondes, who resemble short Swedes. At a long table inside the Friendship Café a chorus of voices blended in the melody of a graceless folk creation. Leo Bar asked for something to eat. He was seated by the fireplace and served some smoked ham, a round loaf of bread with a crispy brown crust, a carafe of country wine and a bowl of boiled beans. After his exhausting flights of imagination the writer now abandoned himself with relish to the simple pleasures of food.

In the meantime, he was being observed with no small interest by a Parisian woman sitting at a table by the wall across from the fireplace and smoking a Dutch cigarillo. He continued eating, free of the slightest suspicion, but all the while he was becoming the object of seemingly casual and passing, yet unmistakable, attention. Once his hunger had been satisfied, he sensed something and began looking around the room until he finally saw the Parisian woman. Exposed stitching along the seams, quilted jacket with some posh fur lining, crushed leather boots: it didn't take much effort to guess that the lady was outfitted by Sonia Rykiel. The height of stupidity—this snobbism of clothes with such fancy price tags. A craving for symbols and tokens of clanship, allowing the immediate recognition of one's own kind—social rites comparable to secret gestures among Masons. Caught off-guard, Leo Bar sat there looking at the Parisian with his mouth half-open, giving the impression of a lame-brained parrot. Small head with highlighted feathery hair—the concentration-camp style. A hint of puffiness in the cheeks and under the eyes, a slight pout to the mouth. Her age couldn't be pinned down precisely, but she had to be over forty. To his horror he realized that he was facing the type of woman who had always attracted him, still did and always would. Oh no, not that!! Not some banal little island romance! But she's spotted me—spotted me as a man who obviously belongs to "her circle." I look the part, after all, don't I?—like one of the mobs of run-of-the-mill Englishmen who go gallivanting around everywhere. That's really what my personal resolve amounts to: don't stand out from the average man, don't reveal an exceptional character. Maybe the lady has simply seen me somewhere, like the brasserie Lipp, La Coupole or the Café Flore? But my god! What if she actually knows me? No, not that, please—not that. Fence yourself off!

He felt that he was striking false poses once again, his legs had veered apart, and he had plopped into a puddle of falsity. Then he delved into the boiled beans. A simple, scrumptious dish! Just what in the hell was she doing here, 2000 meters above sea level in a Corsican village amidst all these little blondes? The deep-red ham looked translucent in a patch of light from the fire. Maybe I've actually met the snob at some soirée? But it's not too likely she'd have escaped my attention, if I had. I'm breaking the bread—this well-browned, crunchy peasant bread with the texture of cake, I munch with the teeth I still have intact. If you'd stuck to chow like this, you wouldn't have lost so many teeth. A glimmering conjecture: something similar to Leopold Bar's own condition had brought that Parisian here. Couldn't she be a writer? A whole group of these George Sands had cropped up, and some of them were even using masculine pseudonyms. I wouldn't be surprised if Emile Ajare turns out to be a female. He pours himself half a glass of wine and dilutes it with water from Artemis's spring. Now there's a drink! He contemplates the tablecloth and the remains of his feast, he's not gazing around, he doesn't raise his eyes, he's behaving perfectly naturally, mumbling a little under his breath, from a travel bag he takes *The Spy I Loved,* an espionage novel purchased at Orly for the trip, and pretends to read like a man engrossed, totally absorbed in the private life of his own independent organism—as simple as can be, unobtrusive and desirous that others keep their distance; then he stands up with his backside squarely directed at that woman's table— aiming his rump right at her, he walks over to the counter and digs into his pants' pockets, keenly aware of the indignity of that rear-end assault (but nobody's making you look at it, madame!), he pays some trifling bill, flings his scarf over his shoulder as he reaches the doorway, and involuntarily, despite himself, he glances back at her table. The table is empty. The coffee cup is empty, and the ashtray contains an extinguished cigarillo, or rather a filter with a long ash, left at least five minutes ago. Ah, so that's how it was? All the better—much, much better. Even better than you can imagine, precious heroine of the Lelouchian pseudo-cinema which, fortunately, is not taking shape.

The bitter pang of overdue freedom, solitude in the mountains. He was standing in the early mountain twilight in the little square of the tiny village Vivario, and at that moment he felt a bit like an arrogant schoolboy in the graduating class, as though his entire life lay before him. That's the way to finish a big meal—full of bitter pride, it keeps you from gaining an ounce. His subsequent actions: he stuck his head inside a barber shop for some reason (Want your mustache trimmed? Thanks, I'll drop by later), he popped into a souvenir shop and bought

a postcard showing the head of a familiar donkey—his future companion in the heavenly mansions, then he went to the toilet, and while re-
lieving himself, he thought about this trickle flowing from the mountain heights into the deepest abyss, quickly losing its distinctive odor
along the way, leaving some unassuming damp blotches on rock, pouring at last into a brook or small river completely cleansed of everything
repulsive, acquiring the purity of Nature's streams in the great circula-
tion of matter. The marvelous flow of mountain waters! Soon the sky
was becoming quite dark, he remembered the hairpin turn and the descent beyond the pass, gave a cough to nudge himself along and got
into the car. Then he discovered that he did not know how to turn on
the lights. He punched various buttons and moved some small levers,
but all he managed to do was activate the distress blinkers. He sure
wasn't going to do any driving with distress blinkers... stupid mess,
that's for sure. What was that guy trying to pull, palming off a defective
car?—conniving fatso, master of the imbecile Juliette! What a low-down
trick, advising him to drive into the mountains in a defective automobile. Perhaps somebody here knows how to turn on the headlights of a
Renault-Cinq? He saw a figure slowly approaching—a person with a
kind of poncho trailing from the shoulders and a hat perched on the
head—a hat like something worn by Bolivian peasants. Excuse me
please, I'm having some trouble, would you by any chance know how
to turn on the lights in this lousy heap? Pivoting in his direction, the silhouette explained in a Parisian voice. Straight into a trap! It was her.
You see—you have to flip the switch—just move it to the right. A hand
with an Indian bracelet entered the car like a soft warm bird and
moved a little black stub. The dashboard burst into light. *Voilà!* He got
out of the car to convey his profound gratitude. The interior of the car
was fully illuminated now, and the silhouette standing beside him became more three-dimensional. A scarf tied tightly around the head,
topped with a rigid hat. A silly frame for a sweet face with a little
pointed nose. Existentialism in action. The stupidest possible plot had
begun to unfold. No use resisting it. I'm driving to Ajaccio, madame,
and, of course, if... you too? how nice, I'd be more than happy to....

And so Leopold Bar found himself once again in the subtropical
seaside zone, on a beach on the gulf of Propriano. Down and down
they had ridden, making conversation the whole time, having readily
found a common language in so-called "Franglais." He'd chatted non-
stop with Florence (could it be her real name?), covering the demise of
literature, the rebirth of cinema, the "new philosophers" (in disagree-
ment with him, she proclaimed Marx a living force), the barricades of
May, the hazards of New York, Russia's crises, homosexual love (she

didn't disapprove but didn't understand—bravo!)... talking, talking so
that they dashed past all the signs without taking notice until they had
left Ajaccio some fifty kilometers behind to the north and reached an
empty parking lot at the deserted beach on the gulf of Propriano,
which was naturally occupied in the darkness with its usual business of
rolling pebblestone.

After leaving her Bolivian and Parisian attire in the car, Madame
Florence in jeans and a blouse was making a tour of the beach in an im-
promptu dance—quite a ballerina! How limber she is. Leo Bar lagged
behind, getting bogged down in the sand, stumbling on a stone, trying
all the while to stay in tune with the night's little plot—holding his stomach in, constantly aware of his awkwardness, thinking his shoulders
were too narrow, his thighs too heavy, and smoking—smoking inces-
santly, not so much because he felt disconcerted but because he was
sticking to the plot, as the man with a flickering dot of light in his teeth.
Gnashing teeth.

"You, I see, are a tobacco fiend, a real chain-smoker," she said laugh-
ingly. Turning the diminutive head, bosom, shoulders, she looked
about eighteen now as the moon flashed through clouds.

"We've hit just the spot for a side-trip," he said like a dolt. The
sound of crashing waves reached his ears from some distance away in
the gulf: there in the turbulent play of moonlight Scylla and Charybdis
were quietly shifting their positions, like molars racked by the pain of
age and overindulgence.

"Here's a chess game. Do you play?" An enormous chessboard lay at
her feet. In the flashes of moonlight the black squares looked darker
than the white ones. Gigantic chessmen, the size of turkeys or cats,
were scattered about, partially buried in the sand.

"Just the spot for a side-trip," he repeated, realizing already that the
phrase would elicit no response and that, in her opinion, they had
stopped just where they should have. Eurylochos, old buddy, plug my
ears with wax! No friends on the scene, the wax can't be molded, the
ropes have rotted, the fatal siren song is coming closer, the gulf's surface bristles with the knife-sharp cliffsides of Scylla and Charybdis: they
converge, my still body slips into the whirlpool.

"Go on, take your pick—black or white?" She lifted a white knight
and then a black elephant-shaped bishop, as though she was grabbing a
cat by the scruff of the neck.

"Which one do you want?"

"I don't care."

"So you mean you don't care whether you win or lose?"

"I don't have any doubts about winning. I'm sure I play better than
you do."

"You study chess theory?"

"Oh no! Sorry, I didn't mean to laugh, that's not at all appropriate. No theory, I rely strictly on practice. Sorry, I'm laughing again—I'm a little nervous. All right, so you're white. Just for the record, what's your name?"

"But I already told you, back there in the mountains."

"Sorry, I didn't catch it."

"My name's Alfred. I'm warning you in advance, my moves are going to be simple, starting with e2-e4... there—e2-e4."

"Sounds like you're a good player. No more talk now, please, I need to concentrate...."

True to her word, she froze in an attitude of concentration, nibbling the nail of her little finger, apparently pondering things as she stared at the board. From time to time she would raise her eyes, looking at Leo Bar and laughing. Her teeth and the whites of her eyes glinted in the intermittent flashes of moonlight. Like a Negress. What funny coquetry, he thought, I haven't seen anything like it for years. What in the hell was a chess game doing here? Obviously it's one of the features of this beach, a game people play in the summer. But just why has this chessboard with these pieces, big as domestic animals, made an appearance in my life? Why is it that wherever I poke my nose, something ridiculous develops? Madame Florence made a move—one which was necessary for launching the four-move combination known as the "Kindermatt."

"Checkmate, Madame Florence."

"Are you joking, Monsieur Alfred?"

Eyes gazing into eyes, a fusion of smiles... A little bit of everything must lie behind the film of this night—sheer enchantment and petty squabbles, champagne, abortions, reasonably sane ideas, hormone pills, independence, humiliation, take me with you....

"No! Really, that's impossible, it's some Mediterranean fraud. You, Monsieur Alfred, are the real corsair—a cheat, a bandit! Let's switch now so you have black."

They proceeded to change places, but as they passed on the same side of the board, they collided, losing their balance: laughter, hands outstretched, quick footwork, thoroughly graceful on the part of Madame Florence, while "Monsieur Alfred" moved like a crab, not devoid, however, of a certain impetuousness. Now I go first! Revenge, revenge!—e2-e4, e2-e4! Your turn, and don't rack your brain. The fact is, I can't even remember how many times in my life I've confronted this position. So you've outgrown surprises, have you? Every surprise is a cliché. But still they lie in wait for you. Who does? Surprises! Not ex-

actly. Winning's made you a smart aleck! Madame Florence, you're
checkmated again, and again in four moves. Monsieur Alfred, you're a
creep, a lout, you're nothing but a brazen A-one bastard and can go to
hell, I can't stand the sight of you!

She fell down on the sand next to the board and burst into sobs. Her
hand thrashed like a fish, sweeping aside the idiotic plastic chessmen.
With a shrug and a stiff vacant smile (he knew this expression quite
well as one conveying a sense of things left undone—an expression he
even liked because it frightened people away), Leo Bar made his retreat, taking a few steps on well-packed sand, and then sat down on a
pile of rank seaweed, clasping his arms around his knees and gazing
into the gulf's obscure murk. Sputters and swishes drifted across the
sea as Scylla and Charybdis withdrew and dissolved into the night, no
less the specters of death than tanks put out of action in the Sinai.

Anguish seized him. An imprecise phrase. He was filled with anguish. But that wasn't quite true. Anguish, genuine anguish, was probably still somewhere on the periphery, maybe it was even withdrawing
right now with those trawlers which appeared in the fog like aching
teeth or crags in myths of the blessed. Goddamn it, a triple mixed
metaphor! The big anguish spilled across the horizon, enveloping all of
Corsica, covering Sardinia; but its two little sisters were sitting here on
the beach—one seizing him and the other filling him. They lacked the
strength to get a tight grip and break him.

"Poor Leopold Bar, you're crying too," uttered Madame Florence,
some distance away. "You poor man, is that any way to play chess with
a woman?"

What a kindred spirit, he thought. Now we'll never part.

In the car she repaired her uncomplicated makeup and put on her
Bolivian hat.

"You keep looking for a daughter, Leo Bar, but what you really need
is mama...."

She had donned Freudian theory along with the hat. Soon he'd get
her back to town, drop her off and forget her. As they dashed along
the moonlit highway, her two frail knees gleamed in the dark. Why
bother with the whole woman, if you could just have her knees?

In the lobby of the Hotel Fesch two men were playing cards, despite
the late hour. One was the Negro from this afternoon, or rather, from
last year, or maybe even the year before last. The other was a young
man, wearing a leather jacket, with limpid scared eyes. Who in the hell
has the limpid scared eyes!—the young man or the jacket? No escaping
literature... The card players stared at Leo Bar as he entered feeling
mean, with a solidly sculpted bearing enhanced by malice. Then the

two men stood up, and the chance to walk past, pretending not to see them, had disappeared.

"Excuse me, Monsieur Bar, I've been waiting all day for you," said the young man, extending his hand. "I'm the journalist Bolinari—Auguste Bolinari."

Leo Bar, choked by the unexpected, found nothing better to do than grab with his left hand the wrist of the hand extended for a shake.

"Let me... even though it's late..."

Now a black hand moved in his direction, and this one was squarely met, palm to palm.

"Let me introduce the American writer Willy Barney. He's an old friend of ours—here on the island, I mean. He always makes his visits the same time you do."

"There's a third member of your party, isn't there?" Leo Bar asked with a hopeful look at a pair of little black ears which would make an appearance above the edge of the table and then drop out of sight again.

"Oh yes!" said Auguste Bolinari in a burst of obsequious laughter. "Let me introduce Charles Darwin."

An astonishing creature appeared in his hands: a black Pekinese with blue eyes like his master's, only more impudent. Little pink tongue, tiny sharp teeth.

"There we have it—the crowning point of evolution," said Leo Bar with an air of profundity.

The local journalist was happy: contact with the writer had been established. He wanted Monsieur Bar to rest assured that there would be no ambiguity about their relations, he promised—word of honor—there would be no interviews, he just wanted to invite you, Bar, and you, Barney, to supper... there's a wonderful restaurant not far away, with really fresh scampi, crab, oysters—all right from the ocean, the boats dock a hundred meters from the restaurant, everything comes straight from trawlers out of the Propriano gulf... Scylla and Charybdis, did you say?... thank you, Bar, that's another present... two like that in the first five minutes of contact... no, no, it's not an overevaluation... let me assure you—no interviews... as a long-time admirer of your work, Bar, and yours too, Barney, I'd just like to show you some provincial island hospitality...

At this point Leopold Bar noticed a mirror reflecting the entire group of faces: the tall American in a tweed jacket and a turtleneck but barefoot; Charles Darwin, sucking his master's finger; Auguste Bolinari himself—short and svelte in tight jeans and his jacket, showing some resemblance to Napoleon, of course, but ridden with modesty; and fi-

nally, his own image—pale pinkish face with the slight double chin, the
mouth half-open, and a wild tuft of hair (his cap had evidently gotten
lost somewhere). A throng of human and animal life on a single square
meter of overpopulated space. A step to the side could redress the balance.

"Excuse me, gentlemen, I respectfully decline the invitation."

"I see that you don't like us," said Willy Barney.

"Not much, I admit."

"What makes us worse than you?"

"Excuse me, I didn't express myself properly. I meant that I don't
much care for *us*—the literati. Do you understand? Not you personally,
Mr. Barney, certainly not you either, Monsieur Bolinari, or Darwin either, of course...."

The American was shifting restlessly on his shoeless feet, clenching
and unclenching his fists. To judge by his age, he must have fought in
World War II or at least in the Korean War. In any case, he'd probably
done some military service, which meant that he regarded a fight as a
good time.

"I was thinking about race," he said.

"Ahhh," said Bar.

"Well?" Barney asked harshly.

"Gentlemen!" exclaimed Bolinari.

"Arff!" piped up Darwin.

"I don't care much for your race either," said Bar, "or any other
race, for that matter. In general, I don't care much for any of this, gentlemen, do you understand? I just don't, I just don't...."

The local journalist stood there mesmerized. The Negro was rocking
back and forth on his heels. LB turned and walked away without saying
good-bye or making an apology. He'd had it with empty etiquette, he
needed to dive under a blanket, catch hold of some slender sprout,
wail a little about the latest loss of solid ground and the demise of the
island of Corsica, forgetting Leopold Bar for a few hours at least. But
instead of turning right to go to the elevator, he went to the left and
walked outside into the dribbling rain on Rue Fesch. He quickly passed
his rented Renault, which had fallen asleep alongside some other little
dozing cars, he found his grimy cap on the sidewalk, put it on his head,
entered a narrow stair-stepped lane, where the only light came from
the lanterns of "private clubs" (the bordellos), then reemerged onto
the Cours Napoleon, a major thoroughfare bathed in an unflagging
nighttime light and patrolled by some of the central government's sub-
machine-gunners, guarding the repose of the separatists. There he
strode along, making entreaties to fate to start the wind and bring a

break in the clouds, with just a few little stars, just some minimal signs of bygone life.

Auguste Bolinari came driving down the middle of the street in a sports car (the guy obviously wasn't hard up) and was waving a newspaper. This is for you, Monsieur Bar, for you! The Negro kept hot on Bar's trail, his fists digging into his pockets and knotted muscles twitching on his cheeks.

"Think you're the only one with biological problems?!" he would yell every so often. "Think you're the only one who loses teeth and hair, etcetera, etcetera?! Get off your high horse, Bar! Think you're the only high-and-mighty man around?"

LB started running and had soon shaken his pursuers. After escaping, he felt regrets about the men he had left behind and the unachieved cozy supper at a small seaside restaurant with confreres of the pen—two wonderful fellows and the marvelous little pooch Darwin, who would have sat on his knees, begging for shrimp tails. A fire would have been crackling on the hearth... He entered yet another empty street with the branches of huge palms hanging in wet rigidity and a bordello's red neon sign growling faintly in the night to announce "Dodo's Place." Now there's the spot for you, if you're no longer capable of simple human associations. Go in and pay for regards!

Dodo turned out to be a Dandie Dinmont toy terrier. What bounciness! From the floor he took a flying leap onto the small table and fixed his round button eyes on Leo Bar. He was all aquiver with unintelligible but intense emotions.

"A martini, Dodo!"

Leo Bar was sitting there alone amidst a couple dozen tables and some eighty chairs. The bordello had either known better days or else was preparing for a brighter future. At the moment it was empty, except for the bandit-bartender, whose gray head loomed into view behind the counter, and a young man of undetermined function who was roaming around the dance floor. He looked too casual to be a waiter with his loose-fitting cardigan, shirt unbuttoned to the waist, bracelets on his wrists, chain around his neck and charms dangling from a cowboy belt. In a bordello like this, with plush-covered chairs, a waiter would be wearing a uniform. On the other hand, a bordello visitor—a customer such as Bar—would not be behaving as this young man was, pacing back and forth with a springy gait, shrugging his shoulders, thrusting out his chest, menacingly curling his lip, muttering something under his breath, walking now and then over to the bar, grabbing the telephone receiver and uttering brief, nervous responses in his conversation—all the while vaguely reminding LB of someone he knew.

"A martini, please!" he repeated his order. Apparently nobody had heard him except for the dog. Dodo! Dodo! The terrier gave a yip and went dashing around the empty, dubious-smelling room, anxious to have his share of the action, but there was no action to be had.

Suddenly the door to the street burst open. Into Dodo's Place walked Auguste Bolinari with his chin held high, coldly reserved and offended. He came over, laid a newspaper on the table and left without saying a word. A copy of today's *Le Monde* lay before L. Bar. Some article had been marked with a red felt-tip pen. Leo Bar's mind guiltily composed a smooth statement: "Auguste Bolinari, you pure-hearted soul and lover of literature, forgive me. The entire existence of degenerates like me is supported by pure hearts such as yourself. But what can I do if you just don't interest me?"

The bartender, limping slightly on a leg made lame in days of brigandage, brought him a martini in a glass with a nasty-looking ring of sugar around the rim. Some suspicious tidbit rested at the bottom.

"Is Dodo old?" asked Leo Bar.

"I'm already past sixty, the boy here's thirty, and the little mutt's ten, which makes him the oldest." The bartender grinned and gave the rickety table a swipe with a scrub-brush which reeked of disinfectant, making the martini wobble and nearly spill. "Life moves right along, sir. It's a relentless thing. Time has a way of..."

"I was just asking about Dodo," interrupted LB. All he needed, to add to his own philosophical tripe, were some words of wisdom from the chief of this den of iniquity.

"We're all 'Dodo,' sir," the man explained, "all three of us."

His smiles, the bows and use of the word "sir" did not convey any particular feeling of good will but simply expressed a professional courtesy, somewhat antiquated in the era of socialism. He had barely walked away, when the thirty-year-old Dodo came over and demonstrated a totally different style.

"You interested in some entertainment?" His hand moved abruptly behind his back, toward his pants' pocket: what was he going to pull out—a gun, a knife? A notebook, it was. "Here's your choice!"

Some color photos fell from the notebook onto the table, displaying specimens of the three principal races of continental land—a Negress, a Chinese woman and a German.

"I'll take all three," said Leo Bar.

"Meaning what exactly?" The young man brought his menacing face close to Bar. The question of resemblance was settled: it was Napoleon Bonaparte with a small nose disfigured during a former boxing career.

"Well, why not?" mumbled Leo Bar. "Let me have all three."

Dodo raised his eyes toward the ceiling, moved his lips as he made a mental calculation and then tore a sheet from the notebook with the exact figure of 1875 francs, "paid in advance."

"Certainly, certainly." Leo Bar took from his pocket the money he had changed that morning and scattered it all over the table in little wads. The sight resembled flotsam on a beach.

A phonograph struck up "Gulfstream," a song from the '30s. Someone opened a door covered with plush to match the walls, and three horrendous girls appeared on the dance floor one by one, wearing transparent burnooses. They were escorted by the toy terrier, Dodo-in-chief. He was having his moment in the sun, performing like a circus pony, prancing jauntily on his tiny old feet in time to "Gulfstream," holding his pointed nose high in the air and casting a look of triumphant pride at the audience—that is to say, at Leopold Bar. After lazily circling the floor a few times, the girls got down to the business of unfastening each other's buttons and snaps, untying bows and ribbons, without stopping their dance. The German became entangled in her lacey underpants and fell onto one knee but then hopped back up and started dancing again with surprising agility and zeal. Leo Bar delved into the newspaper, reading the article marked by Bolinari's felt-tip pen.

"Leopold Bar's new book *Two-Faced but Honest* lays open before us vast empty spaces of this writer's extraordinary spirit, creating the impact of a stalactical cave...," he read. "It would be no exaggeration to say that Leo Bar is probably the most important essayist alive in Europe today..."

"What's wrong? Not interested?" asked the young Dodo, taking a seat at the table. The tiny table rocked under his elbow. His biceps twitched under the cardigan.

"Who says I'm not interested?" asked Leo Bar.

"I said so!!" Dodo's eyes burned through Bar's fragile skin, sounding out every fold with the supersensitive but blind instruments of pure hate. "Maybe you'd like to see something else, mister?"

"I just might," said Leo Bar, laying the newspaper aside. "Don't you have one other whore? It seems to me that the star of your... uh... theater, yes—theater, must be a certain Madame Florence."

What power Dodo had packed in his fingers! In one swift motion he had grabbed Leo Bar by the shirt collar, making a noisy rip.

"You rotten scum, don't you know who Madame Florence is? She's Captain Bouzzoni's granddaughter! Come on, let's go!"

"Where?" asked Bar with interest as he stood up. What a sassy character! What bizarre nerve the man had!

"Where? To the sea!" Dodo was smiling and trembling with pleasurable anticipation of the reprisals ahead.

They went outside. There, as he took gulps of clammy felt-like air under the drooping palms, Bar recalled that in Corsican an invitation to go to the sea carries the force of awful swear words. The islanders had never had any love for the element which made them islanders—that boundless expanse, laying claim to lock, stock and barrel, to their buildings, to their very existence, so they thought.

"You're wrong if you think I'm going to give up without a fight," L. Bar said to Dodo. "I'm two-faced but honest, weak but brave. The vast empty spaces of my extraordinary spirit have the impact of a stalactical cave."

"We'll see about that in just a second," snarled Dodo, brandishing his fists, leading with his right as he threw a series of short punches and a few long ones at the essayist standing a couple of paces away.

"I see you're a boxer," laughed Bar. The thought of resistance was quickly giving way to the idea of capitulation. "The calmer I act, the less hell to pay. Maybe his fists will get stuck in this dough I'm made of?"

"Why are you talking to me in English? Why should I have to speak English with you, you bastard!" Dodo was bobbing up and down, sparring straight away with the five shadows which now radiated from his body along a white wall.

"You prefer French? Were you a champion boxer in the mother country?"

"Phuuu!" Dodo suddenly made a face, as though he had taken a blow to the liver. "I beat Laroque, Lecrème, Charonne, and then for the final I see some Berber show up. Excuse me, I said, what kind of a Frenchman's that—black as a boot? And they tell me, 'You're from the overseas territories, too.' I was a victim of demagogues with their half-ass sneering at working people! Ever since then I've hated the guts of guys like you!"

Dancing in closer, bringing his elbows forward and hiding his face behind imaginary gloves, he started driving the essayist into a corner between two illuminated shop windows, where at least a hundred faces of Napoleon Bonaparte in assorted sizes stood on display. Thoroughly delighted with the existential situation, Bar took a solid poke at Dodo's cheekbone, promptly dislocating all his fingers.

A minute later, Leopold Bar was slowly crawling away, hugging the wall as he moved toward the beach. The obliging Dodo had given Bar a first-rate workout: his face was swollen, his ribs ached, and, worst of all, the near-champion had broken two of his expensive porcelain teeth.

Like the essayist's spirit, his mouth was now reminiscent of a stalactical cave. The fleeing Dodo had sobbed with the shame of the mighty, while LB cried on his hands and knees with the pride of the meek. After all, he had not just given up, turning into a dough-ball, but had waved his arms right up to the end... there had been a fight, rather than a case of assault and battery... he'd been in a fight. The dark night runs a test of her creatures' masculine qualities. The test had taken place. A nocturnal creature with a swollen face cries on the sand, but nobody has seen him yet—a blessing!

"Would you happen to have a cigarette," he heard in Russian. *"Fumer, fumer,* some smoke?" added the giant now towering over him.

Leopold Bar fumbled in his pocket for a pack of Pall Malls which had been badly crushed in the nocturnal test of "masculine qualities." What would Russians be doing here? The man turned out to be a player on a basketball team who had been left behind in Ajaccio after coming down with a stomach ailment, and for a hefty sum they had removed his appendix at the local hospital.

"It was this long," the basketball player said wistfully, demonstrating with his huge palm which was illuminated by the mangled stub of a cigarette.

So now we have Russia, thought Leopold Bar, swaying back and forth, restraining his moans, swaying back and forth, listening to the story of an operation. Only Russia could have topped off this night. Those innumerable Uncle Yashas and Auntie Tosis... LB recollected with anguish his trips to Russia in search of his biological and philosophical roots. How he had burned, how he had tried to penetrate the whole incomprehensible entity, right back to the year Marx died. The mover of minds on a global scale had died a provisional death, but what was Russia, minus his influence? In short order, of course, Marx had come to life again, but Bar no longer yielded to the passing fancies of the Western spirit. He had turned back to the Orient, to the wisdom teeth of all mankind, and he had lingered there until his own personal molars started to hurt. Now the whole matter brought searing pain. Russia, Russia! Cast by some hand to the mercy of fate... But why should I feel sorry for an alien country? I left Russia, but I've left a hundred other countries too and never felt sorry for any of them. Yes, I left Russia behind like a part of my youth, I shaved her off, like the beard I never wore. What's become of them, all those Tolstoevskys? Here was Russia—a boy in a giant's body, greedily smoking a chain of half-demolished Pall Malls and recounting his tale about the removal of his appendix on the island of Corsica.

"Have you ever had appendicitis? It's pretty creepy, having a whop-

per like that inside you. Big as my hand it was! You're probably wondering what I'm doing out here at night on the beach? So, I'll explain.
The operation's given me a colossal case of insomnia. An appendix like
that was a real jolt. I never suspected it could be so big. It's mind-bog-
gling! To tell the truth, knowing that it's *out* adds to the shock. It's a
staggering surprise, a complete mind-boggler!—knowing that some un-
foreseen part of my body has been removed and is no longer there any
more. What else do I have inside me, what other unexpected things?
With this thought in my head, comrade, I'll be flying to Liège tomorrow, we're playing a game for the world championship."

"Which championship?" wheezed Leo Bar.

"The *world* championship."

"Is that really possible, my lad? The world is a monument, a palm
tree, four scruffy dogs, a chipped porcelain tooth, the liner *Napoleon*, a
chestnut donkey, millions of automobiles, and finally your appendix.
Merely touch all that trash, and it pours down on your head. A
Weltanschauung, a philosophy, a disposition of mind—the whole thing
collapses, comes raining down, makes a big snafu! I don't understand
how you can try to win the championship of something so monstrously
rotten."

"Maybe you need some help?" asked the basketball player. "From
the time I was a child, I was raised with the idea that a person ought to
help anyone who needs it, but I've got to admit I'm always glad when
nobody needs it. Thanks for the cigarettes, I'm off. I'll keep in mind
your question about the world championship. But I'm glad it didn't
pop into my head by itself. So long!"

Abandoned by one and all, including Russia, Leo Bar writhed spas-
modically on the wet sand. The murky predawn skies drew near overhead, not a cloud to be seen, not a patch of light—just murk, and it was
drawing near. In the meantime the heavy wet sand was pulling from
below, sucking him into the void. Qualifying as the void itself, the sand
was doing its best to make him sink deeper and deeper, it wanted to fill
the void with the pain-racked body of Leopold Bar.

"O Heavens, my first and last icon, how empty you are, how hope-
less and inescapable your emptiness! How bitter to look at the heavens
at this hour, at this moment, and to realize that I made no mistake,
thinking nothing has ever been up there for anybody." Softly whimper-
ing farewell, Bar shot one last glance at the heavens and realized that
he had made a mistake after all: there *was* something up there. Over
the gulf in the predawn murk a large dirigible was drifting into sight. It
came fully into view from nose to tail and hung suspended—a dark
gray, nearly black dirigible, afloat in the murk in slightly blurred out-

line. It was hanging there before the dawn, before Leopold Bar, high in the heavens above the water, simply hanging there, asking no questions, giving no answers.

Radiant light brought Leo Bar back to a waking state. Everything around him was brightly shining—the dancing waves in the gulf, the glass windows of dancing boats, the crest of the mountainous coast and the white hotels along the quay, moving automobiles, a couple of Coca-Cola bottles dumped in the sand, the sand itself, the flighty tattered clouds, a plane traveling the Ajaccio-Nice route, the boundless sky, and (naturally) the source of all this radiance—the Sun. The essayist got to his feet, fully confident that he, too, was shining or, at any rate, that he had a shine in the whites of his eyes, hidden beneath swollen but shining lids; his brain was shining; and in his stalactical cave (just wait, you bastards at *Le Monde!*) sunshine and ozone were making merry. He took a few steps toward town and then saw the bronze bust of a simple, brave man standing erect on the beach. The pedestal bore the inscription: "Navy Captain Etienne Bouzonni. Died testing a dirigible in December 1907." He looked at the straight nose and the sharply etched chin raised in calm but proud resolution, displaying a trace of kindred feeling. If you believe in Santa Claus stories about the "alter ego," then you might also be prone to believe that a captain like this was alive inside your limp sniveling dough.

He proceeded along the quay and saw the Square of the First Consul coming into sight, followed by the market under regal palms. Up ahead, with her clogs clacking, Madame Florence was walking along the sidewalk in the same direction. She was pushing an oversized stroller containing a pair of baby twins, and in addition she had four dogs in tow—the enormous Athos, as scared as ever, with his legs nearly failing him; that highly courageous but depraved creature, Dodo the toy terrier; the pampered wee Pekinese, Charles Darwin; and the peevish spaniel Juliette. Without accelerating to overtake this marvelous spectacle of a woman with a pair of twins and four dogs, Leo Bar went along with them all the way to the market, where Madame Florence went shopping for artichokes, avocados and kohlrabi, piling her purchases in the stroller at the little feet of the twins, who made soft burbles the whole time, lying side by side with their eyes shining.

"Madame Florence," he called softly.

"Monsieur?" She turned toward him but wasn't quite identical to his acquaintance of yesterday.

"Strong resemblance, but it's somebody else," realized the exultant essayist. The dogs—all four of them—were also looking at him. Strong resemblance, but they were different ones. How amazing! "Excuse me,

Madame! Have a good morning!" he said with a bow and then headed resolutely for the nearest Agence de Voyages. As he came closer, he saw with increasing clarity his reflection mirrored in the travel agent's window. Despite the black eyes and general puffiness of the face, he looked like himself. How splendid to be yourself or at least look like yourself. How splendid to tend to your own business, even if it was only writing some little book. In fact, how splendid it was—ha ha ha!—to write essays, *essays*—poking a bit of fun at your companions in life, both human and animal, because animals, too, derive benefits from books, even if they can't read. How splendid it was to fill readers with anguish and gloom, even if it made them throw your books aside and then turn to caressing one another or their animals, or else go to the market and buy artichokes, or else, finally, to take journeys from capital cities to islands and back again. For after all, there really was more to the world than the gloomy empty spaces of literature.

"Excuse me for bringing the story to such a preposterous conclusion, but could I have you arrange a plane ticket with an extremely complicated itinerary?" Leo Bar asked the Corsican clerk in the travel agency. "Let's suppose, for instance, Corsica-London-Moscow-Singapore-New York-Warsaw-Iceland-Rome-Corsica?"

"Itineraries as complicated as you like, Monsieur," answered the modest little Bonaparte, smiling politely.

November 1977-January 1978, Ajaccio-Moscow

Translated by Susan Layton

SUPER-DELUXE

Vladislav Ivanovich Vetryakov, the same guy who's Slava to his friends and Gibbon to his most intimate circle of friends... dot-dot-dot. You and I look around in confusion: the predicate must be either lost or not yet found, for we still don't know where to put our hero on what dot of the map, in what circumstances and environment, or what action to offer him. So meanwhile, let's handle his nickname: Gibbon, that's a strange one, eh? It is, as we indeed all know, a species of monkey; yet I must tell you there's nothing monkey-like about Vladislav Ivanovich's appearance. Quite the contrary, from the first moment of acquaintance people are struck by his admirable humanity, and we would also like to draw attention to the particular sparkle in his eyes. Such eyes are the mark of a person capable of admiring the objective world and seeing in it not just a heap of things, but also the fascination of various prospects. That's how I'd describe his eyes to the reader. As for the nickname Gibbon, it all began as a joke: he was in the sauna with his closest friends, or rather, they were having a good time drinking vast quantities of Carlsberg,[1] telling anecdotes and stories, and generally goofing around. Tarasian began to imitate an elephant, Lyova a dying swan, and Vladislav Ivanovich dangling his arms down to the floor started to hop up and down in front of the mirror and to shout "I'm a gibbon! I'm a gibbon!" And would you believe it, neither the elephant nor the swan stuck, but "gibbon" did—Slava, the Gibbon. To tell the truth, there were grounds for this nickname to stick to Vladislav Ivanovich: phylogenesis had for some reason meted out to him longish arms and an excessively hairy body, but these insignificant external characteristics didn't hit you in the eye. Especially if rather than fooling around in a Finnish sauna, you were riding in a taxi dressed in a really fine blue flannel suit, lightly tapping a product of the Italian shoemakers' art, peering through fantastic French glasses with an amiable and almost rapt expression as you viewed the world, Odessa's Seashore Boulevard, the statue of the Duc de Richelieu,[2] and the panorama of

the harbor with large snow-white ships at its center. So, having found a
place for our hero, let's forget about the nickname Gibbon in order to
fill our hearts with admiration for this wonderful citizen, Vladislav
Ivanovich Vetryakov, who looks like a theoretical physicist and, moreover, one who has traveled the world. "It's staggering!" said Vetryakov,
"just staggering!"

"What's staggering?" asked the cab driver gloomily.

"Well, all this! Odessa, the port, the ship!"

The cab driver cast a suspicious glance from under his long hair, as
though he were wondering if he had a nut for a fare.

They came to a stop right by the huge hull of the liner *Caravan*.
Vetryakov handed the cab driver a fifty-ruble bill. It was a crackling,
new, rather large note, of a quite pleasant greenish color. Vladislav
Ivanovich had decided long ago that if a person had a taste for money
he should begin with fifty-ruble bills. Ten-ruble bills are just like slightly
off-pink slices of veal; twenty-five-ruble notes are such an indecent size
and have such a repulsive and faded color. One- and three-ruble bills?..
well, I'll tell you frankly, Vladislav Ivanovich didn't have a really clear
idea what use it was for the Treasury to print those under-ten smallfry,
all those rumpled wads of skin, little clods, dead sparrows... no, no,
they all look so ridiculous! A man of taste ought to set his sights exclusively on the design of the half-hundreds.

"No change," the cab driver said and handed the bill back. "Don't
earn that much money in two days even."

"Cheer up, friend! Keep the change!" said Vladislav Ivanovich.

"Now *that's* staggering!" muttered the stunned cab driver.

Having picked up his suitcase and "attaché" briefcase, Vladislav
Ivanovich began to walk up the gangway of the snow-white giant. He
was bursting with song and so was everything around. On board the
Caravan songstress Parkhomenko was singing "Oh, you nights, sailors'
nights!"[3] And Vetryakov sang in his soul a song from his childhood
days in the young pioneers: "In Capetown Port with cacao on board."
The duty-officer was talking on the phone with someone when he took
Vetryakov's ticket. However, once he'd glanced at it, he hung up the receiver and gave Vladislav Ivanovich a respectful and attentive look. It
was, after all, a ticket for the 900-ruble super-deluxe cabin. This way,
please! Be so kind! Please, here's the elevator! Lyuda, show the gentleman, please, to number 02! Lyuda—haughty, pink-cheeked and all a-
crackle, the embodiment of inaccessibility—opened the mahogany
door beyond which a kind of miracle of comfort was immediately revealed. "Just a minute, Lyuda!" "Don't give me that 'minute' come-on,

I'm on duty!" "No, no, you misunderstood me. This is just to celebrate our getting acquainted. Maybe you'll find it useful. I hope you won't be offended, it's just a trifle..." The passenger fussily snapped open his suitcase and in a second the cabin stewardess was holding a box of Madame Rochas perfume, a whole ounce. Oh, mother dear! On her trips abroad Lyuda hadn't even dared to glance at such things. "Well, well, Lyuda, well, I see you're happy, and I'm glad that you're happy, of course, because happiness is very becoming to you."

"My goodness, comrade, what are you... Oh, mother dear, you really shouldn't Comrade..."

"Vladislav Ivanovich Vetryakov, a physicist. I'm a physicist, Lyuda, do you understand? It's really nothing for me."

Lyuda let the physicist into the super-deluxe cabin with a certain amount of caution and, standing a safe distance away, showed him the refrigerator (Italian!), bathroom (entirely Swedish!), color T.V. set (American!), stereo components (Japanese!), and telephone (our make, but on the level of European standards or maybe even higher). "It's really a wonderful ship! But Lyuda, where did they come up with such a strange name for her? The *Caravan*." "What's so strange about that? Don't we have the *Azerbaidzhan* and the *Kazakhstan*? Now there's the *Caravan*..." "Well, I'm glad, Lyuda, that we've become acquainted. I repeat once more that this trifle, this—you agree, don't you, it's not a bad design?—this bagatelle doesn't commit you to anything. On the contrary, if you need something, Lyuda dear, well I don't know, well, it might be anything, say, money, if you, my precious, need money, come to me at any time."

When he was left alone, Vladislav Ivanovich began to arrange all his things in the huge, two- or, perhaps, three-room suite, if you count the bathroom, and why not consider it a room—this blissfully spacious area laid with pink Dutch tile? The super-deluxe! He hung his brown and gray suits, his blazer and Safari blue jeans suit in the closet; arranged piles of English shirts and fine-wool sweaters on the shelves; put away his shoes with the design that "bordered on a work of art," as Gachik Tarasian said; took out the Parisian men's cologne and then cognac, whiskey, and gin. The temporarily careless arrangement of all this represented the most perfect design or, in other words, pop-art. Seized by the ecstasy of existence, Vetryakov begin to jump around on the cabin's fluffy carpet, to flip all the switches and push all the buttons, and with that the cabin came to life, began to sing and light up: a television set featured something heroic, a stereo system played something romantic, and enormous windows opened onto a blue sky dotted with

seagulls and masts. Vladislav Ivanovich began gliding around with a
crystal glass filled with exactly two fingers of Courvoisier cognac, as was
de rigeur, and at precisely that moment the telephone rang, which
aboard the *Caravan* did not mean you should expect bad news, but, on
the contrary, a further improvement in your life. That's exactly how it
turned out: Vetryakov understood immediately by the tone of the voice
that whoever was calling was his kind of guy:

"Welcome back, Slava! This is Marat and Edik calling. Perhaps, you
don't know us, but we know you. Andrei Mikhailovich referred us to
you; Lev called him yesterday. So, uh, everything's on schedule. We'll
deliver the order right away."

In half an hour two fine fellows in jeans and leather arrived, real optimists. Without anybody's help they dragged several boxes of drinks
and snacks into the cabin: Schweppes tonic water, Vladislav Ivanovich's
favorite Carlsberg beer, Beefeater's gin, caviar, smoked sausage,
toasted almonds—everything perfect to a tee. Looking at the order,
Vladislav Ivanovich was filled with a warm, almost exuberant feeling.
No, no matter what you say, the feeling of camaraderie still exists in
this world; as soon as he had mentioned in passing that it would be a
nice thing to have an order delivered on board the *Caravan,* Lev immediately said "It'll be done." Vladislav Ivanovich could well imagine how
Lev had gone through Rosko, and how Rosko made connections via
Vadim Leshin, because it wasn't wise for Rosko to go directly to Andrei
Mikhailovich's level, and so it was Vadim who called Serafima
Ivanovna, and she informed Andrei Mikhailovich on the QT, and only
then, after he had received the go-ahead, did Lyova call Andrei
Mikhailovich directly. No, no matter what the skeptics say, there is still
genuine friendship among men in this world. That's how it happens—
sometimes just a glance at a person, and it's immediately clear whether
you'll go "prospecting" with him or if you'd rather refrain.[5] That's how
Slava himself was introduced to his circle of friends about ten years
ago. Let's see, where was it exactly? While out fishing, in a sauna, or
simply around a table? Some details have been erased from memory,
but the most important one remains forever. Boris the race car driver
had brought him there, and in half an hour Lyova or Gachik, or perhaps Stepan Akimovich himself had said, "Let's drink to Slava! We can
go prospecting with him!" And life had confirmed this: nobody let anyone else down. That's real men for you!

On the sea the steamship *Caravan* was a noble sight! This wanderer,
chartered the world over, usually took Swedes and Englishmen for a
trip to the archipelagos of Polynesia, or Columbians and Argentinians

for a trip in the opposite direction, to the fjords of Norway, and sometimes also visited her native waters to gratify her compatriots. On those cruises, the gaming machines, those so-called "one-armed bandits" were sealed up (because the spirit of profit and the belief in blind fate are alien to our people); a certain something characteristic of them was replaced by something characteristic of us,[6] and *Caravan* set out on the route Odessa-Batumi-Odessa,[7] giving the entire Euksinian Pont and nearby shores the pleasure of observing her presence.

Thus, we have found a proper place in this marvelous, almost dazzling world for our hero and we have provided him with everything he needs. We could now let him out of his deluxe suite onto the deck, for the peripeteia of the story, but before we do this we should perhaps touch upon one detail of his luggage—the "attaché" case, that flat suitcase/briefcase which was brought into worldwide use by James Bond, Her Majesty's Secret Service Agent 007 with a license to kill.[8] However, is it worth it for us to make an attempt to peer into this case and stir up its contents? All the more since Vladislav Ivanovich never counts money himself or rearranges it? There's nothing about Vladislav Ivanovich to remind you of the Covetous Knight,[9] he doesn't really care much about money because, believe it or not, he's not a crook, not a greedy-fingers, not even an artful dodger. He is a friend, a reliable person, an unbiased and brave comrade-at-arms. He is the Prince Myshkin[10] of the contemporary partisan structure, a link in the notorious system of "elemental redistribution"[11] and he is, in the final analysis, just simply a theoretical physicist. His last name is not being kept secret; it genuinely exists: Slava, yes if you please, for friends, yes please; he is always open to friendship. We won't say a word about Gibbon and by no means because it is some kind of criminal nickname, but because it is just his own bad joke which turned out to be very sticky.

So, let's let our hero go on deck and straightaway encounter the ballerina Sokolova. Being very sensitive to cold, she has a shawl draped around her shoulders. In her huge eyes one can see the hope of spending a few days alone. Alas, she's already been noticed by several adversaries of women's loneliness. One of them, definitely a physicist, approaches and blocks her way. What should she do? Well, anyway, at least he's not the worst of them.

"Good evening. Well, here it is, the cradle of humankind. Do you smoke? Winston or Kent? Please! Pardon, but wasn't it you I saw in the ballet program 'White Nights'[12] a few days ago? Oh, what luck, it's a great pleasure to meet you. My name is Vladislav Ivanovich Vetryakov, a physicist. Well, how do you like the cradle of humankind? Yes, yes, of course, I can be more specific. Your Leningrad, for example, is the cradle of the revolution, but the Mediterranean Sea is the cradle of humankind. Our Black Sea, this very sea, is part of the Mediterranean. Well, did you catch my joke? Excuse me, have you already had dinner, Olga-dash-Natalia? Of course I know you are Valentina, but since you've smiled it must mean that you understand humor. We will have dinner in an atmosphere of humor and good spirits, without once mentioning physics or ballet."

The prices in the restaurant turned out to be catastrophically low and the menu clearly humdrum. It seemed to be saying: eat, but don't stay too long. However, Vladislav Ivanovich absented himself for a minute to talk with the waiter Gera, whom he "charged up" to the point of the latter's complete amazement and the table was soon covered with food delivered directly from the hard-currency store.[13] Valentina Sokolova's head was spinning. She is so exquisite, Vetryakov thought as he noticed how the ballerina shut her eyes at the sight of eels and rock lobsters. Wow, am I going to gorge myself on all this, Sokolova thought with her eyes closed.

"What music do you like, Valentina?"

"I like baroque music," the ballerina opened her eyes: hope I didn't spread it on too thickly with the "baroque";[14] that it wasn't too much, the physicist won't smirk.

But he was already walking in a vigorous manner towards the orchestra, towards the seven boys in the Seven Wheels group, those truly distinct optimists of life.

"Hit the baroque, guys!" he requested and "charged" them up so forcefully for the entire evening that the "seven wheels" began at first to spin off in different directions, but then quickly recovered and cut right in to what they were asked for—the rock-'n-roll tune "Memphis."[15]

"Oh, Valentina, Valentina," Vladislav Ivanovich was saying at the beginning of dinner. "I look at you, at your gentle movements, your oval face, your manner of drinking and eating and once more I confirm my credo: down with pessimism! What a grave mistake was committed in the past, in the Middle Ages when in ignorant minds the thought was born that 'there is no happiness in life'! A very unfortunate mistake, Valentina, which is now being corrected by the whole march of history. Well, tell me then, isn't it happiness to eat together? Well, look around: we sail together through the cradle of humankind, the orchestra is playing baroque music, we're eating delicious fish together..."

"And shellfish! Yes, shellfish..." Sokolova suddenly let out a rather strange whirling burst of laughter and held up a lobster by the tip of its claw with her spinning fingers. Her neatly combed bird head was already spinning too.

"And shellfish!" Vladislav Ivanovich picked up the wonderful word in delight. "Yes, of course, shellfish!"

Suddenly, something unpleasant stung Vetryakov as he looked once again at the ballerina's spinning paw. Something was missing. A cold current penetrated that bouillon sea of Vladislav Ivanovich in a thin stream. What was missing? Suddenly it dawned upon him: the paw was minus a ring, a fetchingly beautiful ring. It was necessary as soon as possible to eliminate this injustice, to correct this defect. Vetryakov laughed even more happily: tomorrow in Yalta he'd go to a jewelry store! The anticipation of placing a ring on Valentina's paw even brought him a certain excess of happiness. There are people in this world whose nature it is to fear excessive happiness, who see in it some instability, some elusiveness, but Vladislav Ivanovich was not one of them. He had his credo: man is born to happiness as a bird is to flying!

"Oh, ye gods!" giggled the ballerina.

"Gods of Olympus!" Vetryakov exclaimed as he looked around. They had already started a third bottle of champagne and it could now very well be that one of the passengers might turn out to be from the Olympian assembly.

"You run into acquaintances everywhere, here too," Valentina laughed irrepressibly and teased a group of people who had just arrived and were standing and looking around in the center of the hall. She teased them with her delicate tongue, with her paw which was still missing a ring, and with the lobster claw. "Oh, gods, it's as if I'd never got out of VTO..."[16]

"Representatives of Art!" exclaimed Vetryakov. "What a stroke of luck! We physicists very, very much like to eat with the people of art!"

He launched himself towards three men and two ladies, bowed and scraped, and dragged them along with him, waving to Gerasha with one hand (Give me some advice, friend!), and gestured with the other towards the orchestra (Hit it with the baroque, guys!). He dragged them to his table without paying attention to their bewilderment or slight resistance. "Valyusha, greet your friends! Don't be shy, comrades! The union of science and art, and life itself, prompts us to get together!"

At this point we should stop and rack our brains a bit as to what, within acceptable limitations, is not forbidden even when you're writing a story. There may be a certain anxiety as to whether our situation may seem rather artificial: as soon as the suspicious rich man found his stride on the steamship, the author immediately palms off "art people" on him. Having made this gesture of apology to the readers, I can freely and calmly seat the newcomers, because within the limits of literary convention these "people of art" are somehow no longer people or even figures, but mere phantoms—literary clichés.

One of them, who looked like a lion, was quite old! However, an expression of eternal amazement made him look younger and livelier, because amazement is not a quality of old age or a stiff lion-mask and, therefore, although he resembled a lion, the resemblance wasn't great.

"Melonov!! He's very famous!"

The second was a typical faun with reddish curls which protruded in some spots on his head as if under the pressure of horns. The corners of his sensual mouth were slightly raised, but he looked sad. Since the feeling of sadness is not very well developed in fauns, he resembled a certain sort of atypical faun.

"Razdvoilov!! He's very talented!"

The third was quite sultry; the back of his head was straight and flat, the outlines of his face and figure were decisive and severe. He looked like some toreador. However, for some reason he very often closed his eyes (can you imagine such a habit in a toreador?) and made a lot of unnecessary movements with his hands: for example, he'd put the palms of his hands to his ears, lips and eyes; cross his fingers; or swing now his right, now his left arm. All this is probably not very typical for toreadors, so consequently it was only remotely that he resembled a toreador.

"Charov!! He's very witty!"

The fourth was a lady who resembled a lioness born to be free (she was by no means the match for the surprised lion). Her age and experience on stage had helped her to accumulate a tremendous energy reserve and, of course, a barely restrained aggressiveness. This really made her look like a lioness; the air of danger was all around her.

"Yazykatova!! A terror of a voice!"

The fifth was a nymph, not a mischievous one, but a dreamer. Her softly streaming hair and languishing eyes seemed to wander off somewhere or were perhaps concentrated on one thought—on a daydream of Attic groves—and they made her look like a true dreamer-nymph.

"Svezhakova!! The embodiment of femininity!"

It wasn't clear, precisely, who these celebrities were, either to us or to Vetryakov. But that isn't really essential. The main thing is that they were poets and artists!—It's such a pleasure to see you in person, just like that, in the flesh, and to eat together! Please, don't attempt to pay for yourselves, I beg you, please, don't be offended! Do you have quail on the menu? Gerasha, bring us three platters of quail hen! Garnish and decorate them! Flambé them like they do in France! Wait, wait, hang on... let me send something to the kitchen, here, give the chef this greeting from our table, he deserves it, no two ways about it: he's a real professor of the Academy of Stomachs! Bravo! Bravo! What did you say? The feast of Lucullus?[17] That's really a great joke! Someone suggested a song, any objections? "Let the days of our life flow like the waves, we know that happiness awaits us ahead!"[18] ... Let's drink to... to... let's drink, comrades, to... what should we drink to?... to friendship, comrades! To the friendship of men and women! Let's never part, never, eh? Never, never, okay? Let's meet in Moscow! I invite you all to the Arkhangelskoe! Or to the Tower of the Seventh Heaven, agreed?[19]

"You'll never get in there, to that celebrated 'Seventh Heaven,'" Razdvoilov said.

"What did you say?" Vladislav Ivanovich was taken aback. "What do you mean won't get in? That's just not possible." At that moment he realized that perhaps Razdvoilov, being an artistic person, did not understand the little practical matters of life and, with a wide smile, Vetryakov made a common although somewhat familiar gesture, rubbing his thumb and index finger.

"Not so, bribes aren't accepted everywhere," Razdvoilov winced, "these days there are foreigners, delegations, and tourists everywhere, but...," he coughed and added, "damn it...."

"It's when you don't offer enough that they don't accept," Vetryakov explained in an instructive tone. "For example, if I come upon some obstacle, I begin with a hundred. They don't take one hundred—I give 'em two hundred; they don't take two hundred I give them three. Anybody will take three hundred. You don't believe me? Try it!"

For some reason Razdvoilov took in this practical advice as a joke and burst out laughing.

"So, you are a physicist?" asked Charov. "Theoretical?"

"Both theoretical and practical."

"He is an outstanding physicist!" sang Valentina Sokolova, reeling in her easy chair.

"Then, of course, you know Shalashnikov, Zakharchin, Gerd, and so on?" Charov continued.

"I know a lot, but I'm not allowed to talk about everything," bragged Vladislav Ivanovich with a studied air of importance. He nodded silently, staring straight into Charov's eyes.

"You mean the Problem? Are you assigned to the Problem?" asked Melonov, entering into the conversation.

Vladislav Ivanovich drooped slightly, although he knew that such lulls were unavoidable at parties like this, that there was nothing terrible about it, that in just two or three more steps they'd crest the ridge beyond which happiness would begin again.

"Enough of these stupid questions!" ordered Yazykatova. "Can't you see what a magnificent physicist Vladislav Ivanovich is?!"

The nymph Svezhakova held out her hand to Vetryakov in silence.

There it was, that gesture, that Olympian gift! Yes, yes, of course, let's dance and let's offer each other the movements of our tantalizing bodies.

In the Trade Winds Restaurant on the upper deck of the liner *Caravan,* a dance had been storming in full swing for some time now. Below, in the Albatross Restaurant, the dancing was also stormy. Still further below in the Dolphin Restaurant, the dances were just as stormy and undoubtedly the dancing that went on in the open areas of the stern and the bow were just as stormy. It should be added that in hundreds if not thousands of restaurants all along the Black Sea the dances were indisputably and simultaneously storming in full swing. Moreover, I assume full responsibility for the claim that dances were storming in full swing at that hour all over that enormous region of the country from Dikson to Batumi.[20] The dancing was limited only by the corresponding meridians beyond which dances had already ended in the east and had not yet started up in the west. During recent years stormy restaurant dances have become a distinct phenomenon in our country and, therefore, I may allow myself a short digression. After all, I myself used to dance quite a bit and I remember it perfectly well. I even intend to describe the dances of preceding decades at some future date. Therefore, I have the nerve to say that such body freedom as was found in dances of the late '70s had never been seen before in Russian society. Barriers of age and size were broken down. The seductive sounds of saxophones and guitars drew into the whirling circle huge ladies, falling out of their ruffled dresses, and modest men who, it would seem, should have been more disposed to playing dominoes and, in their turn, out-of-breath captains of our industry who danced alongside asexual longhairs in jeans. Chairs were knocked over and the problems of everyday life were forgotten.

What a soothing and exhilarating freedom of gesture! The rhythm of the rock-'n-roll shimmy is society's way to happiness! Everything is allowed in these frenzied and selfless dancing collectives. Nothing and nobody provokes suspicious glances. There's shouting, noise, laughter. Everybody joins in singing the chorus "Ah, Odessa, pearl of the sea!" It's the marvel of our lifetime—this spontaneous Soviet upsurge of dancing. They say that even foreigners are surprised.

Through the mass of dancers Yazykatova approached the orchestra, striding with the springy gait of a wild animal through a predawn savannah.

"Now I'll rock them in the 'retro' style!" The lady in beige pants leapt onto the stage, leering at Vladislav Ivanovich with a dangerous, voluptuous smile.

While Vetryakov was jumping in the crazy "baroque" dance and following the ecstatic and sinuous body of the dreaming nymph with glistening eyes, he caught a few glimpses of a table at which a heavyweight company of half-breed males from the Caucasus was sitting.[21] And each time he caught sight of this table, a little black trail of residual alcohol appeared in his soul under the dome of happiness, like the vapor of an invisible jet. Vladislav Ivanovich quickly determined that the focal point of the group was a thickset but certainly not fat man with the huge forehead of a Mao-Tse-Tung, the jetblack eyes of a Pugachev, and the bushy sidewhiskers of a Denis Davydov.[22] This man, just like a *bogdykhan* (a Chinese emperor), was stretched out in a Finnish armchair with his body quite relaxed. He was clad in a close-fitting lace shirt through which an undershirt was visible; a black Sochi tie with an ominous outerspace design worked in silver thread slashed downwards like a sword.[23] The others addressed their toasts and told their jokes precisely to him, to this dark-complexioned bogdykhan of mysterious, but related (for such it seemed to Vladislav Ivanovich) physiological structure; he heard them out attentively and solicitously, laughing and stretching his hand to each storyteller for the congratulatory handshake. As Vladislav Ivanovich determined, they were also optimists, of course, but not quite optimists of the same type, not quite from the same circle to which he and his friends belonged. These were rather heavyset and somewhat antiquated optimists and, perhaps because of that, the thin vapor of residual alcohol afterburn appeared in Vetryakov's heavens every time he glanced into that corner. Especially that one brief moment when it seemed to him that the bogdykhan had winked at him almost imperceptibly! Oh no, no, all this didn't deserve his attention! His happiness wasn't disturbed, for his happiness was here, all around him: the "baroque" and "retro," with everything bubbling over!

"No need to be mournful!" Yazykatova sang in a low, knee-buckling roar, slapping herself on the thigh. "The time will pass for separations! For all previous sufferings! The reward will come!"

That's how everything kept going, how everything kept bubbling and boiling until Vetryakov discovered himself alone at a table which recalled the half-destroyed but still breathing Pompeii. The art people had sloughed off somewhere, and the entire Trade Winds was already empty. The lights had gone dim and the waiters and cleaning ladies, exhausted by the partying crowd's maddening pressure, wandered inertly among the tables as if they didn't know how to approach them.

"Gerasha, my precious, if you please—the bill, a cigar and a cognac."

That's what it means to charge up a person properly from the beginning, to awaken the friend in him. Without any haggling over whether, say, "the buffet is closed" or some such, Gerasha brought out a tray with a glass of Martel, a cigar and a four-digit number on a slip of paper.

With the cigar in his teeth Vladislav Ivanovich walked out onto the promenade deck which was bathed in moonlight and glanced around at his sea neighborhood floating at that hour in a cloud of abundance (as one would expect). It was a marvelous plain of deserted sea, ennobled by light from heaven, and the *Caravan* moved across it as powerfully and confidently as the destiny of mankind. And something akin to that cloud of abundance, illuminated by the slightly mournful, but infinitely noble light of the moon, reigned at that moment in Vladislav Ivanovich's soul, and, at that moment, in this cloud of abundance he seemed to himself to be a powerful foreign ship which brings people the gift of goodness and happiness. It didn't matter that he had been stranded right now by Valentina, the nymph Svezhakova, and even by comrade Yazykatova: they had already received from him a certain "charge" of human warmth and were therefore no longer alien to him.

On the deck he caught sight of a lonely figure whose coat collar was upturned. It was Razdvoilov, gazing into the depths of the starry Pont.

"What are our thoughts about, friend?" Vetryakov asked him quietly.

"About Aristotle," was the answer.

"I'm enraptured," Vetryakov pronounced.

"There's something with which to be enraptured," grinned the sad faun. "Take for example his definition of happiness as the manifestation of a soul which acts in harmony with virtue. Do you see here a connection with the notion of freedom?"[24]

"I'm enraptured."

"There is something with which to be enraptured—to have said so much, so long ago."

"I'm enraptured with you," Vetryakov said. "Standing like that on deck with your collar upturned and thinking about Aristotle!"

The faun turned his wide smiling face towards him as if to say: who else is there to think about Aristotle here if not me, the classical goat-legged voluptuary? The faun's ears suddenly seemed to become pointed. What did he hear in that even rumble of the sea? Was it the tapping of a woman's heels breaking down under?

"Excuse me," he moved Vladislav Ivanovich aside and hurried off somewhere into a sparkling shade where there was a fleeting glimpse of something light and fragile.

"What happiness it is to serve art...," Vladislav Ivanovich was saying in the morning into a telephone receiver as he lay in his presidential super-deluxe bed. "You must always be happy, Valentina, because you bring to fruition a manifestation of the soul which acts in harmony with virtue."

"I'm deeply unhappy, Vladislav Ivanovich!" Sokolova sobbed from the depths of the ship. "My joints are growing old. I have never had an ear for music. I memorize my moves like a doll from the village sticks. I hide everything from everyone... except from you, dear Vladislav Ivanovich..."

"Take heart, Valentina, console yourself," he billed and cooed as he looked through the window at the stupendous blueness of the sky. "Up ahead we have Yalta. Just think about us having that yet to come—pearly Yalta!"

Right then and there some metal spring of wonderful anticipation really seemed to cast him upward. Detached from his marvelous mattress (having "taken off," that is, into the air), he caught a glimpse through the window of the undulating blue Crimean mountains and the houses scattered along the slopes, and then he spread out his hands and bounced down again onto his super-mattress just as there sprang to his eyes the clean and friendly face of the floor attendant Lyuda...—"Oh, I've just dropped in to see you, Slava, run by for a little money. The girls are offering stocking-boots..."—followed by a new take-off (but this time with a flip head over heels), a dive into the refrigerator, the burning delight of Carlsberg beer, a quick go under the shower, under a Braun razor, under a Dior atomizer and into the Safari, and..., and... once again all that physics and all that jazz started up.

"According to Aristotle's teachings, every form of matter derives from the unity of four elements: earth, air, fire and water. You find these four elements everywhere, no matter where you stick your nose. A diamond ring is no exception, either, oh no! Of course, it is non-sense to consider a nine-thousand-ruble ring to be more beautiful than the human finger of a woman. You ennoble this material substance with your finger, Valentina, and not vice versa! The four elements are mixed much more beautifully in a woman than in a diamond. I call on Razdvoilov as a witness. Do you agree, poet?"

"I'm stunned by your gesture," Sokolova said, "what sort of salary do you make?" Vladislav Ivanovich took her heart-touching human hand in his own, turned it over like a submissive little bird, and kissed her palm on the mount of Venus.[25] He immediately felt embarrassed by this possessive gesture. "If we must talk about money in light of Aristotle's teachings, then we have to say that there is nothing more primitive with respect to the very process of creation (if, of course, we don't go to the real source—that is, trees) from which money matter is known to be produced, at least according to our scientific circles. Having already moved on to trees, however, we can easily imagine the combination of the four elements in their gigantic trunks. Look how they tower above the waterfall! Well, here we are. We've docked..."

Having delicately outstripped his guests so as to enter the Waterfall establishment ahead of them, Vetryakov quickly charged up the entire personnel—for you! and you! and you! and you, too, my pretty one!—with such lightning-fast shots of optimism that here, once again, we find ourselves in the midst of comfort and tranquility under the quietly rattling crystal mane of a rare phenomenon in nature and, again, we are philosophizing:

"So, you despise money, Slava?"

"No, I respect it, but not more than trees."

"You would've made a good philosopher," Charov cracks a joke.

"What do you prefer: sturgeon on a skewer or shishkebab? I'll make no secret of the fact, my friends, that I have always been attracted to dialectical materialism. I regret that I didn't get any special education in that area. I envy you poets. I deify you. I still cannot believe that we are eating together."

Everybody around the table was laughing and such a relaxed atmosphere was established that they all began to behave eccentrically, to return to the first principles of Aristotle. Let's say, there's a marketplace right before our eyes: earth, air, fire and water are mixed together here and become the embodiment of marvelous vegetable creations with their nutritive souls. We load our hands up with everything, in antique, unlimited quantities: strawberries, cherries, radishes, and, most importantly, flowers, flowers, flowers! The earth gives us its fruit as a gift and we give it our unlimited aspiration for happiness, for beauty. Slava releases flocks of green papers from his sleeve, like a magician. The super-deluxe—crammed full with gifts from the Mediterranean and, alternatively, with goods from the Common Market—is transformed for many hours into a hearth of happiness and artistic, intellectual communication. Trays of roasted meat are brought to the table: lambs and pigs—those possessing two types of souls, the nutritive and the sensory. "Nature is both demonic and divine. Isn't that right, Razdvoilov old buddy? Am I saying it right? Isn't that what Aristotle taught us? People possess three types of souls, my friends: the nutritive, the sensory, and the rational; I'm not mistaken, old man, am I?" "Ha-ha-ha, an extra soul gives us an opportunity to fill our stomachs with both flora and fauna," Charov cracks a joke. "Comrades, in all our passion for classical thought let's all the same reaffirm that we are materialists. We shouldn't forget what it is that's made us what we are, namely, work and struggle!" "What struggle could possibly be under your wing, Slava?" "Gentlemen, I am obliged to declare that I have already lost my rational element," said Melonov. "Let's blend with nature, become plants and animals." "I'm a dandelion." "And I'm a goat!" "And I, dear men, am a caress, a creature still unknown to anyone, I'm a caress—an enormous caress. I want to go to Greece, I want to go to a leafy grove..."

"Slava, why aren't we dancing, why aren't we singing? Suggest something for everyone to sing!"

> No matter what you say,
> There really is no way
> For a king to be wed,
> Even one king, through love!

roared Super-Deluxe No. 02. Vetryakov was whirling all over the fluffy carpeting, bumping all up and down his guests—the invited and the uninvited, the known and the unknown. "What marvelous creatures they are," he thought about them rapturously. "No, no, Vadik Razdvoilov and our teacher Aristotle are right a thousand times over: life is the aspiration of moral earthly creatures to realize the potential which lies within them."

"Vladislav Ivanovich, they say that you are a colossal swindler, is that true?" Yazykatova asked him at one point.

"No, of course, it's not true, Varvara, it is utter nonsense. Judge for yourself! What have we got to steal in physics—a handful of neutrons, a jug of plasma? Who needs it? Everyone already has it. You won't find 'goods in high demand' in physics today, that's all in the past. Of course, if you need anything from somewhere else—a sheepskin coat, say, jeans, a quartz watch—that wouldn't cause me any difficulty. Of course, that doesn't mean I'll steal those things somewhere, Varvara. Even if you wanted to, you couldn't steal such things, and I don't even want to. Stealing is repulsively primitive; it's the base impulsive move of a reptile. Yesterday at dinner or at breakfast or sometime in between Vadik was discoursing upon the upper limit of human feelings. He said that a feeling of friendship is located at the upper limit. I applaud this, Varvara. Friendship is my hobby. A friend is what I am. I work at the upper limit. I have a great number of friends, and I help them to recognize one another, to really get to know each other. By uniting strong characters I arrange the vital design, the pattern of life. Did you understand me, Varvara? The net of human relations had need of a modest unselfish spider and I sometimes play that role. Do you understand?"

"I would understand better if you explained it by means of an example," Yazykatova's exceptional face reflected the powerful work that thoughts do.

"Please, suggest your own example, Varvara."

"Well, here's an example for you," Yazykatova subtly smiled. "My book of memoirs, *Keeping Step with the Song,* is to celebrate my fortieth year as a creative artist and entertainer. Could you fix it up with a publisher?"

"That's not one of the easier tasks, but let me give it a try right now," Vetryakov answered quickly, leaned back in his chaise lounge, closed his eyes and began to whisper something.

In contrast, Varvara Yazykatova turned as tense as a spring on her chaise lounge as, with screwed-up eyes, she followed the movements of his lips and tried to guess where the thought was moving to behind them. An amazing woman, by the way, this vocalist Yazykatova! Vast experience in life helped her to adapt her appearance to any and every trend. Age no longer played even a minor role. In the morning at the edge of the swimming pool she was the very picture of youth—in a transparent robe and with flowers! In the evening, in a restaurant, she was an alluring lioness experienced at sweet battles. And should the conversation turn to questions of social status or to the rankings in art, there would appear before you a stern, asexual and ageless public figure.

So, what could one guess from the way Vladislav Ivanovich's lips stirred? What thought was at work?

"Felix... let's start with Felix... Felix plays on Saturdays with Volodya and Mikhail Yegorovich... we'll reinforce Felix with Seryozha, who will drop by together with Inessa... Inessa and Gordeyev's wife are friends... Mikhail Yegorovich has access to Gordeyev... Gordeyev has access to Storozhova, Svetlana Maximovna, and we'll reinforce her from the other side with Rezo, whom my Gachik will call... Storozhova, already, can handle it... can... already at... can handle it at the level of Kapis... and if Kapis himself withdraws, then..." That's how Vladislav Ivanovich moved, scarcely audibly, around the system, the network of his friendships, and it reminded Yazykatova of a certain pulsating and gelatinous-but-solid mass charged with electricity. "Why there's where Tolya is!" he shouted suddenly at the top of his voice and gaped joyfully with his light-blue, nearsighted eyes wide open. "Varvara, consider the contract already signed!"

"Slava, how free you are with the money," said Melonov on one occasion.

"Want to know why? Because money is an anachronism! Of course, even now it provides for some things, and it's a joy to see how good feelings are revived in people when you give them these green designs, but believe me, friends, money is losing its meaning year by year in this epoch of high demand. I often live for months practically without money... No, no, that doesn't mean I don't spend it; it means that I don't earn any. I sort of forget about it, do you understand me?"

What fullness of life! As he looked from the summits of the Crimean mountains or from the slopes of the Caucasus at the foamy outlines of the land, at the blazing blueness of the sea, and at the *Caravan* waiting below with her ultra-modern inclined masts, smokestack that looked like a sea lion, and the mirror of a swimming pool on her upper deck, Vladislav Ivanovich could actually feel the sensation, as he gazed at all this, of that extraordinary trepidation which is the property of genuine life.

At this particular moment we ought to take note that this man's character was, indeed, like that: he never considered bad weather, slush or penetrating cold to be typical for our planet; he always traversed those periods without retaining any memory of them. The memory of this creature called Vladislav Ivanovich Vetryakov was reminiscent of a kaleidoscope in which only that which is bright and friendly assumes various crystalline combinations;[26] when something amorphous and brownish-gray came to the surface from certain

muddy depths, say, from his childhood (for example, standing in line
for flour during that postwar year of famine; the black-ink numbers on
his frozen paws that were tormented by hangnails), well, right then and
there the kaleidoscope shuddered and the carnival began anew.

"It'd be so nice if all my people, all my friends were to turn up beside me right now! After all, there are people well attuned to sitting at
anyone's table and sharing anyone's company, people whom one
might just as easily call physicists as lyricists:[27] say, for example, Lyova,
or Gagik, or, hey, Stepan Nikolayevich. Now that's true super-happi-
ness: to bring old friends together with the new ones."

Vladislav Ivanovich entered a telephone booth, dropped several 15-
kopeck coins into the automat, and began to dial Moscow. Why
couldn't Gagik, say, or Stepan, or any other friend fly to some nearby
port today, come on board the *Caravan*, and fling himself into Slava's
welcome embrace and, moreover, into this generally joyful atmosphere—into this Mediterranean cradle of humankind permeated by
wellsprings of contemporary views on the world and by Aristotle's philosophy? The telephones did not answer.

"No need to call, Gibbon," Vladislav Ivanovich suddenly heard a
voice say very closely behind him. The one whom he had called
"bogdykhan" behind his back during the whole trip stood in front of
him; he had opened the door a bit and was leaning against the telephone booth.

"Beg your pardon," Vladislav Ivanovich expressed his surprise in a
most polite manner. "You called me Gibbon, ha-ha-ha, and, that means
this is all a joke..."

"There's no need to call either Levka, or Gagik, or Stepan." The
swollen but not dull eyes on bogdykhan's face, almost black from sun-
tan, studied Vladislav Ivanovich's physiognomy. "Let's go for a walk,
Gibbon."

They started to walk along the shore embankment. Bogdykhan
walked a little bit in front of Vladislav Ivanovich, and one could detect
in the way this bogdykhan walked that exceptional trait of being used
to commanding: not looking back at the person he had invited in the
firm belief that the individual he'd invited would undoubtedly follow
him (was simply incapable of not following).

"I've been watching you," the bogdykhan spoke as he walked. "You
are having a good time in the nicest possible way. I approve. Did you
spend a lot?"

"Excuse me... but I... in a certain respect I'm... even...," answered
Vladislav Ivanovich.

The bogdykhan suddenly stopped, took his companion by the crown button on his blazer and raised his index finger, as black and powerful as an ancient Asiatic symbol, to Vladislav Ivanovich's nose.

"Never have regrets about what you have spent on food and pleasure! If you do, no good will come of it for you! Do you understand me?"

"But I don't have any regrets whatsoever...," babbled Vladislav Ivanovich, "... how can one have regrets? What for? Rather, I'm happy, although I would like, nevertheless, to ask you something. You know about our joke, so does that mean you know...?"

"I know everyone."

Once again, the bogdykhan was walking along without looking back at Vladislav Ivanovich, with his powerful belly in front of him as if it were being taken for a stroll.

"All my friends?"

"Everyone," said the bogdykhan.

"But for some reason I don't know you."

"There was no reason for you to know me. Let's go drink some beer together."

They ducked under the canopy of a local cafeteria and sat down at a table to the side. A waiter gave them an attentive look as he ran past.

"Tell him to bring some good beer," the bogdykhan ordered. Maneuvering between the tables Vladislav Ivanovich dashed after the waiter, quickly "charged" him up and there soon stood before them two mugs of fine, not ordinary, beer.

"You remember the French 'pletfurm' shoes?" asked the bogdykhan.

Vladislav Ivanovich gasped.

"You remember the Scandinavian chandeliers? That Italian laceyshmacey? The Swiss wig-shmig?"

Of course, alas! alas!, Vladislav Ivanovich remembered these "goods in high demand," and he also remembered how they were delivered from the South to various warehouses (whether the warehouses stored vegetables or sanitation equipment was of no consequence); he also remembered and even knew approximately where all these luxuries were manufactured and... and with each new word from this bogdykhan, some black-ink bubbles burst in his kaleidoscope, and he even had to shake his head in order to restore the radiance in it.

"Do you have your passport with you right now, Gibbon?" the bogdykhan suddenly asked.

"What?" Vladislav Ivanovich responded, as if he'd just awakened.

"Passport? Yes, yes, of course, it's here, in my pocket."

"Go to the airport and take a flight somewhere. Perhaps to the Baltic seashore or to Tashkent.[25] But don't go to Moscow. I wouldn't advise your returning to the ship, either. Do you understand me?"

The bogdykhan had already got up from the table when Vladislav Ivanovich managed to collect himself somewhat and to grab this unknown but most important friend by the elbow.

"But how can this be? It's impossible. Just up and fly away?!"

"That's my advice, you understand? I took a liking to you—you were having such a good time of it. So I'm giving you a piece of advice. Whether you stay or fly away, that's up to you."

"But everything I have was left there!" exclaimed Vladislav Ivanovich.

"Don't have any regrets about that!" Once again that rocking Oriental symbol of a brown finger arose before Vetryakov's nose. "Never regret what you've spent having a good time!"

"Oh, I have something different in mind, not those material things!" Vladislav Ivanovich gestured hopelessly with his hand. "I am talking about people, about spiritual matters, about the intimacy of relations, friendship, happiness..."

"Aristotle?" grinned the bogdykhan. "By the way, for three years he taught a boy who grew up to become a bandit..."

"Who?" exclaimed the stunned Vladislav Ivanovich.

"Alexander the Great, don't you remember?"

These were the bogdykhan's last words, and with these words he disappeared from Vladislav Ivanovich's life; he walked out of the cafeteria and confidently conducted his stomach into the dense crowd milling under the royal palms.

After he left, Vladislav Ivanovich sat for a long time in the damp and drafty cafeteria, stubbing a Winston into a saucer while the establishment became noisier and noisier and the beer more and more repulsive although, as before, it still wasn't the ordinary kind. Vladislav Ivanovich laughed dramatically at himself, "the chicken's fried, but the lace was French, the platform shoes Scandinavian, and the great Alexander a Macedonian..."

The cafeteria's red-striped tarpaulin drapes were flopping in the wind, a subtropical darkness was bulging up on the horizon, and the white hull of the *Caravan* stood out more and more distinctly in the pre-storm twilight. The electric excitement was intensifying in the crowd along the shore embankment and in the flock of birds in the sky.

Thus, we make preparations to introduce gradually the next literary cliché into the action of our story: an intensification of the drama accompanied by threatening atmospheric phenomena. Gigantic bolts of lightning appear one after another like eucalyptus trees in the black sky before the inert, stolid face of Sukhumi.[29]

On board the *Caravan* flicker fleeting glimpses of merrily frightened people—in the windows of cocktail bars and cabins, from the bridges on the promenade decks. Nothing threatens them there, inside the womb of this ocean giant, and their fears are merely a continuation of the game. Vladislav Ivanovich is standing behind a corner of the harbor control tower, very close to the ship's gangway, which had been desirable and inviting an hour ago but now concealed within itself the uncertainty, alarm, and collapse of his life. The first drops of rain—heavy, like grapes—fell onto his blazer... One must not scorn the advice of a man such as the bogdykhan, if you want to save yourself. Two taxi cabs slowly make a U-turn on the still dry pavement of the shore embankment. Quick—to the hubbub of the airport, into the swarm of boarding and deboarding masses. But Vladislav Ivanovich is motionless. His gaze moves slowly across the decks of the *Caravan.* What will he see there? Maybe, in the next bushy bolt of lightning, a reflection of the diamond on Valentina's swollen, pitiful finger will flash out for a microsecond or, maybe, there will be a flutter of her shoulders sensitive to the cold or of her earlobes—so touching and tiny in the midst of the universe? Maybe, that Flemish opulence of the table and the faces of all his clever and kind friends awaiting his return from the shore will suddenly flash, dreamlike, through the side of the ship, through its steel hulk. Maybe, a lonely figure will appear suddenly to him—someone burdened with life, wrapped in a statuesque tunic that all the same billows in the wind on the launching deck, which is as distant and soulless as a cliff: what loneliness, what bitterness—his contemporaries hadn't understood him, he was driven away from Colchis,[30] for three years he had taught a boy and the boy grew up to become a bandit...

Right then the stormy downpour began to pelt down furiously. As if taking no notice of the sheets of water pouring onto him, Vladislav Ivanovich slowly climbed the gangway to board the *Caravan.*

Having used this tempting cliché, we could have finished the entire story just like that, for it is now absolutely clear what lies ahead for him in the future. Nevertheless, he proceeds to his super-deluxe and we have to follow him, whether we want to or not.

In his cabin there fluttered (this verb is not very precise, of course, with respect to how it characterizes movement, but its metaphorical sense is quite precise), yes, so there fluttered a splendid rosy soul—the floor attendant Lyuda.

"Slava, doll, I dropped in again for some money. I took two hundred, okey-dokey? Oo-oo, you are all wet, Slava, my pet! Well, come
here, taik a baf, a bat.., bas... damn, I've forgotten again where you're
supposed to stick your tongue in that damned English language."

Nimble, womanly fingers; the heated breathing of a woman's care.
"Excuse me, Lyuda, I'm rather in an ambiguous situation, always, when
I'm with you. On the other hand, I don't want to offend you because
you might think that I'm somehow indifferent towards your attributes,
but that's not so at all, I'm not at all indifferent, as you can observe,
Lyuda dear, my darling, but on the other hand... you may think that I
somehow lay claim to you on account of... well, on account of this nonsense, this stupid money and there again I'm afraid of offending
you...." "How could you possibly offend me, Slava, my dearest!" "And
you, Lyuda, you are so dear to me!"

Washed, dried and ennobled by the woman's joyous and fast service, Vladislav Ivanovich walked out into the ship's twilight depths
which were already buzzing with music. Everything was open: all the
cafes, bars, restaurants, dancing halls, and souvenir shops. One could
catch fleeting glimpses of people everywhere. The *Caravan* was already
coursing through the open sea. She had passed the hurricane zone and
the West now glittered with a phantasmagorical sunset extending half
way up the height of the horizon. From the opposite side there approached the enchanting East—no less solid or thick than the West.
Through a window he saw the backs of his friends on the promenade
deck: all the magicians of the arts were present; probably, everybody
was expecting his or her faithful Slava, and everyone was contemplating the sunset. Razdvoilov's touchingly short-fingered paw was traveling quietly along Sokolova's spine. With piercing melancholy, the
thought occurred to Vladislav Ivanovich that for him the coming night
might be the last opportunity in his life when he could make manifest
the acts of his soul in harmony with virtue that's so closely linked with
the notion of freedom. Now he will disappear and buy gifts for them
all, for all those spiritually close to him. A transistor for Razdvoilov, an
Orenburg shawl for Svezhakova, a lacquered Palekh box for Melonov,
some turquoise cufflinks for Charov, a Dagestan necklace for
Yazykatova, and for Valechka Sokolova he'd need to add earrings identical to the rings described above.[31] Oh, how they will be ennobled by
the flesh of her earlobes, skin translucent in a Mediterranean, Venetian
or Genovese sunset. What a design that will make![32]

Everything was done as planned, and the reader can imagine

Vladislav Ivanovich's last night aboard the *Caravan* without the slightest difficulty—all those pre-finale ecstasies. But before us there now looms the problem of a finale, and again my pen tries to avoid existentialist labyrinths, to set off running along the beaten tracks of literary clichés.

Cliché number one. On an early but already dazzling morning the *Caravan* has moored at a dock in the port of Batumi. Among the people on the dock who are meeting friends and relatives on the ship and those who've come out of sheer curiosity are two men on business—OBKhSS officials.[33] Just off to one side is a van with bars on its windows. Vladislav Ivanovich descends the gangway modestly and quietly to face justice. He carries his attaché case in one hand, and in the attaché case are a sweater and toilet articles. The former contents of the chic suitcase no longer concern either our hero or us.[34]

Now he is in the van. There follows a mise-en-scène behind bars. Behind the bar grating are faces, and nearby doves swarm. It is remotely reminiscent of the Russian realistic painting *Life is Everywhere*. Probably, it's not only we, but the hero as well, who make such associations and, therefore, he gently whispers as he glances at the birds, "Life is everywhere..."

He raises his eyes in order to bid farewell to the *Caravan* and he sees three whirling couples on the dancing stage of the ship's stern. Sokolova with Razdvoilov, Yazykatova with Charov, and Svezhakova with Melonov all perform the morning waltz with inspiration, color and selflessness.

"Everywhere there is chic life...," Vladislav Ivanovich thinks quietly, almost philosophically, but no longer says anything.

Cliché number two.

... Vladislav Ivanovich modestly and quietly descends the gangway to face justice. Silence and morning drowsiness reign aboard the *Caravan*. There's routine activity on the docks. The collapse of illusions goes unnoticed. It happens quite often, you must agree: amid the swarming masses of people who move along routinely, there is often present one person inside whom something thunders sacrificially and desperately, but silently. And suddenly, some powerful, unanticipated sound swells behind the scene of capitulation. It is precisely "The Song of a Singer Off Stage"; it suddenly breaks across the Batumi docks in gigantic decibels. Either a drunken sound technician has cut in with it or the energy of the literary cliché has simply materialized by itself:

With passion and languor,
The flame of desires
Stormily throbs
In seething blood!

At that very moment Vladislav Ivanovich sees his friends running towards him, he sees their beautiful eyes, their hands outstretched to
him, their palms turned outward in a gesture of desperate compas-
sion... "Slava, Slava, we love you, you are honest, you are good... an ap-
peal... the jurisdiction..."

"No, no, my friends, don't worry," smiles the happy Vladislav
Ivanovich, "I'm actually somewhat... of a substantial crook..." Diamond
tears glisten on the women's cheeks; Valentina Sokolova—that small,
fragile and forever dear creature—sensitive to the cold and suffering
from polyarthritis—clings to his chest in a farewell embrace.

"Slava, I will wait for you..."

Cliché number three: the rebellion of individualism—march to the
beat of your own drummer![36] The *Caravan* was not successful in escaping the storm; moreover, she fell right into its eye, where she was spun
around by terrible and uncontrolled centrifugal forces and, after that,
the currents of individualistic intention dragged her stern into the
Bosphorous and further—into the Dardanelles—and cast her for a long
time amid the countless islands of the Aegean archipelago until she
could overcome the raging elements and restore herself on an inflexi-
ble course for Batumi.

Contemporary technology triumphed. The liner made its exit—slic-
ing the stormy waves—not having lost, as a matter of fact, a single atom,
a drop, a tiny bit... except for one of her passengers whom nobody
needed anymore, as a matter of fact, because he now represented the
type of individuum who's mutinied.

Meanwhile, as he wiped his glasses and soared in the waves of the
Aegean Sea, the proud and gloomy Vladislav Ivanovich thoughtfully
meditated on a commune-inimical meditation.

"There are no longer individuals in our world; there are only human
systems. By supplying people goods in high demand I am, in essence, a
scoundrel bucking the system. The path of humankind is predestined
by the laws of nature. I will not reform, no matter what the epoch. Let
me be judged here, in the cradle of humankind. Let any social order,
even that of the most primeval age, judge me."

Towards morning the storm calmed down and the water became
warmer. Vladislav Ivanovich managed to doze off a little bit on his back

as he lay on a quietly powerful but soft wave. When he woke up he saw that he was approaching an island with reddish-brown cliffs which displayed all of their folds beneath the rays of the rising sun. Here and there in these geological folds stood white figures who looked like statues; some were standing near the water and some higher up. They were a dozen strong men dressed in white and seemingly sculpturesque clothing that stirred in the gentle breeze: the trial by jury, the philosophers of the Lyceum School....[37]

With that, having tired of literary compromises, we finish the story.

1978

Translated by Joel Wilkinson and Slava Yastremski

RENDEZVOUS

It was a very long time ago,
in the mid-sixties...

He was recognized by everyone belonging to the intelligentsia. The young women from the intelligentsia acknowledged their recognition of him timorously, but the most intelligent ones greeted him with an all-understanding smile. Young experts with rhomboid-shaped pins who came to town on special work assignments made a real public show of their unabashed and enthusiastic recognition of him. They sent bottles of champagne to his table, trying whenever possible to present him with the Brut label, but if that wasn't available, at least a Dry label: "Now then, comrade waiter, you be sure to say that it is from the fellows at Box 14789 Security-Plant."[1] There was a certain haughtiness evident in the recognition of the older specialists, followed later by a serious attempt to establish closer contact so that matters of importance could be discussed in detail. As for foreigners with any degree of intelligence at all, they were always, all of them, profuse with their respects. Foreign professors flocked to see him—tugging nervously at their tweed jackets and tottering, obsequiously but helplessly, in the labyrinths of our powerful Russian tongue; their purpose in consulting with him was to clarify some vitally important question, which they would then develop with all due attention to its importance into articles for scholarly journals and thereby make their contribution to solving the enigma of the Russian soul.

He was recognized, as well, by a lot of individuals in other spheres of society. All those who kept up-to-date on trends and events in contemporary life nodded respectfully to him. Regular policemen and traffic cops from the GAI Traffic Control Department knew him, too.[2] And even the doorman at the Nashsharabi Restaurant remembered his face.

Some half-baked Salieris,[3] spiteful people, put on airs of not recognizing him or, if they did acknowledge him in some way, it was by showing disgust. They'd say that they were already boored-tooo-death with him, that to mention him was offensive and ohh-soo baa-nnal. They'd persist in talking on and on about him, repeating how offensive and banal it was to discuss him, and then they'd launch into such malicious gossip and fantastic anecdotes about him that in due course it became clear what a truly important figure he was for them and their shrivelled and dried-up lives.

But, right now, he was trucking along in his walrus-skin ski-boots purchased last fall in Reykjavik and the coat that was popular for Moscow's gray and white winters, along a soft muddy surface—Gorky Street on New Year's Eve.[4] At this moment, walking in a dense crowd and rarely recognized—only by occasional shouts of greeting—this pensively lanky fellow had suddenly fallen into a melancholic trance.

And, suddenly, publicistic journalism struck him as boring and unnecessary and, equally suddenly, his soul began to pine for the still distant spring, for the encounter which he'd been waiting for all his thunderous life.

You see, he had never given much thought to himself. It had been fights, clashes, refutations, speculations, advancements, and tears of reconciliation in everybody's eyes, but where oh where is there now a teardrop for me, a little one of my own, where are you then?

That Tahitian girl at the poetry reading who, with her softly sparkling Tahitian eyes, had cast frequent glances at him from the third row.... He had seized the opportunity then to shout to her: "You're a Tahitian flower, you're a lotus! And I'm a Russian juniper! Got it? I'm a Russian juniper! Do you understand what a juniper is?" She had nodded to him from within a whirlpool of faces and stretched her slender arm out to him, but the crowd was already carrying him off in the opposite direction.

There, near a gift shop and with the snow falling hard, verses about the Tahitian girl began to take shape and, suddenly, right then and there, having become totally oblivious of his presence before a nationwide crowd that was awed by the sight of him, Lyova Malakhitov, the thirty-three-year-old darling of the people, composed a poem about a Russian juniper:

> I'm a juniper tree, a juniper tree small in stature,
> And you—a tiny, scarlet, Tahitian flower...
> I'm a little juniper tree, up to my neck in snow:
> My berries profit bears who venture where they grow.
> But you, there on some Tahitian shore, must know!
> Don't believe the press, its lies and vanity!

"He's composing!" the crowd whispers.
"Soon he'll let it rip!"
"Lyova, let's hear it!"
"Lyova, quick, strike while the iron's hot!"

Having finished the verses and felt a tremulous shudder, he spied the large number of shining faces all around him. His heart skipped a beat and his blood, pulsing with rapture, started to clamor like bells; he threw open his coat, removed his flap-eared Urals style winter hat he'd bought in Montreal, and began to read....

The big uproar quite recently was the "match of the century." Lyova defended the goal of our country's national hockey team. His defense of the goal was daring and decisive against the attacks of vicious Canadian and American professionals, the all-star team of the Star League. One trio of the Stars' horsemen-forwards was captained by Maurice Richard himself,[5] hockey player numero uno, and an old friend of Lyova's since that emergency landing on the island of Curaçao.

Here's what had happened: at the end of the third period Richard was awarded a "bullet" penalty-shot, that is, a one-on-one duel with our team's goalie, Lyova Malakhitov, the people's darling.

There stood Richard, bent over, with his frightful hockey stick thrust forward. And there stood Lyova, in his goalie's mask, looking like a clown. There they both stood, in a sound vacuum which was unexpected after fifty-nine minutes of tumultuous roaring.

The score's 2-2. Richard's "bullet" will be the last chance for the Stars to win. It's a sure thing, 100 percent odds.

Now the terrifying Richard has started skating towards Lyova. Richard the terrifying and powerful, flashing his platinum teeth, with a pirate's earring in his disfigured ear and a chromium-plated head: he moves to the attack slowly, his muscles bulging like those of the armored Lancelot—Richard the Terrifying, the world's leading gladiator. By no means is he just some Kelowna Packers amateur or other.[6]

"You're coming at me, Maurice," thought Lyova, "you're coming at me, you shaggy red Canadian bison, as Semyon Isaakovich said. O teammates of mine—Loktyev, Almyetov and Alexandrov, Mayorov brothers and Vyacheslav Starshinov,[7] o momma dear, my modest librarian, and you my gray-haired Urals and my nursemaiden Volga, o Nina, my saintly and inaccessible wife, and dear comrades from all sections of society, here I am, standing here before him, a skinny clown, a wretched Pierrot, a simple little shepherd boy from the Urals. Maurice, there's no mercy in you, you've forgotten about everything, Maurice. Do you recall at this second that emergency landing in Curaçao? Do you remember how our Boeing tossed and turned as it fell towards the ocean, and all my gals, my beloved stewardesses, heroically combated our queasiness, and how we leveled out just above the ocean and barely held out to reach Curaçao, and how you and I that night went to a bar with those brave gals from the KLM airline, and, in the bar, how we were recognized and given an ovation, and I played Paganini on my miniature Stradivarius and you, Maurice, shared your expertise in wrestling, and the proprietor, deeply moved, presented the two of us with little triangular watches for which there's no equal on this earth. Where's your watch, Maurice? Mine's in the dressing room. And where's your momma, Maurice, the little cashier for the Salvation Army in your native Quebec? Ah-ha-ha, Maurice, you're about to make a feint and then you're going to hurl that puck as if it were a chunk of your own ruthless soul, but I, the skinny clown, will nab it ruthlessly and it will throb in my glove until it stops zinging, yes, I will nab all 100 of your hopes and we will go our separate ways in peace.

Then, the following took place: suddenly, Lyova lunged forward and fell onto the puck. Richard skated through him splendidly, gliding brilliantly over the ice. The puck flew off against the sideboards behind the goal. Lev shot after it like a rocket and with his lean, trim stomach pressed Richard's bisony buttocks against the boards. Together, they both slammed down on the ice and the puck, like a top, spun off a short distance. Afraid to stand up on their legs, they both maneuvered their stomachs around and, suddenly, our Lyova swirled halfway around impetuously and covered the puck. Scattering sparks, the chromo-horrific Richard slowly skated up to Lyova, now back on his feet, gave him a tap on those pale Ural eyes with his stick, heaved a sob in an apparent recollection of Curaçao, and clasped him in a bear hug. They both began to cry. The picture of the kiss they gave each other was printed in all newspapers of the world; even the *Jen min jih pao* published it, although its true, under the rubric "Their Morals."[8]

A thickening twilight altered the day's coloration. The light began to turn dark-blue, with streaks of white, and then grew to be whiter and whiter; snow fell in flakes the size of a handkerchief. Distinctly, one by one, the kerchiefs glided down and the dark-blue sky, already almost black, barely peeped out between them here and there, only peeped, and Lyova had turned white all over, and even wobbly like Father Frost.

He ran up to a snow-covered telephone booth, tore open the door and hid from view. It was an ordinary glass-and-snow shield, but inside it was gloomily warm and comfortable, and there was a smell like that of innocent sin (a thousand memories!), and here everything rose up before him in the little holes of the telephone receiver—beginning with the childhood stuff ("Is this the zoo? No? Well, why's there a monkey on the phone, then?") and ending with that of the adult male of today (a call home to my wife Nina, the saintly and inaccessible).

"Nina?"

"What's the matter?"

"It's me, Lyova."

"What's wrong?"

"Uh-h-h... well... I... don't think... Ninochka, it's just Mishka Tal and Tigran... we were glued to our chairs, you understand? Ninok, Nitush... we were analyzing Bobby's last game."[9]

"Why should I care?"

"Well, of course, you're thinking...."

"I'm not thinking... ('that I've been with some chicks...') anything! (... 'Athenian nights, I know...') I'm not thinking anything ('... you don't believe me, you...')! I'm not thinking anything!... ('you think that...').

"...I'm a scoundrel, a cut-loose ('... When at last...') type, but I really love... ('...when, at last...') you, you're saintly, but I'm a pitiful sort... ('...when, at last... will these sobs end?')."

Silence....

"Ninok, what are you doing?"

"Reading."

"What?"

"'Stavrogin's Confession.'"[10]

"Why the ooh?"

"That's interesting."

"Have you read it?"

"Ninochka!"

"You're lying!"

... silence, in the booth an aside in an almost inaudible whisper: "No prophet in his own country...."

"You have your glasses on...?"

"Yes."

"That's my sweet *Bubo Bubo*."[11]

... silence....

I'll use this third pause to tell the story of their love and union.

It's been seven or eight years since they met on a distant Siberian construction site to which Lyova Malakhitov, at that time a truly young youth activist, had come with some undefined goal.

Lyova, then a fly-by-night progressive, was strolling along a viaduct and saying the kinds of things one was supposed to: "Well, then, guys, how's it going? Say, gals, how are things?"—sometimes he would also turn cold, freeze in his tracks, and strike a serious pose—he had caught a vision of Yermak's campfires on Siberia's immense horizon. And soon after his arrival, things started going well at the construction site with the education of the masses in political and social-work activities.

After he'd spent a night conferring with the engineers, Lyova managed to move off dead center one of the crews working on a most important section of the dam.

On one occasion, as he was standing with pole in hand on a wildly tossing raft and racing down the wildly impetuous river, as he was standing with his pole thrust among the breakers and the boulders, as he was standing with his pole in a thundercloud of spray, in the rainbows—drunk with happiness, not booze—as he was standing with his pole on the raft, he suddenly caught a glimpse of a complicatedly lonely gantry crane on the riverbank. It seemed at first that blue searchlights had been installed on the cabin roof, but it was just Nina's eyes. Nina, a minimally educated but dreamy girl, was then working on a tower-crane isolated in the taiga. How often she had dreamed, screwing up her eyes at the river, of the arrival in a cloud of spray of a fairy tale-beautiful and young-looking *Komsomol member*, and here he goes and appears, Lyova Malakhitov!

For Lyova, it was a matter of but a single minute to maneuver abruptly in between the cliffs, to beach the boat at the base of the steel giant, and to prostrate himself at the feet of searchlight-eyes Nina.

They remained, just the two of them, in the cabin of the crane until nightfall, yackety-yakking and heave-hoing, loading and moving the boulders from one place to another in order not to just sit there without doing some work.

Now it was already after the brightly shining day had changed into a flaming red sunset that Nina and Lyova turned up alongside the future hydroelectric porter station. And there, inside a turbine rotor, they made love for the first time.

Long afterwards, a number of tales about their wedding circulated far and wide across the vast expanses of Siberia.

Well, for example, it was said that...

In Moscow Nina spent her time educating herself. Unexpectedly, she manifested exceptional or, to speak more simply, fantastic capabilities. Nina gulped down book after book. No matter what time of night he happened to rouse, Lyova would see her reading, her forehead propped up against the table lamp. First, she went through the classics, then contemporary foreign literature. Simultaneously, she mastered three European languages. And with that achievement she gained entry into the company of the most serious people in Moscow and in this circle she passed judgment, with the proper condescension, on contemporary Russian literature. Then came philosophy—Hegel, Kant, the study of Zen Buddhism, a return to Christianity, and then a new breaking away from it, nighttime tears on the pillow next to the tranquilly snoring Lyova, nighttime tears over the fate of humankind, early-morning seriousness with glasses on her puffed-up face (my sweet Bubo Bubo), attempts to read out loud and the criticisms of her world-famous husband.

In the circle of serious people they talked about Nina's husband with a kindhearted little smile: What do you expect? He's a student idol, fate's spoiled child, poet, hockey and soccer player, musician, construction designer, and, what else? Leonardo da Vinci, hee-hee-hee? Nina suffered and criticized poor Lyova because he led such a flash in the pan life. Lyova's pillow was perpetually flying from the bed onto the sofa. And Lyova would sit in darkness, on the sofa, tug his ears reddened by champagne—no words, o my friend, no signs—and cry.

The reading skills which he possessed were no less than those Nina had and, what's more, he possessed a photographic memory and could, like V. B. Shklovsky,[12] recall everything he had read by heart. But he couldn't devote himself wholly to reading, to immersing himself in philosophy, to sitting at home nights when calls were coming in right and left—Lyova, play..., Lyova, write a..., perform a..., Lyova, design this or that, make a quicky flight here or there, help with this, come to the rescue of..., chew 'em out good... Lyova!

Yes, Ninochka criticized her Lyova for his lack of seriousness, but not at all from jealousy of some imagined crowd of blondes, brunettes, or redheads who, it goes without saying, hang around fellows such as Lyova. These supposed hordes, legions of profligate women, didn't disturb her at night, didn't cause her to grit her teeth at all or to be tormented by insomnia; all that was just nonsense, beneath contempt. She was a person with a solid education and a philosophical mind. Lyova's lack of seriousness—now that's what distressed her!

"Did Oistrakh call, Ninochka?"

"No."

"Well, who did?"

"Stravinsky called from Paris."

"What did he have to say?"

"For Christ's sake!" (Sometimes, something like that just popped out—memory of days in the taiga.)

"Ninok, I beg you, what did Igor have to say?"

"Oh, he's writing a bass solo for you. Do you really sing bass?"

"Nina!"

"You always sang tenor."

"You're having your fun again, eh, Nina? Why are you making fun of my bass voice? After all, that's what God gave me and He alone will take away"... (A plaintive sobbing.)

... Silence to the sound of bu-bu-bu, an elephantine rumble of contre basses (the love of contre basses for all other instruments is well known), the honeyed flow of a flute and a strained forte piano in 2/4 time.

"Where are you off to now, Lev?"

"A New Year's party."

"Ahh-khh!"

"What's that, Ninochka, darling?"

"No strength left to say."

"You've got to understand, they asked as a special favor... the kiddies are expecting it... kids from the Philharmonic, Zoya Avgustovna... well...."

"Ahh, to the devil with all of you!"

Siberian woman: telephone receiver bangs on the hook at the other end of the line in Izmailovo![13] Siberian woman: a running leap and her face buries into the pillow! Siberian tears on "Stavrogin's Confession," and to the devil with 'em all!

As for Lyova, he left the telephone booth and ducked around a corner onto a relatively quiet square where there were patches of unblemished powdery snow; he and a fellow walking four excellent Boxers on a leash exchanged bows, then he ducked under the archway to the courtyard of a gloomy apartment building, and reappeared from there with the courtyard attendant's shovel.

At the rear of the square, about one hundred meters from the memorial statue, there was a hill of snow that reached shoulder height. Lyova cheerfully went at it with the shovel. Scoops with the shovel uncovered a light-blue Moskvich, purchased last year in Rome.[14] The courtyard attendant, a woman, rushed out of the gloomy building.

"Oh, I was wondering what scoundrel swiped my shovel. But it's just you, Lyova, eh?"

"Console me, Marfa Nikitichna!" Lyova exclaimed and pressed his face against her immensely padded shoulder. He had a short cry.

"Here, here, Lyova, why're you, come now... why're you!" the attendant began to squirm as if she were being tickled.

"Thanks, mommy, o mommy mine," he shouted, making no sense at
all.

"My second mommy," he thought, gazing at the attendant's back as
she walked away with the shovel. "No, the third," he corrected himself
as someone else came to mind. "My third mommy: a Russian woman!"

"Marfa Posadnitsa!" he shouted, making even less sense than before.[15]

He turned on the ignition and the little Moskvich began to tremble
feebly.

"My dearest, my true friend," Lyova whispered, kissing his Moskvich
on the windshield, steering wheel, speedometer and ashtray. "My kittie-
cat, puss-puss," and the car zoomed forwards.

Inspector Major Khrapchenko bowed to the pale-blue Moskvich
from his sentry box near the Telegraph Office, Inspector Lieutenant-
Colonel Polupanchenko waved to him on Manezh Square, and
Inspector Lieutenant-General Fesenko shook hands with Lyova at the
entry to the Kremlin's Bronnivitsky Gate.[16]

Lyova parked his "puss-puss" alongside Bronnivitsky Gate and entered the Kremlin on foot.

At Bronnivitsky Gate there is a constant wind current of unusual
force and under the gate's archway the whistling and roaring is like that
in an aerodynamic wind tunnel. And the snow which falls into its zone
sticks together and flies like a solid mass; in it human figures, pelted in
the face and in the back, gyrate helplessly.

Thus, the wind and snow pelted against Lyova, under his "popular"
coat and thermal sweater. Having overcome the resistance with difficulty, having fallen down flat several times onto the cobblestones, and
yet forcing his way into the Kremlin, Lyova swerved around the corner
of the tower to catch his *breath*.

Right beside him the wind was howling and moaning, but just above
his head the snow was swirling peacefully.

Lyova pressed his back up against the ancient brick and turned rigid
as he suddenly heard Blokian music:

> Hurricanes blow,
> The sea murmurs low,
> Snow flees the blast,

> In a moment an age hurtles past,
> We dream of a blest shore at last![17]

In a gap in the dark clouds—my God!—a star suddenly flickered; it winked encouragingly.

Through the glass-marble facade of the Palace of Congresses there shone a candled fairy-tale world: gigantic fir trees in pendulant silver filaments; red, yellow, and light-blue balls and pointed ornaments, bonbonneries, huge fluffs of completely white cotton, and, yes, everything else you might or might not imagine!

Here, right from the start, representatives of Moscow's kiddies fell into the solicitous hands of masked entertainers—buffoons, gray-wolves, Red-Riding Hoods, bunny rabbits and baby foxes, Barmaleis, crocodiles, Aibolits, Buratinos, and Behemoths—*the leaders of the Young* Pioneer organization in the capital and artists from the Central Children's Theater.[18]

The whole atmosphere was charged with anticipation—they were waiting for Father Frost. Zoya Avgustovna immediately led Lyova off to the dressing room, rushing him along the hallway and chastising him mildly for his tardiness. There was a conversation between them. This is what it was:

"Zoya Avgustovna, do you remember... once... in the Crimea... I... I'm possessed... you'll understand...."

"Lyova, doll, put the beard on, right away. The kiddies are waiting."

"Then hoist to the mast your rough sail...[19] Give me a kiss on the cheek... motherly like... right away, I'll...."

"Lyova, doll, the coat and boots...."

"And your coat of invincible mail, mark with a cross on the breast...[20] Zoya Avgustovna, I'm possessed... for I, too, am a human being.... Do you remember, there was a storm?"

"Oh, you forgot the padding! Lyova, doll, unbutton the coat and put on the padding. Hee-hee-hee, that'd be an act now—a skinny Father Frost!"

"You know my Nina, don't you, Zoya Avgustovna... saintly, inaccessible... she's castigating me for a lack of seriousness... I'm anxious about it... I... I...."

"Straighten the beard. That's right. Marvelous. Your sheepskin. The bag. Your trumpet. *C'est magnifique.*"

Massive, rosy-cheeked and with a nose like a potato, Father Frost stood at the threshold of the dressing room and sighed.

"Is it really my life or did you just appear to me in a dream...."[21]

"Lyova, doll, bless you, man!" Zoya Avgustovna began to shout, her eyes goggling in horror, "Bless you! Don't think about anything now! Put yourself into it!"

Puffing obediently and good-naturedly, putting himself into the role, Lyova Malakhitov—Father Frost—ambled along the corridor.

Bear cubs—activists of the Central Young Pioneers' Palace—in bells and ribbons, hopped all around Father Frost.

> Children, children, form a circle,
> Form a circle, form a circle,
> We are friends, yes, you and I are,
> And I love you!—ecstatically shouted Lyova.
>
> Quickly, children, wipe your nose.
> Wipe your nose, oh, wipe your nose,
> He's brought presents, our good host,
> Lyova, jolly Father Frost!—the children shouted

beside themselves with joy.

Dancing jauntily around the circle, Father Frost took in tow a multiracial band of kiddies, among whom a fair number were little Laotian and Cambodian princes.

Soon the gold trumpet was snatched from his bosom and Lyova began to make it sing in such a way that Armstrong himself would have been envious. Indeed, the great Satchmo had already envied Lyova—at last year's Newport Jazz Festival when he alone had vindicated the honor of our music. Louis turned absolutely green on that occasion, and then all gray before he once again blossomed with happiness and returned to being a kindhearted brown Louisianian; the heavenly Ella Fitzgerald dashed on stage and gave Lyova an expansive kiss, and Duke also bubbled over with kisses, and then they all four played together. And how!—several hundred people in the Newport crowd were carried off the field with heart attacks.

Lyova pranced around the tree with his trumpet, his beard and locks flipped and flopped, his padding fell out, and wide pleats of the baggy Father Frost suit flapped lightly and freely in the air. Gifts flew out of his voluminous bag—Eastern sweets, fruits, experimental mechanical toys. The children clambered onto his shoulders; a pair of tots had been sitting on his head for some time already, hanging on by his ears.

Zoya Avgustovna and the Palace Manager were in tears. The tree-trimming party had been a success.

"They criticize him in vain," the manager said, "the critics, paralytics, gnash their molars on him in vain...."

"You think so?" asked Zoya Avgustovna, drying her eyes with light flicks of her lace kerchief.

"I had in mind the caustic lashings, the overkill," the manager corrected himself. "Criticism, of course, is necessary, but not with such voluntarism, mark my words, that's how it'll be."[22]

"In the Philharmonic we keep an eye on everyone," Zoya Avgustovna icily ended the conversation.

Aside from the general gaiety and commotion there stood two mummers—the Buzzard from *The Tale of Tsar Sultan* and the witch Baba Yaga.[23] They were talking in husky masculine voices, talking and glaring intently in Lyova's direction.

"What in the deuce is he jumping around here for, like an idiot, like a hypocrite?" asked Baba Yaga. "What in the deuce is he shaming our whole generation for?"

"And you, in what deuce?" Buzzard sniggered unpleasantly.

"I? In the deuce of Pollitrovich and Zakusonsky!"[24] Baba Yaga exclaimed. "But as for him, he's got everything going for him!"

"Don't get excited," Buzzard rasped, "I see you have some scores to settle with him."

"My score with him is on behalf of our generation!" Baba Yaga cried out fervently, even frightening himself somewhat with the vastness of this idea, but he continued once he'd clenched the bit between his teeth:

"A personal score, too! You remember what the poet once said: 'the best of our generation, take me for your trumpeter!'[25] Who else could be our trumpeter if not this Levka with his talents, but he just clowns around. Our generation is strict, 'fellows with upturned collars,' as the poet said...."

Baba Yaga kept talking in this vein for quite some time, but Buzzard, having crossed the wing-hands over his chest, followed Lyova's movements with his flaming eyes.

"Let's get out of here," he finally said. "They no longer need us here. The forces of evil ought to withdraw."

They left the Palace proudly and majestically—like sad demons, exiled spirits—and for some time they strolled together through the square that crackled with frost.

At about this time the snow stopped falling and a small lake formed an intricate shape in the dark clouds in which the moon appeared, its reflection lackluster on the frost-rimmed cobblestones, the cupolas of the Ivan-the-Great, Archangel, and other cathedrals, the cupolas of the little Church of the Enrobement. Baba Yaga continued to develop his views, but Buzzard kept his silence.

"An amazing individual," said Baba Yaga, "Ghiaurov's bass, Yehudi Menuhin's bow, Konovalenko's reactions, Yevtushenko's pen, Popenchenko's fist, a gifted weaver of verses, and talented in everything, absolutely everything.[26] No matter where you go, he's there—everywhere, Lyova Malakhitov—the star attraction."

"Exactly right," thought Buzzard.

"But this clowning around, these ah-s and oh-s, this exaltation," continued Baba Yaga, "sometimes I think, just imagine, it's not a game, maybe, not a bitching state of affairs, perhaps it's because of a pure heart or something god-like, eh?"

"Exactly right," thought Buzzard and a trifle internally he gnashed his internal teeth.[27]

"Seems it's time," he said, "the party's ended."

They set out together for Bronnivitsky Gate. Buzzard shot a look at Tsar Cannon, and with a sly and malicious joy recalled previous years and the nights he'd spent in the muzzle of this gigantic weapon.

"Time for what?" asked Baba Yaga, "what do you have in mind?"

"Well, haven't you been dreaming of currying Lyova's favor?" Buzzard laughed loudly, "dreaming of basking in his rays, dreaming of getting on familiar terms with him, of sassing him around a bit, dreaming that a few more of your acquaintances will see you together with him? Isn't that right?"

"And just what are you dreaming about?" the barb-tongued Baba Yaga shouted, "isn't it exactly the same?"

Buzzard burst out in a roar of internal laughter with his deep vocal cords.

Happy, red-cheeked, and panting, Lyova strolled towards his car with *travesti* from the Central Children's Theater surrounding him. These tiny actresses—perpetual bunny rabbits and baby foxes—usually return to their feminine selves with difficulty, and by no means do all of them totally return: they peck like fledgling birds; they buzz like a swarm of bees; they smell sweet like flowers; they twist and fidget like their heroes—the bunny rabbits and baby foxes.

"Ai-ai-ai! How little you are," the surprised Lyova cried, "tell me girls, it's probably marvelous, eh, living on the verge of absolute Lilliputianism?"

"Lyova, take us with you! We want to go with you!" the actresses shouted.

"I'll take all of you with me! How many are there? Seven, eight? Everyone crawl into the Moskvich! I'll take you all home."

Near the car two men were waiting for him: one was a ruddy-faced, blue-eyed, and self-searching type; the other a sardonically quiet individual with eyes like dark tunnels, where there shine the yellow lights of a locomotive.

"Hello," the men said.

"Greetings," Lyova replied politely. "I hope you recognize me. Do you? In any event, I'll inform you that I'm Malakhitov. I myself was a volunteer militia man and not a bad one, either, you can believe me. As you see, I'm not doing anything reprehensible. The girls? They're my comrades from work."

"Hey, Levka, don't you recognize us?" the ruddy-faced one said. "Gotten conceited, eh?"

This little word "conceited" was a genuine curse for Lyova. Once he heard it used, our public's darling began to fidget and babble, stuff like "Aw, dammit, forgive me old man, it's my damn visual memory, old man, say, old boy, gettin' what you can?" et cetera. At such times he was rescued by the words "old man" or, depending upon the circumstances, other derivative phrases which he'd mouth, like "old boy," "old buddy," and "old buddy boy." So it was that Lyova began to mumble now:

"Aw, damn it, old men, it's my damn visual memory—old boys, say, old buddies, gettin' what you can?" In reserve there was still "old buddy boys."

"That's it, gramps," the ruddy-faced one rejoiced. "It's not nice of you to forget old pals. Our generation must support one another, pops."

"True, old buddy boy!" Lyova proclaimed, deeply touched by this simple thought. "Here, let me kiss you!" He bussed the powdery cheek of the ruddy-faced one and turned impetuously to the gloomy one. "And a kiss for you, too, allow me!" He kissed the steely cheek and his lips stuck to it, like what happens in childhood when you kiss a sled runner and your mouth becomes frozen to it.

The situation turned rather bizarre: Lyova tried, but could not pull his lips off the steely cheek; the gloomy owner of the cheek stood still, smiling sardonically. Finally, with an abrupt twist of his head, he set Lyova free.

"'ell, then," Lyova muttered in embarrassment. Little drops of blood came to the surface on his lips, but that was of no consequence. The main thing was a feeling of friendship, which unlocked Lyova's soul and left it wide open as he watched the little actresses skipping along and the two people of his own "generation," that rosy-cheeked old friend and the gloomy but likable Mephistopheles. What a pity not to be able to spend the evening with these fellows, he thought, but I really must go home to Nina, beg her forgiveness, immerse myself in her stern intellectual life.

"My friends, our union is beautiful!" he exclaimed. "Some time or other let's spend an evening all together."

"Okay, let's do it right now," Gloomy pronounced in a squeaky, but surprisingly tender metallic voice and, with equally surprising sincerity, gazed into Lyova's eyes.

And once again a bizarre phenomenon took place: Lyova's pupils seemed to freeze, stuck on the cold and yellow train lights immobilized in the two tunnels.

"What a brilliant artistic personality," thought Lyova as he tried hard to wrench his intent stare away from the lights, "what a pity we can't do that right away... have a serious chat right now, open our souls to one another, become of one mind. Verily, verily, one life's not enough for a person...."

The snow maidens, bunny rabbits and baby foxes danced in a circle and sang in their thin voices:

> Our kind Lyova Malakhitov,
> You have a soul that's candid!
> Malakhitov, Lyova, you are kind,
> You're a sacred cow of....

Ruddy-faced, having taken him by the shoulder, hooted into his ear:

"But do you, Lyova, remember Kolka Xenokratov, the one who sat in the back row and chewed paper? Just imagine, he's a laureate now! And Kuzya, remember him? How about his riding into class on the back of the principal, no less... you remember? Just imagine, he's a book reviewer... on his sixth wife already!... No, brother, our generation...."

Lyova jerked his head, trying in vain to tear his eyes away from the yellow flames. "There's a real nuisance for you," he thought, "I don't even remember the last names of these most distinguished fellows of my generation. Have I really gone and got conceited? Shame, shame...."

"As a matter of fact, why couldn't we set off somewhere right now?" he exclaimed. "Let's whip over to the Nashsharabi, watcha say, old buddies, old pals?!"

The yellow lights backed off with a jerk and shifted into faintly discernible dots. Lyova freed himself and jumped into the Moskvich. Chirping raucously, the travesties found themselves places in the back seat, and Lyova's peers took seats next to him. Already overwhelmed with a stimulating wave of joy, Malakhitov switched on the ignition.

"Won't take," Moskvich suddenly pronounced with a cough.

"Don't shame me, don't shame me, don't shame me, pet," Lyova mumbled heatedly and rapidly as he fawningly but unobtrusively stroked the steering wheel with his tongue.

"Won't take; that's that!" Moskvich turned stubborn. "I'm no tank or tractor that's fit to haul such freight. Let one of 'em get out...."

"But who, who?" Lyova asked.

"He'll know himself...."

It stands to reason that this dialogue wasn't heard by anyone in that honorable company, but Gloomy Peer just happened to guffaw loudly and climb out of the car.

"Don't want to cramp anyone, fellers, so I think I'll just get there on my own. Ciao!"

With these words he dashed off towards the nearest churning eddy of the snowstorm and disappeared. Immediately, the Moskvich started up and drove off to the world-famous Nashsharabi Restaurant along well-beaten paths.

O Nashsharabi, Nashsharabi, you've eclipsed Maxim's and the Waldorf Astoria!! O, you Mecca of our century's sixties! Is there a heart—whether from Moscow, Leningrad, Siberia, the Urals, or, yes, of any human being, even a Dane—which doesn't flutter when entering through this archway with tiger faces and ox-eyed beauties, through this archway which retains and blabs out so many secrets, which has heard so many oaths and toasts and has even been embarrassed by bragging lies, through this archway where the "wild melody of the clarinet" and the biological howl of the saxophone swing,[28] where the stupefying scent of the house specialty—Seywha (calf ears and chicken rumps in a sauce made with a Caruso cocktail)—drives even the experienced gourmets of Barbizon to distraction, is there a heart that doesn't flutter?

It's not at all known what means of transport Gloomy Peer used, but he was already awaiting Malakhitov's company near the restaurant, standing a bit to one side of the line left over from last year, in which people were caked with snow.

"This one with you, Levka?" the doorman Murat Andryanych asked.

Andryanych was such a hefty fellow that he thought nothing at all of addressing even the most respected citizens informally, though he would exchange polite, reciprocal niceties with those whom he didn't let in, that is, with practically all humankind.

"With me, with me, Andryanych!" Lyova exclaimed. "Greetings to you, Andryanych from Thor Heyerdahl!"[29]

"Notify Thor I reciprocate, my regards," Andryanych whistled.

Such greetings, I tell you—the warm signs of human concern—were more dear to the old man than the most generous tips. For is the meaning of life really in the tips one gives? Ponder that one yourself!

With little travesties clinging to him, Lyova entered the vestibule of the restaurant, arm-in-arm with his peers.

"Malakhitov with his children," the line whispered respectfully, "seven daughters...."

"And those two, who are they, his brothers?"

"Friends. One's a boxer from the GDR and the other's Cosmonaut 10."

"Cut it out, comrade. They're Malakhitov's colleagues."

"Think you know more than anyone else, eh?"

"Can you imagine it? I do. My wife's sister...."

The evening hadn't turned out to be a failure for the people in line after all.

"There we were, chewing the cud and not wasting our time. We saw for ourselves how Lyova Malakhitov made his entry with seven Japanese girls. What a sight—handsome, shapely, in a thermal sweater made of semi-conductors. Ooo-eee, Lyova's sweater was made to order by Levi Strauss himself at the Philips plant, and it's permeated throughout with platinum wires that heat you up or cool you off, when ya wanna, depending upon the outside temperature...."

Reserved, yet with dramatic flair, Lyova walked through the buzzing crowd.

"Oh gals, Malakhitov's shown up!"

"So maybe it's even trite, but I like him. Son of a bitch, he's good looking!"

"Salute, Lyova, doll! Doesn't see me! Got conceited, the rattler!"

"Pardon me, but now there's a genuine walking anachronism, a fossil! All that super-gifted talent of his, his exaltation... No doubt about it, his time has passed... He's a pterodactyl, a mammoth...."

"They say he's become a sozzler."

"Hell, no! He's married a fifth time! Got married in Latin America!"

"Gotta ask, think maybe he'll do a song?"

"Mr. Syracuzers, Malakhitov's shown up. Do you want to be photographed with him?"

"What do you think, would it be acceptable if I, a proper lady, were to invite Lyova to dance? Oh, I'm just joking, joking!"

"Good fellow, a case of Claret for Malakhitov's table! And keep the change!"

"Have you seen his new sculpture?"

"Primitive!"

"You're a snob! Personally I always reread his marvelous 'Discourse on Cooking Salt...' before going to bed."

"Oh, girls, I'd give myself to him with my eyes shut, only its frightening...."

"Mr. Malakhitov! Oi, sorry Levka. I just let my tongue absolutely run off awagging. I'm Shurik, from the Society for Cultural Relations. We've met. Remember, in Damascus?! You asked me for a light. Hey, listen, the Argentine cattle magnate Syracuzers and his girlfriend, the daughter of Maharajah Adzharagam, want to drink a toast to you and have their picture taken with you. Professor Willington from Cambridge has plans to present you with his all-weather..... Of course, you understand how important it all is."

"Comrade Malakhitov, Jean-Luc Godard and Marina Vlady[30] have been asking for you."

"An anachronism, a walking fossil...."

"Hello, hello, hello, friends—ladies and gentlemen! Hello Tanya, Natasha, Claudine! I remember, I remember everything, how could one forget, Marisya...."

With these words Lyova conducted his retinue to a free table. Fifteen minutes hadn't even gone by when the stately waiter Leon appeared beside the table.

"Seywha?" he asked with his customary sullenness.

"Good memory, Leon!" Lyova grinned fawningly. "Seywha for everyone, à la Malakhitov, with vegetable oil, dill, vinegar, and that Japanese 'sooi' sauce. The chef knows."

"That won't wash," Leon snapped curtly.

"What?!" Lyova shouted, glancing at everyone in his retinue one by one. "You see? It's the beginning of the end!" Then, having propped his head on his fist, he pronounced bitterly: "It's falling, my popularity's falling...."

"Your popularity, comrade Malakhitov, is in no way falling," Leon said sullenly. "We don't have any vegetable oil in the kitchen."

"Well, then, serve us... serve us your Seywha," Lyova said tiredly. "See here how mine is already standing on end, in a tuft?" he asked, pointing with his finger to a triplet of crow's-tail tufts on the back of his head....[31]

Having placed the order and tossed a crafty green glance at the dining room, and having convinced himself that everyone was looking at him, Lyova knitted his brow seriously and started up a conversation about the fate of members of his generation and about life in general.

"Everything returns full circle, old men, but life—that's a serious matter. You agree? Our lifespan is short, but we still complicate it with all kinds of stupid actions. True? Take Ortega y Gasset, who writes that a new reality has risen up, different from both natural inorganic and natural organic reality;[32] however, we find in Engels' works that 'Life is a form of essence of albuminous bodies,'[33] and the thought is full circle. But recall now our youth, 'And whither does the azure Nereids' songful sorrow beckon us? Where is she, the magical Hesperides' goldening distance?'[34] Well, that's from Vyacheslav Ivanov... Yess-ss, old pals, but humans are free beings and they can create a better life. That's my own contribution, though. But maybe it's not mine after all, no matter. I remember how we conversed with Sartre in Las Vegas...."

Rosy-cheeked Peer, whose surname turned out to be Babintsev, was enjoying himself. Lyova Malakhitov in the flesh, Lyova Malakhitov himself, had braced his elbows on the table and furrowed his famous forehead into a grid of wrinkles and was conducting a conversation with him, and what a conversation—a conversation about the meaning of life! And the eyes of prominent individuals were directed at them, including even at him, Seryoga Babintsev, who very recently, for the sum of 6 rubles 54 kopecks, had been hooting at a children's party as Baba Yaga.

Gloomy Peer, the owner of an extremely strange calling card which identified him as "Yu. F. Smelldishchev,[35] Modern Dances," listened to Lyova very attentively, trying to catch the thread of his thought; he looked with a frozen grin at the tablecloth and, after every spiral in Lyova's speech, clicked peculiarly—it seems, with his tongue, as if he were counting off something.

And as for the baby foxes, bunny rabbits and kitties—they were at the pinnacle of bliss. With quivering little noses they were snaring the smell of Seywha, with their entire skin they were feeling the looks of great men; they were also bobbing up and down, fidgeting, doing pirouettes, whispering in giggles, and only occasionally would the more serious little faces, recalling the historicity of the moment, turn towards Lyova, nod at the word "Sartre," and restrain their effervescence with all their strength of will.

It has to be said that even Lyova was pleased with the start of this evening.

There he sat with sympatico contemporaries, people of exceptional acumen, and conducted a pleasant and serious conversation with them, without carrying on disgracefully, or guzzling champagne, or kissing everyone who happened along—they were sitting and conversing like your ordinary intellectuals.

Alas, this didn't continue for long. Soon, under the pressure of universal love, general understanding, a hail-fellow-well-met attitude, and even effrontery, Lyova could not restrain himself and, as usual, plunged into dissipation. He made the round of tables, surrounded himself with bosom buddies, guzzled down a bottle of cognac and about half a case of champagne, sang, of course, his favorite song— "Don't put out the fire in your soul, put out the fire of war and lies"— improvised, of course, on the saxophone to the melody of "How High the Moon," danced the Caucasian dance by himself, taunted the cattle magnate Syracuzers with anti-bourgeois innuendoes, accepted the all-weather cap from Willington, returned that gift with one of his own— the thermal sweater, accidentally fell headlong into a bowl of Spearchucker soup[36] on the table of his polite hosts from the Caucasus, and, to all-around raucous laughter, told the Princess Adzharagam that women like her were once thrown into the "appropriate waves" in Russia, reached an agreement with the wizards of the leather ball about the next day's practice, and promised the builders of a box-numbered oil refinery to catch a flight tomorrow to Tiksi[37] so as to investigate the complications there. In a word, it all resulted in the most ordinary of chaotic Nashsharabi drunken muddles. At times Lyova went icy, turned cold, or was covered with goosebumps as he pictured to himself how, at this moment, "my sweet Bubo Bubo" is rustling pages, meditating on the humble words of Tikhon and on Stavrogin's bravado,[38] but... once more, from all sides glasses were handed him and shouts were heard: everyone wanted something from him.

Suddenly, that evil little word "anachronism" reached his ear and he froze as if caught in a lasso, in the middle of making an impetuous movement.

"How's that? Me, it's me that's an anachronism? Me, Malakhitov, I've outlived my time? I'm a pterodactyl? Is that what you said, friends?"

Light-blue eyes blinked in assent, but a pointy little beard cocked itself straight up:

"Yes, namely you. But we're no friends of yours. Don't you love the truth, Malakhitov?"

"Hey, how can that be? Hey, what's going on here?" Lyova surveyed the dining room again with his eyes. It was all astir and, in places, stormily seethed. Everything spun round and round before him.

At this moment, Charlie Willington, having been driven nuts by freedom, was putting on a bizarre exhibition in the center of the room as he poetically thumbed his nose:

> I, Professor Willington,
> Despise the Pentagon
> For its wadded purse,
> And bubonic-plague curse!
> Why spill people's blood?
> Better to "Make Love!"
> I totter, as with the flu,
> My kids are hippies, too,
> But I myself—a handsome beast!
> Russhians, brothers, all zee best!
> Who gives a spit we've got gray hair,
> Peace will conquer, will conquer war!

At another time Lyova might have kissed the professor for such a marvelous song, but right now the shaken "anachronism" only superficially applauded this daredevil from Cambridge and surveyed the dining room again with his eyes, searching for salvation. And suddenly, it seemed to him that it was there!

Two pairs of huge, affectionately calm eyes looked at him from a marble corner. In his head flashed Khlebnikov's words: "As waters of distant lakes behind the dark boughs of a willow, the sisters' eyes were silent, but they were beautiful."[39]

Lyova wasn't mistaken: directly at him, darkening with affection, shone the eyes of two sisters, two scholars, Alissa and Larissa. Beautifully placed heads swayed back and forth, and the sisters' breasts fluttered, just like the Gulf of Joy and Tranquility in the midst of the whipped-up sea of Nashsharabi. Lyova dashed off. "Can a little spot be found here for a walking anachronism, pterodactyl, mammothsaur?" he babbled in faltering speech.

"Sit down, Lev," the sisters answered simply.

"Girls of Russia!" the idol mumbled through his teeth, dunking a small tuft of his forelock into the Rkatsiteli wine[40] in the glass before him—"they will not spurn you or deceive you. Maybe, you... you are the feminine ideal of which Blok, Tsyolkovsky,[41] and I have dreamed all our lives... Maybe, you both... you are personifications of the Beautiful Lady, you... I love you. And words like that aren't spoken in vain!"

Meanwhile, the next incident took place in the restaurant. Syracuzers and his girlfriend replaced Professor Willington in the limelight.
Princess Adzharagam, dressed in a sari that was iridescent like a spot of
crude oil, was swimming like a peahen, that is, just like a Georgian
woman, and was manufacturing purely enigmatic, Indian movements
with her arms. Meanwhile, the bull of the meat industry, having thrust
out his stony belly which was strapped in a raspberry-colored vest, was
acting silly as he smoked his forty-dollar cigar. The sight would have
been tolerable if the multi-millionaire hadn't suddenly begun to sing:

> Hardly anyone here will say, I dare,
> He seriously knows about billionaires.
> Yet, meanwhile, right here's Odessa's grandson
> Who's a master, wheeler-dealer businessman.
> I like gobbling up the little nations,
> Without any foolish hallucinations.
> And I inundate the continents
> At exactly the right moments!
> With their bitter groans, Papuan lieges
> Eat up only pseudo-sausages;
> The English people gulp down neat,
> But despairingly, pseudo-meat...
> I just love the cataclysms
> And the paroxysms of capitalism!
> I have dreams of profits with my eyes shut;
> No, not of any losses—I despise their guts!!

On another occasion, Lyova would have given the high-handed
shark a worthy rebuke, but now he only growled: "There you have it,
the morals of a yellow devil! No matter how much caviar you feed
them, they've still got greedy appetites."[42]

Having said this, he once again turned to the sisters:

"Alissa, Larissa, would you be able to love me?"

"Oh, stop it, what nonsense!" the sisters broke out laughing. "How
can we love you, Lyova? We're writing dissertations about you. Now
I'm the philologist and I'm writing a study called *From Sumarokov to
Malakhitov*, and I'm the chemist writing a study on *Certain Problems of
Coagulation in Light of 'Discourse on Cooking Salt'*.... Would you be able to
answer a series of questions for us?"

"But what about love?!" Lyova asked, perplexed. "And what about
the idea of the majestic Eternal Feminine?"

"Oh, stop it," the sisters began giggling. "How can you love your dissertation topic?"

"How so?" Lyova uttered longingly. "And why not? I mean, hey, ain't I a human being, too?"

He got up, wobbly. Princess Adzharagam swam past. Lyova, half exhausted mentally and physically, swam after her.

"Madame, my dame, am I not really a human being? Couldn't you, tired of the luxury and whimsies of a multi-millionaire, love me—a simple, poor, prominent fellow? However you like—carnivorously or platonically—just love me!"

"In general I don't have anything to do with men, especially during the first week of a full moon," the princess answered in Hindi.

"Oh why, oh why don't women love me?" the public idol cried, stopping in the middle of the room.

A burst of laughter was his answer. The baby foxes and bunny rabbits, having already dispersed throughout the dining room, roared with laughter with all the rest.

"Oi, no more or we'll die laughing! The women don't love Malakhitov!"

"Gals, I'd give myself to him with my eyes shut, only it's frightening—it's Malakhitov, after all!"

"The women don't love him! I'll die!"

A creampuff-bodied lady, the director of the Photographic Studio in Stoleshnikov Lane, hooted:

"Comrade Malakhitov, would you be surprised if I were to invite you to dance?"

"Invite! Invite me!" Lyova begged.

"No, I could never dare do that! I do have a favor to ask, though, Comrade Malakhitov: Come to our studio with your championship medals!"

Lyova flung himself to one side, searching within the guffawing dining room for an empathetic, deeply touched face. In vain. The whole Nashsharabi thundered, the night was a success! The joke that "women don't love Lyova Malakhitov" whizzed around the room like a ball of lightning, smiting everyone on the spot. And as for the confidant of schoolday shenanigans, Seryoga Babintsev, he was bathing in the rays of his own fame already and telling inspired lies to the young specialists who sat around him: "Lyova and I clambered all over the Caucasus, old man. Once, at Klukhorsky Pass we drank ourselves blotto."[43]

And only one person, Yuf Smelldishchev, having crossed his hands over his chest, was standing next to the serving table; in his Mesopotamian eyes Lyova again spotted the approaching yellow flares. Responding unconsciously and uncontrollably to their call, Lyova began to draw near, but he was seized by the hand by an elder comrade—his longtime instructor in billiards, horse-racing, and descriptive geometry—Helmut Osipovich Lygern, now director of one of the film studios. They embraced with a kiss.

"Helmut Osipovich, I've had a frightful day today," Lyova said bitterly. "I learned that I've become a walking anachronism and that women definitely do not love me. You, as an old comrade of mine, ought to have some understanding...."

"That's ashes and smoke," Lygern brushed it aside, "your 'Large Swings' received the grand-prix in Acapulco. Have you heard? Now that's hot stuff! And you're grieving about women! Listen, Levka, you have any new ideas along our line, about cinematography? We've waited a long time."

"New ideas?" Lyova laughed ironically. "Everyone demands new ideas from me, and you're no exception, Helmut Osipovich." He laughed again, this time mischievously. "Here's a new idea for your enterprise. You ought to set fire to Studio 6."

"Set fire, how so?" Lygern asked matter of factly, already scribbling the "idea" into his notebook.

"Soak it in kerosene and put a match to it."

"Sensible," Lygern mumbled, "sensible, sensible...."

Two bleached blondes ambled past them and gazed intently at Lyova, with perhaps more than a look of business interest.

"But why, why! don't women love me, Helmut Osipovich?!" Lyova cried out, in genuine despair.

"That's nonsense, I'll arrange it for you," Lygern mumbled, developing Lyova's idea in his notebook.

Lyova jumped up again and tore off through the length of the dining room into the buffet, to Roza Naumovna, whom he always held alive in his memory as a lady of pleasant exterior and kind personality, even though Roza Naumovna was already, at least partially, an old woman.

"Women don't love me, Rozochka, little momma," Lyova cried, being crowded by the shapely Nashsharabi waitresses. "No one loves me except an unattainable Tahitian girl.... You say I've got a wife, Rozochka? Not a word about Nina, she's saintly.... She's perpetually chastising me and there's cause to do so! Take, for example, today—instead of quietly drinking tea with her and having a conversation about Dostoevsky, I'm here again and everyone wants something from me...

everyone is laughing... but the women don't love me...."

"You ought to take off for the Volga, Levchik, for the Yenisei, to the rafts," his snackbar attendant admonished him sincerely, "nearer to the sources...."

"And you, do you love me, little momma—Rozochka?"

Roza Naumovna smiled at her recollections.

"I love you, Levchik, but now I'm already like a mother to you. Or, more exactly, like an auntie...."

"I know, Lyova, why the women don't love you," came a familiar gritty voice behind Lyova's back which sounded like a knife scraping across a skillet. Smelldishchev, yes, it was he who took Malakhitov by the elbow and led him into the restaurant's cambric-velour "changing room" and sat him in an armchair and bent over him.

"Okay, why?" Lyova mumbled and tried hard to laugh it off. "Just why, Yuf, old puddy, don't women love me?"

"Because you are not handsome!" Smelldishchev bellowed out quietly.

Lyova screeched, like a wounded gull.

"What did you say? Yuf, you mean that seriously? Malakhitov is not handsome?"

"Yes, if one must look truth in the eyes, you are very unattractive," Smelldishchev axed away cruelly. "Women love thick wavy hair, but you, Lev, have got a scrub brush on top. Women adore black or light-blue languishing eyes, but yours, Malakhitov, are buttons, not eyes. Women, of course, like short Roman noses, but your shnozzle, admit it, is even beneath criticism."

Not saying a word more, Lyova dashed out of the "changing room" towards the toilet. Smelldishchev, having grinned with satisfaction, sat down in an armchair and began to wait.

Meanwhile, the joke of the century had already spread to the kitchen and auxiliary rooms of the Nashsharabi. Forgotten, the "seywha" boiled and boiled—the cooks were rolling on the floor from laughing so hard.

"Whaaat? Is he really having bad luck with the broads?" the chef, Chibar, asked as he poured half a pail of water onto the parched dry "seywha." "But there's been talk that he exchanged four thousand for hard currency."[4]

"In general, now, he's got broads hanging everywhere," the waiter Leon said, sucking at his bad tooth, "each is more frightful than the next and the jabber that comes from them—just rotten philosophy. Such 'sophy that your bald patch would corrode before you could figure it out.... Yuck, I hate it!" he ended, with unexpected passion.

Fifteen minutes later Malakhitov reappeared in the "changing room." He was walking with his head lowered, with the face of a clearly unhandsome man.

"You were right, Yuf, old puddy," he blabbed thickly. "I examined myself from all angles. All true—the straw brush, the buttons, and the nose—nothing special.... No wonder women don't love me. What the hell, it's never too late to discover bitter truths. Yes, Malakhitov's an unattractive man."

"But meanwhile, through me, a certain lady has arranged a rendezvous with you," Smelldishchev said, his voice vibrating with tension.

"That's all in the past now," Lyova said. "How could I possibly go to a rendezvous with a mug like mine?"

Weakened, he lowered himself onto the canopy bed of pile velvet; his head began to spin, his eyeballs were filled with lead, the surrounding reality began to be transformed into fog, and out of this dreamy fog the vibrating voice of Smelldishchev once again floated to his ears.

"And meanwhile this lady picked you out from among hundreds of others! Let's go!"

....

He pitched the popular coat onto Lyova's shoulders, pulled the "flapears" on over his head, and shoved him out into the whistling, storming Moscow night. Like mudded yellow spots, occasional lamplights lit the way in the whitish fog. Wildly and incoherently, the trees on the boulevard creaked and creaked.

"Where in hell are we going?" Lyova asked. "What district does she live in? Hey, wait up, Yuf, old puddy, why are you grabbing me like that? Where's my puss-puss then, eh?"

He eyed the line of snowbanks, trying to guess under which one of them his Moskvich was sleeping. Yuf held him in steely embraces. A police patrol car rode past noiselessly. Lyova suddenly felt, for some reason, like calling for help, but he just marveled at the absurdity of this thought.

"There's my Moskvich!" he cried out. "There's my joy!"

"That beasty won't take us anywhere," Smelldishchev gnashed his teeth. "Let's search for some other transportation."

He suddenly grabbed Lyova and raced him through the blizzard, yes, so rapidly and forcefully that no transportation, seemingly, was necessary. Lyova barely succeeded in shifting his almost unnecessary legs and kept muttering something about the rush being in vain—say, is it worth it, for me to rush, with this external appearance?—but the wind whistled and howled.

Yuf gave him no reply, but he somehow did growl strangely and frighteningly in a voice boiling with anger. Then he twisted his head around and flashed his right eye—behind them loomed the headlight of a police motorcycle. Yuf impetuously crossed the square, leapt behind a corner, and having straight away saddled an asphalt roller left by workers for the night, pulled Lyova to him with a jerk. The roller moved off slowly, then built up to a speed which was abnormal for its build, and accelerated along the axial thruway—under the automatic traffic lights. Patrol cars encountered this strange crew twice, but it didn't even enter the policemen's minds to stop it. Once they'd noticed Lyova's lanky figure on the roller, the officers only laughed kindheartedly: Malakhitov's clowning around again....

"Yuf, old puddy, where oh where're we, hee-hee, rolling off to? Now where's this lady of yours? Pulling my leg, eh?"

"There'll be a lady, there'll be one," Smelldishchev uttered as if forcing himself, and glanced at Lyova with one of his Mesopotamian eyes and laughed internally.

An almost forgotten foundation pit from a construction project closed down at some point has existed at the outskirts of Moscow since time immemorial. For several decades all kinds of legends circulated about this foundation pit and the construction project, but then the tales came to bore Muscovites and were forgotten. However, one was preserved. It reads:

> In a remote epoch there lived in Moscow maybe a merchant, maybe a prince, maybe a bandit from the high road, or, in short, a well-to-do man. This man had a love—maybe a German, maybe a Tartar, maybe an Egyptian—who passed on to eternal peace with God. The merchant decided to immortalize this ma-daame, and namely—by building a very high palazzo. A palazzo half a kilometer in height, like the contemporary, our favorite Ostankino, [45] and on the top for this palazzo to have the figure of a laaaday—lifesize height, that is namely a casino in the breasts, and, in the head, itself a bit larger than a four-story house, the administrative offices of his (button-making) firm. The finger of that lady was ought to be pointed to the sky and on the finger a ring or, in essence, a round balcony along which our swindler had intentions to go for walks. Here's what kind of crime was being plotted against healthy thought and human good taste. The funniest thing is that the project would have been realized, but revolution washed away the countless wealth of the prince and flung him personally beyond the borders of our world. Since then there has remained near Moscow a round, sinister foundation pit with some sort of stakes, lakelets of tainted water and bundles of birch trees which have grown up through the concrete.

And it was precisely here that Smelldishchev led our idol, Lyova Malakhitov.[46]

The depressing site appeared in front of Lyova. Like a lunar crater, only filled with snow and with bundles of rusty armatures of a sinister configuration jutting up here and there. New construction projects in the capital were already approaching fairly near to this bad place: no further away than one and a half kilometers there loomed the skeleton of nine-story buildings, where occasional windows of weirdo nightowls and the neon signs of hairdressing salons were lit up. A warm, human world was very close, but here the wind howled with such convincing terror that Lyova understood there was no road back.

"What devil possessed me to agree to this rendezvous?" the despairing, belated thought flashed through his mind. "Indeed, how many times have I sworn not to agree to a rendezvous of this sort...."

"So the lady, it seems, didn't show up, Yuf?" he said with a nervous laugh. "Well, given the little lady's absence, we can split and go home, eh?"

Smelldishchev didn't answer. He stood exposed to the wind, stretched his hands out at his side in rapt concentration, like a rocket before take-off.

"Let's wait five minutes or so to cleanse the conscience and then scram," Lyova said with simulated courage as he jumped up and down and clapped his mittens together. "Otherwise, you know, old puddy, this freezing lambaster will drill its punches right through to the bones."

Smelldishchev rose up into the air. The stupefied Lyova watched as "old puddy Yuf" slowly but surely soared higher. At about thirty meters from the earth, Smelldishchev stopped his movement and, having spread wide his extremities, hung above Lyova like a helicopter. This, undoubtedly, was really a security-guard helicopter or, to speak more precisely, a tipster. Her tipster.

"So that then, I see, is what sort you are, Malakhitov the rather famous." Lyova heard behind him a voice not devoid of pleasantness. He turned slowly around and saw....

On a block of ferro-concrete sat Lady. In spite of the night's darkness, Lyova could discern all the features of this Lady absolutely clearly, and therefore we, too, will have to describe this person's external appearance and dress in detail.

She was rather large. An excellent boa of black fox-fur covered her voluminous bosom. One hand of the Lady, dry and disfigured, with sclerotic veins, was decorated with expensive rings and bracelets, the other, similar to the arm of a heavy-weight weightlifter, was corseted to the shoulder in a black glove. The Lady's stomach was covered by very thin chiffon through which there shone the most diverse tattoo designs, beginning with a primitive little heart pierced by an arrow and ending with a most intricately needled frigate. From the shoulders, in majestic folds, there fell a cloak of pile velvet. Lady had the heavy face of a free-style wrestler, but it set off beautifully the Cupid's bow shape of her crimson lips. Her hair was permed in pretty little ringlets and her head was crowned with a fashionable hat that looked like a propeller.

"Recognize me, Malakhitov?" Lady asked in a cordially patronizing tone.

"It stands to reason, I recognize you," Lyova answered in a quivering voice.

"Why then do you abhor me?" Lady asked in an emotional woman-like fashion. "Aren't I really a beauty?"

She stood up and drew closer, limping in the felt boot on her dry leg, but, by way of compensation, hoisting her other one—naked but for the pink garters—in a can-can step. She flapped her cloak and, with a suddenly stony face, assumed the pose of a powerful athlete. Then, evidently unable to endure the strain, she grasped her side and oohed, but quickly regained her composure and gave Lyova a smile that promised a lot.

"Why then do you abhor me?" she cooed tenderly.

"I don't abhor you at all," Lyova mumbled haltingly. "I don't abhor you, not one little drop."

"You abhor!" Lady bellowed, bared her good teeth and suddenly burst into sobs. "Do you really think of me, Lev? Did you actually remember me during that match with the Canadians? Why don't you refer to me in your poems? Ahh, I can't find any feeling for me in your violin and saxophone improvisations, but at times...," Lady suddenly frowned menacingly, roared with a menacing voice—"at times you even spurn me, and I, after all, love you sincerely...." Having cast him a fleetingly crafty look, Lady lifted her little skirt a bit, as if to fix a garter on her healthy, full leg. And, as a result, a thigh was exposed from which there grew a wriggling little worm.

"Why, oh why, my friend, *lieber Freund, cher ami,* do you shun your Lady?"

She hobbled forward still closer to Lyova, brought her Roman face near—the one now significantly more weighted down (if one doesn't consider the lips), and held out her healthy arm in the black glove.

"Why?"

"Because you are Stinking Lady!" Lyova shouted with a tremble, but not without a small amount of courage, too.

He waited for a thunderous outburst, a deafening hiss, a blow, an eruption, whatever, but nothing followed. Lady, having lowered her arms, stood in a kind of helpless, almost doomed pose. Only in her face did certain changes take place: slowly, her mouth and eyes widened, and in them there appeared a yellow light.

"Understand," Lyova began speaking hastily and inconsistently, "I don't have anything against... I even... in my opinion, more than once... of course, you know... I expressed myself respectfully, but you request passionate love and this I... am not able... physically not fit... as for 'stinking,' I take that back... it slipped off my tongue, forgive me, you simply... are not to my taste... partially... although I also acknowledge certain of your charms... you...."

The eyes and mouth had already dazzled him. He glanced upwards in horror—above him, extremities outstretched, hovered four Smelldishchevs.

"Nope, I won't kiss you!" Lyova cried out furiously and fell on his back into soft, powdery, white snow, into the deep pit. "Go to Nashsharabi! There'll you find yourself a suitor...."

He will never, never kiss even the hems of this Lady's dress. She's not his Lady. This is a Nashsharabian, underground, rotten, second-hand, delirious, under-the-counter, camphor-reeking spawn of the spider tribe which has strayed through the back streets of Moscow since ancient times. Let her promise you alcoholic, tumultuous fame and lure you with casks of soft-black caviar, the most delicate suede, and the least rustling of silk hats, with furs of otter and nutria skinned alive, but know!—you lay a finger on her and there's no getting away, she will suck from you everything, your mind, honor, youthful cleverness, talent, and your love. It's better to perish!

He no longer noticed that Lady, having lost all interest in him, was ooh-ing and ahh-ing as she hobbled away—grasping at the rusted armature. Nor did he see how the Smelldishchevs attached their hooks to a concrete slab and lowered it onto his powdery warm pit.

Morning was remarkable for its unexpected brilliance and ruddiness—"frost and sun, a marvelous day."[47]...Lyova came to and spotted a narrow strip of sunlight which filtered like a needle through the concrete tombstone.

"Wow, I went and overdid it yesterday," Lyova frowned. "Shame, shame.... What the hell? Where in the devil have I ended up?"

He tried to raise the slab, but it stands to reason he was not so fortunate. He tried to dig out under the slab, but neither the snow nor the earth even stirred.

"Hey, what's with me, huh?" Lyova thought with fear. "What sort of foolishness is this? To tell the truth, can't feel the cold at all. Must shout, shout, notify fellow humans that Malakhitov's covered by a concrete slab... after all, I've got practice today, got to be photographed in Stoleshnikov, and Nina.... O God!"

Suddenly, quite near, motors revved up and hoarse voices were heard to say "heave! ho! start it up, in reverse" and a lot of unprinted and unprintable expressions. Lyova watched as steel cables were attached under the slab and then an automatic crane revved up its motor and lifted the slab into the light-blue sky.... Lyova scrambled out of the pit and saw that the whole "crater" was full of bulldozers and cranes and workers moving sluggishly here and there. Apparently, the city authorities had taken measures to clean up the evil emptiness and to build on it something useful and pleasant to the eye.

"Thanks, guys, you rescued me!" Lyova shouted to the workers. "I overdid it a bit last night, who doesn't now and then...."

The workers didn't pay the slightest bit of attention to this famous person. They stood at the edge of the pit and morosely looked downward. Lyova shrugged his shoulders and took off for the city. He walked with a lightness surprising even for him, as if he were swimming through the air. With pleasure he watched people rushing to the metro and the puffs of cigarette smoke in the crowd and the newspapers rustling in people's hands. It was pleasant for Lyova to see these faces so robust in the bitter frost, to feel himself a part of the crowd, and he promised himself to begin from this time on a new life.

A strange thing happened in the metro. Lyova popped all his five-kopeck coins into the automat, but the go-sign just didn't flash. Behind him people were pressing forward, grumbling in bewilderment. Lyova shrugged his shoulders and walked through the turnstile freely—the machine didn't even register his passage.

In the train an elderly skier sat down on him. Lyova sensed no uncomfortableness because of this; he was merely taken aback at the skier's lack of propriety. There was something surprising in this—to come right up to a person and simply sit down on him.

"I didn't settle up"—the frightening thought suddenly flashed through Lyova's mind. "I didn't settle up yesterday at the Nash-sharabi." He rushed to the exit and, already in the doors, caught the reflection of the ill-mannered old man who was sitting in the very same pose, with his pear-nose on exhibit.

In spite of the early hour, the dreamers were already on patrol near the Nashsharabi. Lyova gave a start from habit, but obviously the dreamers had totally turned to salt from their expectations—they didn't even crane their necks towards the nation's idol. Andryanych also didn't raise an eyebrow to answer Lyova's greeting.

Lyova entered the foyer and was amazed at the quiet and freshness which reigned there. All tables were arranged in long rows, covered with starched tablecloths, and set with a modest, clean-looking breakfast: smoking pots of coffee, crisp rolls, cream, jam. There was no hint of the rancid smell of yesterday's "seywha."

At the tables sat Lyova's friends and associates in complete silence: soccer and hockey players on the national teams—Mayorov brothers, Starshinov, Yashin, Chislenko; the poets Yevtushenko, Voznesensky, and Rozhdestvensky; Tigran Petrosian, Spassky; Jean-Luc Godard and Marina Vlady; John Updike, Arthur Miller; Dmitri Shostakovich, Academician Lavrentyev; Armstrong and Ella Fitzgerald; the cosmonauts Leonov and Armstrong-Aldrin; Sartre; Vysotsky and Konenkov; Vitsin, Nikulin, and Morgunov... and many other well-known and kind persons."[48]

Lyova stopped on the threshold, raised his hand unsurely in greeting, and his soul contracted—he had never experienced a more frightening moment.

And suddenly, far back at the rear of the dining room, a little door opened....

Someone tall, tan and feminine, with luminous dark-blue eyes and in a white dress—wasn't it his wife, Nina, saintly and inaccessible?—moved towards him and there was love in her eyes.

"Am I really saved?" thought Lyova. "Really saved, saved, saved?"

1968

Translated by Joel Wilkinson and Slava Yastremski

VICTORY
A STORY WITH
EXAGGERATIONS

In a compartment of an express train a grandmaster was playing chess with a chance companion.

The man had recognized the grandmaster immediately when the grandmaster had entered the compartment and he was immediately consumed by an unthinkable desire for an unthinkable victory over the grandmaster. "So what," he thought, casting sly knowing glances at the grandmaster, "so what, he's just a runt, big deal."

The grandmaster understood immediately that he was recognized and sadly resigned himself: can't avoid at least two games. He immediately recognized the man's type. He had often seen the hard, pink foreheads of people like that through the windows of the Chess Club on Gogol Square.

Once the train was moving, the grandmaster's companion stretched with an expression of naive cunning and asked indifferently:

"How about a little game of chess, comrade?"

"Oh, I suppose so," the grandmaster muttered.

The man stuck his head out of the compartment, called the conductress, a chess set appeared, he grabbed it with an eagerness that belied indifference, scattered the pieces, selected two pawns, clenched them in his fists and showed the fists to the grandmaster. On the bulge between the thumb and the index finger of his left hand there was a tattoo: "G.O."

"Left," said the grandmaster and he cringed slightly, imagining blows from these fists, either the left or the right.

He drew white.

"We've got to kill time, right?... you can't beat a game of chess on a trip," G.O. chattered as he arranged the chessmen.

They quickly played the Northern Gambit, then everything became confused. The grandmaster looked at the board attentively, making small, insignificant moves. Several times, all the possible checkmate moves of the queen appeared like lightning before his eye, but he extinguished these flashes by lowering his eyelids slightly and submitting to the weak inner drone of an irritating, plaintive note, like the buzz of a mosquito.

"Khas-Bulat, you are bold, but how poor is your hut..." G.O. hummed on one note.

The grandmaster was the embodiment of neatness, the embodiment of simplicity of dress and manner, so characteristic of insecure and vulnerable people. He was young, he wore a gray suit, a white shirt and a simple tie. No one but the grandmaster himself knew that his simple ties bore the label House of Dior. This small secret had always been, somehow, a source of comfort and warmth for the young, reticent grandmaster. His glasses, too, had served him often, hiding the uncertainty and shyness of his glance from strangers. He regretted his lips which had the habit of stretching into pitiable little smiles or quivers. He would gladly cover them from the eyes of strangers but this, alas, was not accepted in society as yet.

G.O.'s playing shocked and hurt the grandmaster. The pieces on the left flank were crowded together forming a bundle of cabalistic charlatan symbols. The whole left flank stank of the bathroom and chlorine, of the sour smell of barracks and wet kitchen rags, with a whiff of the early childhood smells of castor oil and diarrhea.

"You are Grandmaster So-and-So, right?" G.O. asked.

"Yes," confirmed the grandmaster.

"Ho, ho, ho, what a coincidence!"

"What coincidence? What coincidence is he talking about? This is just incredible! How could this have happened? I refuse, accept my refusal," the grandmaster thought quickly in panic; then he guessed what was the matter and smiled.

"Yes, of course, of course."

"Here you are, a grandmaster, and I fork your rook and queen," said G.O. He raised his hand. The knight-provocateur hung above the board.

"Fork in the behind," thought the grandmaster, "Great little fork! Grandfather had his own fork and nobody was allowed to use it. Ownership. Personal fork, spoon and knife and a personal phial for phlegm. Also remember the 'lyre-bird' coat, the heavy coat of 'lyre-bird' fur, it used to hang at the entrance; Grandfather hardly ever went out on the street. A fork on Grandma and Grandpa. It's a shame to lose the old folks."

While the knight hung over the board, the phosphorescent lines and dots of the possible pre-checkmate victims and raids flashed again be-

fore the grandmaster's eyes. Alas, the dirty-lilac flannel sticking out on
the knight's neck was so convincing, that the grandmaster shrugged his
shoulders.

"Giving away the rook?" asked G.O.

"What's one to do?"

"Sacrificing the rook for the attack, right?" asked G.O., still hesitat-
ing to place his knight on the desired square.

"Simply saving the queen," muttered the grandmaster.

"You're not baiting me, are you?"

"Oh, no, you are a strong player."

G.O. executed his cherished "fork." The grandmaster hid the queen
in a quiet corner behind the terrace, behind the semi-crumbled stone
terrace with the slightly rotted carved little pillars, with a pungent smell
of rotting maple leaves in the fall. Here, one can sit it out squatting
comfortably. It's nice here; in any case, the ego does not suffer. He got
up for a moment, peeked from the terrace and noticed that G.O. had
removed the rook.

The intrusion of the black knight into a senseless crowd on the left
flank and his occupation of (b-4), in any case, demanded further
thought.

The grandmaster understood that in this variant, on this green
spring evening, the myths of youth would not suffice. It is all true,
there are jolly fools wandering in the world—sailor Billy, cowboy Harry,
the beautiful Mary and Nelly, and the brigantine is raising its sails; but
there comes a moment when one feels the dangerous and real proxim-
ity of the black knight in square (b-4). Ahead was the struggle—complicated, intricate, entrancing and calculating. Ahead was life.

The grandmaster took a pawn, got out a handkerchief and blew his
nose. The few moments of complete solitude, when both lips and nose
were hidden by the handkerchief, put him in a banally philosophical
mood. "So you keep striving for something," he thought, "and what
then? All your life you are striving for something; victory comes but it
does not bring happiness. Take, for example, the city of Hong Kong. It
is distant and quite mysterious, but I have already been there. I have already been everywhere."

The loss of a pawn did not upset G.O. much; after all, he had just
won a rook. He responded to the grandmaster by the move of the
queen, which brought on heartburn and a sudden attack of migraine.

The grandmaster surmised that there were still some joys in store
for him. For example, the joy of the prolonged moves of the bishop
along the whole diagonal. Dragging the bishop lightly across the board

could substitute, to a degree, for a headlong glide in a skiff along the sunlit and slightly stagnant water of a Moscow pond, from light to shade, from shade to light. The grandmaster felt an overwhelming, passionate desire to conquer square (h-8), that square, that mound of love, with transparent grasshoppers hanging above it.

"That was clever, the way you got my rook and I missed it," said G.O. in a bass voice. Only the last word betrayed his irritation.

"Forgive me," the grandmaster said quietly, "perhaps you should return the moves?"

"No-no, no favors, I beg of you," said G.O.

"I will give you my sword, and my horse, and my gun...," G.O. began to hum, deep in considerations of strategy.

The tempestuous summer holiday of love in the field failed to please and, at the same time, disturbed the grandmaster. He felt that the externally logical but internally absurd forces would accumulate in the center very soon. As before, he would hear cacophony and the smell of chlorine, as in that damned memory of the distant corridors on the left flank.

"I wonder: why are all the chessplayers Jewish?" G.O. asked.

"Why all?" said the grandmaster, "for example, I am not Jewish."

"Really?" said G.O. with surprise and added: "Please, don't think that I mean anything. I have no prejudices on that account. Just curious."

"Well, take you, for example, you are not Jewish."

"How could I be?" muttered G.O., sinking back into his secret plans.

"If I do this, he'll do that. If I take one here, he'll take one there, then I go here, he responds like this... Anyway, I'll finish him off, I'll break him down, anyway. Big deal, grandmaster-cheatmaster, your muscle still can't match mine. I know your championships: prearranged. I'll squash you anyway, let your nose bleed."

"Well, I've lost an exchange," he said to the grandmaster, "but that's O.K., it isn't evening yet."

He began the attack in the center and of course, as expected, the center immediately turned into an arena of senseless and terrible actions. This was non-love, non-meeting, non-hope, non-greeting, non-life. The chills of flu and, again, the yellow snow, the postwar discomfort, the itching all over the body. In the center, the black queen kept croaking like a raven in love, raven love and, besides, the neighbors were scraping a tin bowl with a knife. Nothing proved the senselessness and the elusiveness of life as definitely as this center position. It was time to end the game.

"No," the grandmaster thought, "there is still something besides this." He put on a cassette of Bach's piano pieces, calming his heart with sound, pure and even, like the splashing of waves. Then he went out of the summer cottage and down to the sea. The pines were rustling above him and there was a slippery springy floor of pine needles under his feet.

Remembering and imitating the sea, he began to analyze the position, to harmonize it. His soul suddenly felt pure and light. Logically, like the Bach coda, came the checkmate to the black. A dim and beautiful light lit the opaque position, now complete, like an egg. The grandmaster looked at G.O. He was silent, bull-like, staring into the furthest positions of the grandmaster. He did not notice the checkmate to his king. The grandmaster was silent for fear of destroying the magic of the moment.

"Check," said G.O. quietly and carefully, moving his knight. He could barely contain his inner bellow.

... The grandmaster let out a scream and began to run. After him, stamping and whistling, ran the landlord of the summer house, the coachman Euripides and Nina Kuzminichna. Ahead of them all, catching up with the grandmaster, bounded the unleashed dog, Dusky.

"Check," repeated G.O., moving his knight and swallowing air with painful lust.

The grandmaster was being led along a passage in the midst of a silenced crowd. Someone was following him, barely touching his back with some hard object. A man in a black overcoat with S.S. insignia on the lapels was waiting for him in front. One step-half-a-second, another step-a second, another step-two... Steps leading upward. Why upward? Such things ought to be done in a ditch. One must be brave. Must one? How much time does it take to put a stinking burlap sack over one's head. Then, it got completely dark and difficult to breathe, and only somewhere very far off an orchestra was playing with bravura "Khas-Bulat, the Bold."

"Checkmate," G.O. shrieked like a copper horn.

"Look at that," muttered the grandmaster, "congratulations!"

"Ugh, ugh, umph, I'm all sweaty, just incredible, it happened, god damn it! Incredible, slapping a checkmate on a grandmaster! Incredible, but a fact!" G.O. broke out laughing. "I'm quite a guy!" He patted himself jokingly on the head. "Oh, you grandmaster, my dear grandmaster," he buzzed, putting his hands on the grandmaster's shoulders and squeezing them with familiarity, "my dear young man... The poor little nerves gave out, right? Admit it!"

"Yes, yes, I broke down," the grandmaster confirmed hurriedly.

G.O. swept the pieces off the board with a wide free gesture. The board was old and cracked, the polished coating was lost in places, exposing yellow tired old wood, with fragments of round stains left long ago, here and there, by glasses of railroad tea.

The grandmaster stared at the empty board, at the sixty-four absolutely dispassionate squares which were capable of accommodating not only his personal life, but an infinite number of lives. And this endless pattern of light and dark squares filled him with adoration and quiet joy. "It seems," he thought, "that I haven't committed any really treacherous acts in my life."

"Suppose I were to tell about this, nobody would believe me," G.O. sighed.

"But why shouldn't they? What's so extraordinary about this? You are a strong player with willpower."

"No one will believe it," G.O. said. "They will say I am lying. What proof have I got?"

"Allow me," said the grandmaster, somewhat hurt, staring at the hard, pink forehead of G.O. "I will give you convincing proof. I knew that I would meet you."

He opened his briefcase and took out a gold medal as large as his hand. An inscription was engraved beautifully upon it: "The bearer of this defeated me at chess. Grandmaster So-and-So."

"It remains only to add the date." He removed a set of tools from his briefcase and engraved the date, also beautifully, in the corner of the medal. This is pure gold," he said, presenting the medal.

"You don't mean it?" G.O. asked.

"Absolutely pure gold," repeated the grandmaster. "I ordered a lot of these medals and I shall replenish my stock continually."

1965

Translated by Greta Slobin

THE STEEL BIRD

A TALE WITH DIGRESSIONS
&
A SOLO FOR CORNET

Where the infantry can't pass
Nor armored train race by
Nor heavy tank crawl through
The Steel bird will fly.
(Battle Song of the Thirties)

Enter the Hero, and an Attempt at a Portrait

It would appear that the hero of my tale appeared in Moscow in the spring of 1948, at any rate that is when he was first observed on Fonarny[1] Lane. It is possible that he had inhabited the capital even earlier, no one denies it, maybe even a number of years, there are plenty of blank spots on the city map, after all.

A sharp smell of mold, of filthy damp underwear, a mouse-like smell struck the folk crowded round the beer vendor opposite No. 14 Fonarny as the hero walked past. Their nostrils were invaded by decay and foul weather, disintegration and putrefaction, by the twilight of civilization. Even seasoned veterans who had marched from the Volga to the Spree were stunned, so out of keeping was this smell, this sign of preposterous destructive forces, with the Moscow spring evening, with the voices of Vadim Sinyavsky and Claudia Shulzhenko, with the peaceful lowing of captive BMWs and Opel-Admirals, with the abolition of ration cards, with reminiscences of retreats and advances, with the

beer, the rust, but astonishingly tasty sardelle,[2] with Deputy Minister
Z.'s wife, whose charming hands had fluttered the first-floor curtains
literally one minute earlier.

The smell conjured up something that not even the most desperate
times had produced, that a normal person would never dream of, not
even hell, something far worse.

The stunned episodic characters stared mutely at my hero's frail
back, and at this moment he stopped. Even ex-paratrooper Fuchinyan,
a man of snap and precise decisions, was taken aback by the sight of
our hero, his pale, somewhat hairy hands, with their two string bags
and the scraps of yellow newspaper poking out the holes in these string
bags. The string bags dripped something dark onto the asphalt. Even
so, Fuchinyan resolved to rouse the crowd with a joke, to terminate the
oppressive situation, to get his cronies in formation for the rebuff.

"Now here's a little rat," he said. "If I were a cat I'd gobble him up,
and that would be the end of him."

His cronies were about to roar laughing, were just about to line up,
but just then my hero turned to them and choked off their laughter
with the inexpressible sadness of his eye sockets, deep and dark as rail-
way tunnels in scorching Mesopotamia.

"Could you please tell me, Comrades," he said in an ordinary sort of
voice which still gave each of the beer drinkers the shudders, "how to
get to 14 Fonarny Lane."

The episodic characters were silent, even Fuchinyan said nothing.

"Would you be so good as to indicate No. 14 Fonarny," said the
hero.

"Something is dripping from your bags," pronounced Fuchinyan in
a hollow jerky voice.

"No wonder," the hero smiled meekly. "This one is meat," he raised
his right arm, "and this one is fish," raising his left arm. "Omnea mea
mecum porto," he smiled again and there was a gleam of light in the
Mesopotamian tunnels.

"No. 14 is across the street," someone said. "That entrance there.
Who do you want there?"

"Thanks," said our hero and crossed the street, leaving two dark
trails behind him.

"I've seen him somewhere before," said one.

"I've met him too," said another.

"His snout is familiar," said a third.

"Enough!" cried Fuchinyan. "You know me, I'm Fuchinyan!
Whoever wants a beer had better drink, anybody who doesn't, needn't.

Everyone knows me here."

And, notwithstanding the terribly edgy atmosphere, they all began drinking beer.

The Doctor's Recollections and a More Detailed Portrait

The history of his first illness and my part in it is a mystery to me to this day. First, I don't understand how I, an experienced clinician and generally acknowledged diagnostician, was unable to make a diagnosis, or even a working assumption, on the nature of the illness. I have never seen anything like it—there was nothing to kick off from, not the slightest starting point for the development of a medical thought, nothing to catch on to at all.

Before me lay the naked body of a comparatively young man; the subcutaneous fatty layer was a little wanting, but in general near average; the cutaneous coverings were pale, dirty and unhappy (I remember going cold with horror when I made mental use of this highly unmedical term, but later things got much worse), breathing was even, there was no wheezing, all I could detect was the alveola's fussy whisper and the soft twitter of the hemoglobin absorbing oxygen; the heart beat was distinct and rhythmic, but it became quite clear to me, while I was listening, that this was a suffering heart (we doctors laugh at a lyrical term like "suffering," for anyone with the slightest education knows that spiritual sufferings develop in the cortex of the large hemispheres, but in the given instance it was a spiritually suffering heart, and again I was overcome with fear). The stomach was soft and smooth to the touch, but the sigmoidal intestine showed signs of a strange playfulness (this threw me completely); the peripheral blood vessels were examined on the extremities under a layer of skin, and suddenly on the right thigh I read the blood formula, just as if it were typed on a form from our hospital: L-6500, ROE-5mm/hour, NV-98 (the formula was normal)—that is, an objective examination yielded no sign of physical suffering, and only in his eyes, in their deep sockets, in the ancient cave city, raged pneumonia, military tuberculosis, syphilis, cancer, and tropical fever all rolled into one.

In the first place there was all that, and in the second place I have no idea why I didn't send him to a clinic but instead leaped outside into the night and ran all over the place rousing my colleagues in my hunt for penicillin, which was very scarce then.

When I got back, I bent over him with the syringe containing the precious penicillin, and one of the countless women surrounding his bed babbled behind me:

"Doctor, it won't hurt him very much, will it?"

My own hands were trembling with pity for this creature, and the paltry injection I was planning to give him seemed almost like a laparotomy, but nevertheless I remembered my medical calling and ordered:

"Turn over onto your stomach."

He instantly rolled onto his stomach, I couldn't even work out which muscles were exerted to make this movement possible.

"Pull down your underpants," I said.

He pulled down his underpants, baring buttocks of a very unpleasant appearance, resembling the edge of a forest where stumps had been grubbed out prior to a forest fire coming through.

"Poor thing!" gasped the women from behind.

When the needle entered the upper right quadrant of the right buttock my patient began to tremble, at first ever so gently, then his whole body began vibrating violently, something popped and gurgled inside him, something whistled, sweat stains spread across the pillow, but this lasted no more than a minute, then all abated and he was calm.

"What is this?" I thought, slowly pushing forward the plunger of the syringe. "What secret chains have suddenly forged me to this horrible behind, this transcendental being?"

When the procedure was over the patient immediately turned over onto his back, and his eyes lit up bright yellow, like the headlights of approaching trains. He smiled meekly, even humbly.

"When will we be having another jab, Doctor?" he asked me.

"Whenever you want, my friend, any time of day or night, the first beckoning of your hand, the first call, no matter where I am," I replied in all seriousness.

"Thank you, Doctor," he thanked me simply, but I immediately felt warm inside.

"Thank you, dear Doctor, you have saved him," whispered the women, closing the circle. We all fell silent in order to remember for ever the majesty of this moment.

Nevertheless, I couldn't resist measuring some of his body proportions with a tape measure. For years I kept this data secret, and recently it was classified by the Committee for Coordination of Scientific Research.

Chapter 1

Nikolayev, Nikolai Nikolayevich, manager of the houses' on Fonarny Lane, was busy sorting out a dispute which had flared up between the occupants of Apt. 31, No. 14, Samopalova, Maria and Samopalov, Lev Ustinovich.

The case was simple enough both in essence and ramifications, but savage and militant, with no foreseeable reconciliation.

Maria and Lev Ustinovich had once been husband and wife, but had separated some ten years before the war on account of an extreme rupture at the cultural level. The house manager understood this well and sympathized with Lev Ustinovich and respected his resolve and strong will, because for a quarter of a century now he had also been oppressed by the low cultural level of his better half.

That was long ago and long forgotten, and now, of course, the former couple didn't even remember that they had once twined in tender embraces and forgotten themselves in fits of unrestrained mutual passion. Now they sat before Nikolayev and looked at one another with heavy stale ill will. Maria, a cottage-industry worker, was stout and dark-faced, whereas Lev Ustinovich, manager of a hairdressing salon, was the exact opposite—desiccated and fair.

At that time, ten years before the war, Samopalov had brought into the house one Zulphia, a woman of eastern origins, and sired her four boy-devils, and all those years Maria had struggled along with Samopalov's first-born, her daughter Agrippina, whom she kept, raised and made into an assistant in her difficult domestic trade.

The essence of the dispute came back to Lev Ustinovich's complaint that Maria, who had formerly earned her living by inoffensive embroidery, had now acquired a loom, whose rattling did not create any conditions whatsoever for relaxation for Samopalov and his family. The arguments on both sides had already been exhausted, except for the main trumps which were kept in reserve, and the two sides were merely exchanging meaningless retorts.

"You're a slob, Lev Ustinovich," said Maria.

"And you, Maria, are a self-serving narrow egoist," countered Samopalov.

"Your Sulphidon makes more noise than my loom when she's bashing your head against the wall."

"My God!" choked Samopalov with indignation. "What slander! And

I have forbidden you, Maria, to call Zulphia Sulphidon."

"And what about your kids bawling at night?" Maria wasn't letting up.

"The floors shake when your Agrippina walks!" shouted Samopalov, stung.

"My Agrippina is like a turtle dove, as for you, Lev Ustinovich, you might pay attention to people's protests, clearing your throat mornings in the toilet and making such noises that it's impossible to go past into the kitchen."

"That's not true!"

"It is so!"

"Children!" called Samopalov, and instantly his four swarthy boys, the best gymnasts in No. 14, ran into the house manager's office.

"Agrippina!" shouted Maria and into the office swayed her incredibly plump fair-haired daughter, the spitting image of Samopalov.

"It's a disgrace, Lev Ustinovich," she blabbed, "the way you victimize Mother and me in communal matters, it's beyond endurance."

Samopalov's children by Zulphia—Ivan, Ahmed, Zurab and Valentin—surrounded Agrippina, yelling, and the house manager Nikolayev couldn't make out a single word.

The irresoluble situation that had arisen in Apt. 31 depressed Nikolai Nikolayevich beyond words, this great storm of passion merely saddened him, but God forbid that he should give the slightest indication of sorrow or alarm, after all he was the administrator, the law and the terror, the word and deed of Fonarny Lane. How could he help these people, what could he rouse them to? At that time the term "peaceful coexistence" did not exist. The only thing he could do was put one of the Samopalovs in prison, but strange as it may seem, that didn't even enter his head. What could be done, what measures could be taken, on whom could he lean? As everybody knows, the role of the public at that time was reduced to zero: it was necessary to act alone, to administer, divide and rule, with the whip and treacle cake, or whatever.

"Quiet, everybody!" he commanded softly, and the Samopalovs fell silent, because they knew that even though Nikolai Nikolayevich appeared slow moving, he could be tough and occasionally capricious.

"I order you from this day to cease dissension and quarrels," said the house manager severely, adding in a gentler tone with an inward smile. "After all, you are relatives."

"But what about that loom? The loom should be smashed!" burst in the hot-headed Ivan, but he was restrained by the more rational Ahmed.

"Comrade House Manager," began Samopalov, bringing out his hidden trump, "the loom, as I see it, is a typically capitalist means of production, and in our country, as I see it...."

"Oooh, Lev Ustinovich! Oh, you so-and-so!" Realizing the point of his speech, Maria let fly, "as if you didn't hold on to your means and take clients at home, why, you shave the deputy minister in his flat, you rake it in on the side, and you want to besmirch a poor widow!"

"Just a minute, what sort of a widow are you?" retorted an outraged Samopalov. "I seem to be still alive. None of my wives have been widows yet."

"Mama has a certificate from the co-op for the loom," wailed Agrippina, in floods of tears,

"I won't give up the loom, certificate or not," declared Maria. "I'm a Soviet citizen and I'm not going to give up my beloved loom. I'll write to Stalin, our father."

"Don't you dare!" shouted the house manager at this juncture with unfeigned anger. "Don't you dare take Generalissimo Stalin's name in vain! What is this? As if Joseph Vissarionovich need be bothered with your squabbles and your idiotic loom."

The quarrel subsided and the Samopalovs left the office.

Nikolai Nikolayevich, brushing away melancholy thoughts, established some basic order in his place of work, closed the office and set off home. He too, like the Samopalovs, lived in No. 14, which had been built in 1910, and so was faced with tiles that gleamed in the sunset. The house had six stories, one main entrance with a bizarre canopy overhead, a working, if prerevolutionary, elevator, central heating, telephones and other such conveniences. There were 36 apartments in the house and 101 accountable tenants. In a word, this house was the pride of Fonarny Lane, and indeed remarkable for the whole Arbat[4] area.

When he had finished his supper, read the *Evening Moscow* and fed his superb goldfish, Nikolai Nikolayevich sat down on the ottoman, drew the cornet-à-pistons out of its case and called to his wife:

"Klasha, lock up!"

His wife, accustomed to such commands, locked the apartment entrance without demur and fastened the chain. Nikolai Nikolayevich raised the instrument to his lips and softly, most tenderly began to produce the melody "... And squadron by squadron, the cavalrymen tighten the reins and fly into battle."[5]

At this point Nikolai Nikolayevich's small secret had better be revealed. Before the war he was soloist in the Gorky Park woodwind orchestra, and in the war years, despite breaking his neck to get into the

front lines he was assigned to the orchestra at the front. Cornetist
Nikolayev's playing won many a military commander by the purity of
its sound and its major key quality, and so by the end of the war he had
earned the rank of major. Guards major. On leaving the service he realized there was no way back, a Guards major couldn't, had no right to
be a frivolous cornet-à-pistons player, even in the C.P.C.R. or the orchestra of the Bolshoi Theater. Having blotted out his past, Nikolayev
appeared before the Raikom[6] and requested an administrative job. And
so he became a house manager. Naturally, none of the inhabitants of
Fonarny Lane knew about Nikolai Nikolayevich's past, and those of
them who heard the pure major notes of an evening assumed it was the
radio.

True, occasionally Nikolai Nikolayevich would begin to stray into a
minor key: such was the nature of his work, it would dispose anyone to
melancholy reflections, even to philosophy. And then these very secret
evening rehearsals became the source of Nikolai Nikolayevich's melancholy, a source of recollections of a bright, happy life, of that animated
collective labor to which the rank of Guards major prevented him from
returning.

Nikolai Nikolayevich was an accomplished musician and had
achieved such a degree of unity with his instrument that sometimes the
cornet-à-pistons would begin to express those deep thoughts and feelings of its master to which house manager Nikolayev did not normally
give rein, and which he at times did not even suspect in his makeup.

And so now it was with the aim of distracting himself from sorrow
that Nikolai Nikolayevich began rendering the rollicking cavalry song,
but slipped without noticing it into a queer and none too jolly improvisation.

"How did it happen, how can it be, why is there discord in the
Samopalov fam-i-ly?" sang the cornet. "Poor, poor Stalin, my unhappy
leader, beloved father, dear heart of iron."

It should be observed at this juncture that Nikolai Nikolayevich, in
addition to the prevalent filial respect for Stalin and worship of his
qualities of genius, experienced the most ordinary pity for the leader,
that is, he felt almost fatherly towards him, as he would toward a child
of his own torn from its parents by inhuman destiny, or towards an or-
phan. Sometimes he had the feeling that the leader was tormented by
his comrades-in-arms and ministers, as well as the 220 million Soviet
people plus all of progressive mankind. Of course he was afraid of
these feelings and suppressed them, but now and again they would
break out via the cornet-à-pistons.

"Dear people, you are not crocodiles, why then do you shun friendship and love? Aunty Maria, run your wretched loom a bit quieter, don't disturb others. Dear barber Samopalov, remember how tenderly you once caressed Maria, remember the child, share your living space,[7] always keep the laws of society. Don't write to Stalin, dear Maria, don't hinder the poor man thinking and creating. Have pity, my dear, on the standard-bearer of peace, our dearly beloved son and father,"sang the cornet.

"The theme of the leader is magnificent," said someone behind Nikolai Nikolayevich.

It would be difficult, no, impossible to describe Nikolai Nikolayevich's state the following instant. His physical movements were extremely unbecoming: firstly, he dropped the cornet, secondly, he fell to the floor, thirdly, he farted, fourthly, he attempted to hide his instrument under the ottoman bolster and only fifthly and finally did he turn around.

Before him in an indecisive pose stood a man holding two string bags. Something dark dripped from the latter onto the parquet floor.

"What? What did you say?" exclaimed Nikolai Nikolayevich.

"Don't worry," said the man, "I merely said that you gave a very moving and original rendition of the leader theme. I have never heard it treated like that before."

"How do you know what I was expressing? What kind of paradox is this?"

"I just happen to understand and love music," replied the man with the string bags very seriously.

"Then you understand my cornet?" Nikolai Nikolayevich was still conducting this dialogue in rather high, almost falsetto tones.

"Yes."

"Are you a composer?"

"No."

"Who are you then?"

"Benjamin Fedoseyevich Popenkov."[8]

Nikolai Nikolayevich was silent and simply stared at the newcomer. The latter stood before him, frail, unclean and stinking, in a soiled and frayed suit, which was however made of good prewar Champion cloth, a field shirt under the jacket, minus a single medal or decoration, but wearing two prewar badges—a MOPR[9] and a Voroshilov Gunner.[10] Nikolai Nikolayevich pinched himself hard on the behind, but all in vain, it was solid reality.

"Please understand," the silence was broken by the man called

Popenkov, "what you were playing was very close to me. It was my life, my feelings, my sufferings. Take the Samopalovs, to whom the cornet appealed so movingly, I don't know them, but they must be wonderful, wonderful, *wonderful* people!" he cried, "but can't they really come to any agreement? And what you were playing about Stalin, that's right here," his chin nodded towards the area of the heart.

"Something is dripping from your bag," said Nikolai Nikolayevich gloomily, all the strings in his soul ajangle.

"No wonder," Popenkov smiled meekly. "This one's meat"—he raised his right hand, "and this one's fish"—he raised his left hand. "Omnea mea mecum porto, or translated, all I have I carry with me."

"Are you just out of prison?" asked Nikolai Nikolayevich. He still hoped for salvation.

"No," replied Popenkov, "I haven't had the slightest connection, not even family connection, with enemies of the people."

Nikolai Nikolayevich felt crushed, pitiful, almost naked, almost a slave.

"What can I do for you?" he asked, still frowning, grasping for his position.

"Nikolai Nikolayevich, Comrade Nikolayev," began Popenkov piteously, "I come to you not only as to a man, not only as to a musician, but as to a house manager. You are a wonderful, wonderful, *wonderful* man!" he barked.

Here he squatted down and looked up at Nikolai Nikolayevich from the deep hollows of his eyes, and Nikolai Nikolayevich was touched by the desert heat, so powerful was the sorrow in these eyes. The next instant Popenkov, leaving his string bags behind on the floor, leaped high into the air, even too high, rubbed his hands madly and landed.

"Nikolai Nikolayevich, I am asking for refuge, shelter, a roof over my head in one of the houses entrusted to you."

"But you know about the passport system," mumbled Nikolai Nikolayevich plaintively, "and then where could I put you, the way it is they are occupied beyond capacity."

"Nikolai Nikolayevich, I'll lay my cards on the table, I'll tell you everything," Popenkov began hastily. "I have walked a long way here, I have been through a lot, I flew here, driven by loyalty and love for a certain person. For a year now... that is, I beg your pardon, for a week now I have been living down amongst the foundations of the Palace of Soviets. And now I have finally worked up the courage to come to him. My cards are on the table—I am talking about Deputy Minister Comrade Z.! The fact is, dear Nikolai Nikolayevich, that I saved Z.'s life several times. I sacrificed myself for his sake, and he said 'Benjamin, come and live with me, you'll be my friend, my brother; a part of my very self.' And here I am, and what do I see? A wife, a young beauty, beauty, a *beauty!*" he cried, "antique furniture... I was very happy for him. But Z. didn't recognize me, more than that, he was even frightened of me. I don't understand how anyone can be afraid of me, a small pitiable man. In short, Z. showed me the door. Believe me, I am not judging him, Z. is a marvelous, marvelous, *marvelous!*," he cried, "man, I see his point—responsible position, mental and physical hypertension, a young wife, and so on, but what am I to do now, because that was my last hope."

Popenkov squatted on his heels again and looked up at Nikolai Nikolayevich from below, and if the house manager had had any concept of the geography of our planet he would have compared the sorrow of his eyes to the ancient sorrow of Mesopotamia or the sun-scorched hills of the Anatolian peninsula. But since he had no such object of comparison, the intangible sorrow of the eyes affected him more powerfully than any learned geographer or historian.

"You say that you have suffered, that you have lived down in the foundations, and I still don't know where to put you," said Nikolai Nikolayevich in a shaky voice. "Of course you realize that I can't very well lean on Z., he's way above me."

"Yes, yes, me too," concurred Popenkov.

"He only lives here, you know, out of a sort of eccentricity, and because his wife likes the prerevolutionary molded ceilings, essentially he lives here on Fonarny Lane only out of a sense of democracy and I don't know what to do about you, Comrade Popenkov," Nikolai Nikolayevich was completely nonplussed.

"Don't feel awkward about it," Popenkov said encouragingly, "I'm not fussy, you know. Any left-over space would do. Your entrance, for example, is spacious and just fine..."

"The entrance would be impossible, the district inspector is very strict, you know. The yardkeepers I could manage, but the district inspector...."

"A-t-t-t-t- A-t-t-t-t-," Popenkov began thinking, clicking his tongue loudly, "A-t-t-t-t-.... The elevator! Your excellent spacious elevator! It would suit me just fine."

"The elevator... is for general use," muttered Nikolai Nikolayevich,

"Well, of course," agreed Popenkov, straightening up. "Believe me, I won't disturb anyone. You can give me a cot and I'll set it up in the elevator only when I have checked that all are present, that all the birdies are in their little nests, and I'll be on my feet at six a.m. and the elevator will be at everybody's disposal. In the event of any extreme nocturnal need, first aid, or say, a visit from our comrades from the organs,[11] I will free the elevator immediately, flit straight out. How about it? Well, Nikolai Nikolayevich? I can see you've come round already. Well, one last effort. Remember, dear friend, what the cornet-à-pistons was singing. Dear people, you are not crocodiles, why then do you shun friendship and love...."

"Well, all right, I'll give you a cot, but be so good as to remember that the elevator is for general use," growled Nikolai Nikolayevich, who always growled like that when meeting someone halfway. "Let's go, Comrade Popenkov."

"Wait a moment!" exclaimed Popenkov. "Let's have a few moments of silence. Moments like these should be captured."

Nikolai Nikolayevich, in a complete trance, as if he were under hypnosis, silently captured the moment.

Having done this, they went out into the hall. Klavdia Petrovna glanced out of the kitchen and froze, her mouth wide open, seeing her husband scramble up to the top cupboard after the cot. Popenkov looked at her sorrowfully from the top of the ladder.

"Here is your cot," growled Nikolayev. "But take note, it's only meant for one: the springs are weak."

"Nikolai Nikolayevich, you are a wonderful, wonderful, *wonderful!* man," Popenkov began his descent with the cot under his arm. "Tell me, how did you get in?" Nikolayev asked after him.

Popenkov turned round.

"The usual way. Don't you worry, Nikolai Nikolayevich, I won't let on about your cornet. Not a whisper, silent as the grave. I understand that each of us has his little secrets, I for example..."

"Thank you, you needn't let me in on your secrets," said Nikolai Nikolayevich gloomily, looking askance at the string bags, which were still dripping something.

When he had shut the door he laid into Klavdia Petrovna.

"Why on earth don't you shut the door, mother, when you're asked?"

"Kolya, dear, have a conscience, I locked it the moment you began to play, and fastened the chain."

"Then did he fly in the window or what?"

"That's true," gasped Klavdia Petrovna, "it couldn't have been through the window. Perhaps I forgot, got caught up with things in the kitchen. I'm getting old, Kolya, sclerosis... Who was he?"

"From the organs," growled Nikolai Nikolayevich to stop further questioning.

His wife was well-trained and said no more.

That evening on their way toward the elevator several of the tenants noticed a sorrowful figure with two string bags and a cot in the dark corner of the entrance hall, but some passed by without noticing. Popenkov acknowledged the tenants with a submissive nod. When the last tenant, the flighty Marina Tsvetkova, having adroitly given the slip to the officer who had seen her home, had taken the elevator up to her floor, and when the officer had stopped capering around the entrance and railing against Maria's treachery, Popenkov brought the elevator down, set up his cot in it, ate a little meat, a little fish, and assumed a horizontal position. In this position he thought with a feeling of deep gratitude about the house manager Nikolayev, with kindly feelings about Maria Samopalov, whom he as yet knew only from the cornet song, with slight reproach about Deputy minister Z., with some agitation of the latter's young wife, with a touch of playfulness about the fleet-footed Marina Tsvetkova, and then he sank into dreams.

His dreams were unchecked, almost fantastic, but we won't enlarge on them just yet, let us just say that if for most people sleep is sleep with or without dreams, for Popenkov sleep was a sort of orgy of dreams.

In the morning, at six sharp, Popenkov cleared out the elevator and took up his position in the corner, submissively greeting the inmates as they left the house. So it was on the following day, on the third, the fifth and the tenth...

Naturally all kinds of rumors, conjectures and speculations were circulating, but they eventually got back to the house office and stopped there.

A conversation something like the following took place between Nikolayev and Deputy Minister Z.

"Listen here, Comrade Major," said Z., "this guy from the entrance, he hasn't said anything to you about me, has he?"

"He said that he saved your life more than once," replied Nikolayev.

"There are a lot of people who have saved my life, but I don't seem to remember this one," mused Z., "no, I definitely don't remember him."

"Perhaps he'll save it yet," suggested Nikolayev.

"Do you think so?" again Z. was thoughtful. "He couldn't be dangerous, could he? I'm not a nervous type myself, you know, but my policeman is agitated."

(Police sergeant Yury Filippovich Isayev was on permanent guard on the Deputy Minister's landing.)

"I don't think he's dangerous," said Nikolayev, "what's dangerous about him? An unfortunate man, sensitive, understands... er... art."

"Then that's all right," Z. dismissed it with a wave.

Well that's about all, this is where the first chapter ends. It should only be said that everybody soon got used to Popenkov, and many were even inspired to sympathy. Soon he was admitted to some of the apartments. He was a good listener, he sympathized with people and a fair number of the inhabitants opened their hearts to him. True, the working class, headed by diver Fuchinyan, looked askance at Popenkov and wouldn't let him anywhere near them.

The Building Inspector's Report

The double door to No. 14 opens outwards, is 3 meters 52 centimeters wide and 6 meters 7 centimeters high. The door is manufactured from the wood family known as "oak," has copper handles in the form of a reptile, "the snake," on both sides.

Above the door hangs a light in a colored metal grid, the grid has 24 cells, the bulb (100 w.) is working.

Note. The oaken surface of both sections of the door has a carved representation of the fruit of the vine, seriously damaged in the lower parts. Three centimeters from the external handle a three-letter inscription[12] carved out with a sharp instrument has been concealed by three parallel strokes by order of the house office, however can be deciphered under close examination.

Passing through the door we have before us an oval-shaped area, known as the main entrance hall, measuring approximately 178.3 square meters. The figure is approximate, since it is as difficult to measure the square area of an oval as of a circle. The height of the dome-shaped ceiling of the "main entrance" is 16.8 meters at its highest point. The floor consists of a tiled mosaic of oriental, or more precisely Mauritian character (consultation at the Oriental Institute). The tile stock of the floor has been damaged, about 17.2% of the total number of tiles.

A light fixture in the form of an ancient Greek amphora with handles hangs from the ceiling by a metal cord (consultation with the A.S. Pushkin Museum).

This is not functioning and represents a danger to life and limb, on account of the worn nature of the cord, but in view of the absence of the requisite ladders (12m.) in the house office, it cannot be removed for transfer to a museum.

Lighting of the "main entrance" is effected by means of four light fixtures, two on each side, each having three light sockets. Of the twelve bulbs eight are functioning. The light is diffuse, dull yellow. The far right plafond is damaged (broken) on the left corner, thus directing the light into a niche on the left side of the door, about 1.25 meters from the latter. The niche has an arched top, is 2.5 meters high, 1.5 meters wide. Formerly the niche housed a hollow cast-iron sculpture of Emperor Peter I, of which only the 1.1 meter high boots, known as Wellingtons, remain (consultation with the journal *October*).

Color of the walls to a height of 1.6 meters is dark blue, oil paint mixed with turps. Above this point and all over the dome are fragments of badly damaged frescoes (1914 A.D.), that is curls, extremities, folds of garments, female mammary glands, etc., elements of Greek mythology (consultation with the journal *October*).

Note. To the right and the left on the dark-blue background of the walls are chalk inscriptions and drawings, erased by order of the house office, although the said inscriptions and drawings were not harming anybody.

Daytime lighting of the "front entrance" is effected by means of six windows with colored glass, three windows on each side. The windows rise to a point, are 4.5 meters high, 0.5 meters wide, situated 0.7 meters off the floor at a intervals of 0.8 meters from one another. The panes on the left side reflect an oriental, more precisely a Japano-Chinese subject, that is: geishas, rickshas, water carriers, tea houses, gunboats (consultation with the Soviet-Chinese Friendship Society).

The windows on the right hand side reflect a medieval Franco-Germanic subject, that is: knights, minstrels, fair ladies, animals, horses, side arms (consultation with the Soviet-French Friendship Society). The lower section of the second left pane is reinforced by a sheet of ply 0.5m x 0.7m, the lower section of the first pane on the right is reinforced by a sheet of cardboard 0.5 x 0.9.

The area is heated—four central heating radiators, with three sections each, set along the walls.

At the far end of the oval-shaped area is an elevator shaft housing a working elevator. On the doors of the elevator are four enamelled white plates 0.2 x 0.4 c with black letters. The signs say: "Look after the elevator—it preserves your health," "Unload children first, then yourselves," "Dogs prohibited," "The elevator is not a lavatory!"

The inside of the elevator is a box, area 4 sq. m., 2.5m high, painted brown, containing a square mirror, unevenly broken in 1937.

To the right of the elevator begins the first flight of a white-marble staircase, numbering thirty-eight steps, of which sixteen are damaged. At the very base of the stairs is a hollow cast-iron figure 1.25 high, absolutely unidentified by the specialists. In the figure's right hand there is a lamp, which several of the inhabitants attempt to use as a rubbish bin, when they know quite well that the lamp is fixed solid and can't be tipped up and what will happen if the rubbish reaches the top?

Part for cornet-à-pistons

Theme: Good day, capital, good day, Moscow! Good day, Moscow sky! These words are in everyman's heart, no matter how far away he is... Improvisations: Poor unfortunate, he lay in the foundations, suffered long years. He saved the Deputy Minister, only to be cast out by him, where then is gratitude? There is no justice, there is no justice, they can ruin the fledgling. Poor stinking wretched transient, who are you? Have you a residence permit,[13] have you a mother, have you a passport? Terrible fledgling, live in your elevator, only keep tight about me. If you should tell, it will be dreadful for me, I shall be silenced forever. The terrible burden of authority oppresses night and day. A post in management is a great thing, a terrible thing....

Sudden end to the part: Morning meets us with coolness, the river meets us with the wind, curly head, why then do you not welcome the gay whistle's song?

Chapter 2

What had happened? What was wrong? There was banging and shouting on every floor, a nocturnal working bee in No. 14 Fonarny. Sergeant Yury Filippovich, stupefied with terror, pounded at Z.'s door, fell into the flat and began trembling in the Deputy Minister's arms.

"What's the matter, Yury Filippovich?" asked Z., back only half an hour from a night conference. "What's happened?"

"I don't know, blessed father, I don't know, blessed mother... The banging and the shouts," muttered Yury Filippovich.

Leaving his guard to his spouse, Z. dived for his cherished Browning.

Samopalov's children came spilling down from the sixth floor. Maria in her fright threw herself on Lev Ustinovich's neck. Zulphia clutched at him from the other side. Only Agrippina, duffer though she was, immediately armed herself with a coupling bolt ready to defend her mother's loom.

Doctor Zeldovich from the fifth floor emerged onto the landing already dressed in an overcoat and warm scarf, carrying a suitcase. His family likewise made ready in the space of a few minutes,

It had all started with that flighty Marina Tsvetkova galloping down four flights of the marble staircase like a frightened antelope and all but tearing off its hinges the door to Nikolai Nikolayevich's flat. At this time, it being the dead of night, Nikolai Nikolayevich was sitting in the lavatory, concealed from his family, and was playing his cornet. On the sly, almost inaudibly. The cornet piece was interrupted by unbelievable godforsaken banging and crashing.

"Comrade Nikolayev!" yelled Tsvetkova.

"Him, Your! protégé! there! in the elevator!.."

"What's the matter with him?" roared Nikolayev like a bear.

"In... convulsions!" shouted Tsvetkova, opening wide her already huge eyes.

"Save him, good people!" roared the cornet player in a panic.

The whole house was roused and everybody streamed downstairs, some in pajamas, some in dressing gowns, some in underpants, in whatever came to hand. In one minute the vestibule was crammed with a buzzing crowd, resembling the Roman forum. Those who pushed nearer to the front could see Popenkov writhing on his cot through the open doors of the elevator.

"Doctor! Get a doctor! Comrade Zeldovich!" shouted people in the crowd.

Doctor Zeldovich steered a course through the corridor that had formed to the elevator, and then the convulsions ceased and Popenkov lay quiet, his arms stretched out along his sides.

This unpleasant occurrence (the convulsions, the severe attack) took place several months after Popenkov moved into the elevator. Until then the life of the house had flowed comparatively peacefully, calmly, almost without a hitch, at any rate without any overt troubles.

As has already been stated, the inhabitants quickly got used to the submissive figure with the cot, patiently standing in the darkest corner of the vestibule near the radiator. And the figure meanwhile was adapting to its new place of abode.

Above all he had to master the vestibule, to interpret its secret nocturnal life. In the dead of night Popenkov observed things very closely, silently, not interfering until he had completely got to the bottom of their contradictions.

The fact is, the oriental mosaic was in direct and irreconcilable conflict with the ancient Greek amphora hanging directly above it. It would clink its tiles at night, changing the figures of its mosaic in order to create an indecent word, thereby offending the ill-mannered amphora for good, and the frescoes too, all these lumps of unbridled flesh, in short, the whole ancient world. Alas, all the ornament's efforts were in vain, either there was not enough time, or something else, just as with the ceiling's nightly attempts to organize the scattered parts of the body into one whole.

And there was ferment in the stained glass panels, a restrained simmering of passions. A flat Gothic figure, perhaps Roland or Richard the Lion-Hearted, being seated with fair ladies, was sending kisses to the geisha on the other side, who in turn had turned to the knight the enticing triangle of her naked back and was smiling over her shoulder, utterly scorning the samurai and water carriers.

"Ojo-san, tai hen kirei des' ne," whispered the knight in Japanese.

"Arigato," replied the geisha, gently as a little bell. "Domo Arigato."

An enigmatic figure on the staircase (it might have been Diogenes, were it not for some of Aladdin's features) kept straining to go out for a walk, but at his first movement the snake on the inside stretched and hissed, and the one on the outside beat its head furiously against the door.

Then naturally they were all devilishly interested in the luckless amphora, nobody knew what was inside it. The knights and samurai assumed that it was wine, and what man doesn't dream of wine? The fair ladies and the geishas were convinced the amphora contained a sweet-smelling substance and dreamed of massaging themselves with it. By morning speculation on the amphora had gone to extremes.

Only Popenkov knew for certain that there was nothing in the amphora but half a century of dust, thirteen desiccated flies, two spiders dying of starvation, and a Herzegovina Flor cigarette butt—goodness knows how that got there.

On the whole, this nocturnal life was not to his taste. He had some reason to suspect that if it went on much longer, there would be a general shift, and the samurais would dash for the fair ladies and the knights would get in amongst the geishas, the gunboats would land the "tommy" troops, the lad with the lamp would go out on the town, the ornament finally form its cherished word, the amphora would naturally be broken open, the snakes, God forbid, might find their way into his cot and the world he intended to rule by virtue of being animate might collapse altogether. So one day, in the heat of the vestibule orgy, that is at five a.m., he sprang up from his cot, scattered the already deranged mosaic and leapt into Peter's boots.

Naturally everybody took fright, gasped, began whispering in corners as to who and what, what kind of a bird this was, but Popenkov hushed them, jumped up (somewhat strangely, since he jumped together with the boots), tore down the Greek amphora, smashed it to smithereens on the floor, and, back in his niche, proclaimed:

"There's your despicable filthy dream, there's nothing in it but dead flies and half-dead spiders, and I'll finish smoking the butt, a Herzegovina Flor doesn't turn up every day. Is it clear now who's boss?"

With these words he jumped out of the Wellingtons, picked up the butt and puffed away on it for a good hour, lying on the cot.

They all fell silent and froze for ever and ever, even before his specific instructions, only the ornamental design coiled obsequiously and attempted to crawl up and lick him on the foot in gratitude for his having dealt with the amphora, but Popenkov brushed it away with his heel and wouldn't let it near him.

In the morning Maria Samopalov was first down, she was off to the co-op to deliver her work.

"Well, well," she said when she caught sight of the broken amphora. She thought about it and gasped.

"The cord wore out, Maria Timofeyevna, what can you do, time erodes even the most solid metal," remarked Popenkov philosophically.

"It could have come down on my head," Maria calculated.

"According to the probability theory, quite likely," concurred Popenkov.

"It could have slammed Lev Ustinovich," Maria screwed up her eyes.

"Easily," nodded Popenkov. "Imagine, one minute there was Lev Ustinovich, and the next he was finished."

"It could have crowned Nikolai Nikolayevich...."

"Not only him, it could even have been Deputy Minister Z.," Popenkov entered in enthusiastically.

"Yes, if one of the top bosses came to our house it could have crashed down on him," Maria went on speculating.

"Exactly. That would have been a real disaster," Popenkov grew sorrowful.

"Anybody at all could have been killed," said Maria, summing up.

"You are quite right," agreed Popenkov.

"And what about you, you weren't hurt, Benjamin?" enquired Maria.

"I got by, Maria Timofeyevna. I was sleeping peacefully, Maria Timofeyevna, when suddenly I heard a crash, practically an explosion! Shades of the war, and I began shaking with horror. Surely not again? Surely the imperialists couldn't do it again... Do you understand?"

"I wouldn't put anything past them," growled Maria. "The light should have come down on Churchill's head, or Truman's."

"I subscribe to your sentiments," said Popenkov, opening the door for Maria. "It looks as if you are on your way to the co-op, Maria Timofeyevna?"

"I am delivering my work," replied Maria importantly. "It mightn't be much, but I do my bit for the state, not like your barbers. In a pinch a man can get by with a beard, but he can't manage without textiles. The other day I was walking past Kindergarten No. 105, they've got a bit of my embroidered linen on their window, it's real heartwarming."

"Permit me to have a peep at your work," asked Popenkov.

They went outside and Maria, even though she was very suspicious, unwrapped her bundle and showed him part of the linen. Popenkov, his arms folded on his breast, stared at the cloth.

"Why don't you say something?" Maria was surprised. Popenkov brushed that aside.

"Of course, we are only handicraft workers, invalids," whined Maria, "we're a long way from these...."

"This is art!" suddenly exclaimed Popenkov fervently. "It's real art, Maria Timofeyevna. You are a talented, talented, *talented* person," he cried out.

"Spontaneity, expression, fi-li-gree. You ought to go further. You could produce," his voice dropped to a whisper, "old French tapestries."

"What tapestries? Are you out of your mind, Benjamin? You'll get me into a predicament," Maria was getting anxious.

"Don't worry, I'll explain everything. Let me come with you," he seized the bundle with one hand and Maria with the other. "I'll help you, I'll get the reproductions, and you and I will make tapestries. I don't need any remuneration. I would just like people to have beautiful old tapestries."

He led Maria along the winding Fonarny Lane, persuading her to take up old tapestries, simultaneously going into raptures over the charms of the lindens in flower, the flight of swallows (a keen dagger-like glance above), and the clear June day. From time to time he would jump into the air, rubbing his hands excitedly. Maria merely groaned under his pressure.

The reader is quite right to ask who is this Benjamin Fedoseyevich Popenkov, where he came from, his cultural level, what he is by profession and so on and so forth. If he isn't given this information the reader is within his rights to assume the author is leading him by the nose.

I could fall back on some naive mystification and really lead the reader by the nose, but literary ethics above all, so I am forced to declare that I know nothing about Popenkov. Water in clouds is dark. I have the feeling that in the course of the narrative some kind of a portrait of this character will emerge, however approximate, but the story of his origins and various other data are most unlikely to ever float to the surface.

The first tapestry was naturally sold to antique-lover Zinochka Z., young wife of our good Deputy Minister. The tapestry was beautiful, although of course it had suffered from the effects of time, whatever you say, almost two centuries have gone by since it was produced by anonymous craftsmen in Lyons. A pastorale was depicted on it, slightly reminiscent of Bouché.

Zinochka actually gasped when Popenkov brought her this tapestry. So did the Deputy Minister, when he learned what it cost.

"It's unthinkable!" he said, immediately calculating in his head that about two months wages would go on the acquisition of this object. "Zinochka, it's unthinkable, it smacks of bourgeois decadence."

"What are you talking about, darling?" said Zina in astonishment and came towards him, her shape visible through a transparent negligee.

The Deputy Minister immediately flew into the abyss, the tenth wave closed over his head, a typhoon raged.

"Mind you, it's very valuable," he said, when some time had elapsed.

After the sale of the tapestry friendly relations were established between Popenkov and Zina. The Deputy Minister was hardly ever home, he lived for his department, and Zina naturally was bored, and in need of live human company. Occasionally in a state of misanthropy she would despatch Yury Filippovich to walk the dog and summon Popenkov up to talk about life, the sad nature of human existence.

"For goodness' sake, Benjamin Fedoseyevich," she would say, reclining on the sofa in her dressing gown, with Popenkov sitting on the edge, "Here I am, young, beautiful... I'm not ugly, am I?"

"How can you ask! How can you?" said Popenkov indignantly.

"No, I'm not fishing for compliments," Zina dismissed his protest with a wave of the hand, "it's only lack of confidence in myself, doubts, anxieties.... You understand, I am young and not ugly, I've got everything—a beautiful apartment, money, my own car, foodstuffs, why should I be so unhappy, why aren't I satisfied with life? Perhaps I am a superfluous person like Pechorin?"

"I understand you Zina, I am familiar with all that," said Popenkov sadly, gazing at the floor, "it's as if we were the same person. We are drawn to the heights. We are superior beings, Zina,"—for an instant he raised his eyes and scorched Zinochka with the fire of Mesopotamia.

"In '43 I gave myself to a pilot," said Zinochka. "He was the first, he took me savagely, inhumanly. It happened on the riverbank in a downpour, but he was like a tiger, like...."

"Like an eagle,"prompted Popenkov, "after all, he was a pilot."

"He was a pilot then, now he's a Deputy Minister," nodded Zina sadly. "He's a friend of my husband's, he visits and drinks vodka with Z., he's changed."

Popenkov would get up, pace the carpet nervously, rub his hands, turn sharply to Zinochka... Ooh, how she appealed to him, ly-y-ing there unafraid.

Then there would be Yury Filippovich's cough and the dog's bark. Zinochka would get up off the sofa, tell Popenkov all sorts of trivia to do with the delivery of antiques and see him to the door. Because of Yury Filippovich and the dog, their meetings began to take on a sort of unnecessary ambiguity.

At night Popenkov would command the frescoes on the dome to move, to piece together the scattered parts of the body. He didn't give up hope of assembling Zina's tempting figure, but kept getting freaks, sympathetic enough to look at, but "typically not the real article."

Two people were much later than the rest coming home, No. 14's number two charmer Maria Tsvetkova and the Deputy Minister himself. In those days, as everybody knows, the windows in the ministries and departments shone all night in the center of sleeping Moscow.

Z. always entered the house energetically, slammed the doors hard, crossed the vestibule in military strides, waking Popenkov as he went.

"How is life for the young, Savior?"

Popenkov jumped up, opened the elevator door, refrained from answering this question, which hurt his pride, but would ask humbly:

"Will you take the elevator?"

"It won't be required," Z. would say and fly up to his first floor apartment on strong legs.

Tsvetkova would tap with her wedge-heeled shoes, the current season's model. She wore a white woolen coat, like Claudia Shulzhenko, and a Marika Roekk hairstyle.

In the war years a girl like Tsvetkova was the dream of all the warring countries, that is, of all civilized mankind. She had something that disturbed and inspired hardened fighting men, that connected them with normal human life, and if this was symbolically labeled "Lyudmilla Tselikova," "Valentina Serova," "Wait for me, and I will return,"[14] and on the other side of the warfront "Marika Roekk," "Zarah Leander," "Lili Marlene," and in the sands of the Sahara and in the Atlantic "Deanna Durbin," "Sonja Henie," "It's a long way to Tipperary," in real life it was Maria Tsvetkova.

The war years were for her a time of tender power, of romance, sorrow and hope. Her boys, her beaus, were flying over Königsberg in night bombing raids, tramping the highways of Poland and Czechoslovakia, surfacing in submarines in the cold Norwegian reefs. By one such hero, actually the only one she had really loved, Tsvetkova had a daughter. The hero didn't return, he died after Germany's capitulation, somewhere near Prague.

Tsvetkova was still lovely in 1948, but her style had altered a fraction, almost imperceptibly. She continued to accept the attentions of officers, because their shoulder-straps and decorations reminded her of the not-too-distant past, and because "youth was passing," but as for civilian dandies in long jackets with box shoulders—they got zero attention and a pound of scorn.

The officers would see Tsvetkova home, she would get into the elevator with bouquets of flowers, and tap one wedge heel as they went up, hum "The night is short, the clouds slumber," barely notice the cot with Popenkov, and never react in any way to his compliments regarding her figure and general charms.

Whereas Popenkov added Tsvetkova to his dreams, practiced black magic on his dome and mosaic, and in general, if we are to be quite honest, experienced great anger towards the human race.

That night Tsvetkova entered the vestibule tipsy and gay, covered in dahlias, poppies and other flower buds.

"Permit me a sniff," requested Popenkov and buried his face in the bouquet, almost touching Marina's breast with his bony nose.

"You really should visit the bathhouse, Popenkov," said Marina, "you smell most unpleasant. Would you like thirty kopecks for a bath? Here's thirty kopecks and a peony for good measure."

"How am I to interpret your gift?" asked Popenkov, stuffing the flower and money into his bosom. "As a sign of interest or a sign of pity? If it's pity, then I shall return it; pity lowers a man, and man has a proud ring about him."

"Are you a man, then, Popenkov?" Tsvetkova showed naive surprise and pressed the button for her floor.

Popenkov shuddered with proud and powerful feelings he himself didn't fully understand.

"You are a flighty creature, Marina, I know everything about you," he said, getting a grip on himself.

"You don't know anything about me," Tsvetkova suddenly grew sullen, "and I'm not at all flighty, I'm very down to earth, and you don't know a thing about me."

They went up.

"I do know," said Popenkov.

"Ha-ha," said Tsvetkova, "you don't know anything. For example, you don't know who I'm in love with, which man I have adored from afar for a long time, I love Deputy Minister Z., so there!"

The elevator came to a halt and Tsvetkova attempted to get out, but Popenkov pushed the ground-floor button, and down they went.

"What do you think you're doing?" asked Tsvetkova.

"Just this," giggled Popenkov. "But what about Zinochka Z.?"

"Zinka, that so-and-so heifer!" cried Tsvetkova. "When Z. moved into our house he liked me better than Zinka, but I dropped him, because he was a Deputy Minister so he wouldn't think that I loved him just because he was a Deputy Minister. Fool that I am!" she burst into tears and pressed the button for her floor.

Up they went.

"Curious, curious," pronounced Popenkov. "So you were seeing Z. then?"

"So we were seeing one another, what of it, so we went on trips together, but we haven't been seeing one another for a year now, and I don't want anything from him," Tsvetkova was still crying.

"Don't cry, my dear," said Popenkov, putting his arms around Tsvetkova and unobtrusively pressing the ground-floor button, "don't cry, unhappy, delightful, *delightful* woman," he cried, opening his eyes wide. "Unrequited love, how well I understand it, that's the story of my life, we are creatures with a similar destiny..."

Down they went.

"Let go of me, you foul-smelling fellow!" Tsvetkova suddenly came to and pressed the button for her floor. "Have you gone mad or what?"

She tried to struggle out of Popenkov's embrace, but his arms were like steel. She felt the incredible superhuman strength of his arms and was even afraid.

"Let me go!"

Down!

"And if it is exposed... haven't you thought?... the excesses?... Zinaida's wrath... and if it were made public?... What if I take it around the various departments... eh?"

Up!

"Let me go, you wretch! You nut... miserable booby," and a slap across the face, "idiot... let me go, I won't be answerable for what I do... I... I work for the newspaper... as a secretary... I'll write a piece about you.... What a scoundrel you are... let me go!... that's it."

Down!

"In misfortune I... kreg, kreg, karusers chuvyt... hemorrhoids... how can I see?... fit, fit, rykl, ekl, a?"

Up!

"You nothing... you scourge, you animal! My tears are not over you! My lover was a pilot, a hero twice over! Get out of the way!"

Down!

"In the paper... about me?... chryk, chryk,... grym firaus ekl... in brackets... why not take pity... I ekl buzhur zhirnau chlok chuvyr... kuri-kuri... a weak organism...."

Up!

"Are you out of your mind? You're quite mad! Ha-ha-ha-ha-ha-ha-ha-ha-ha-ha-ha-ha! You can't fool me!"

Down!

"Lyk bruter, kikan, kikan, kikan..., pity and love... I thirst like an eagle... order... liton fri au, au... we'll fly away... fit, fit, rykl, ekl, a?... over the ruins, over the houses... flowers, Marina... ekl...."

Down, down, she was no longer in control of her arms, her laughter had died away and her tears dried up, whereas the elevator was as full of electricity as a Leiden jar, and kept falling, falling, then rocketed upwards into thick blackness, into a wretched sky, and she felt as if she herself... any minute... just like her beloved pilot or tankman... the one who hadn't returned... any minute would meet her end, but just then Popenkov crashed onto the cot and went into convulsions.

The women of No. 14 set up a rescue committee and took turns at the patient's bedside.

In the morning they brought semolina, cream and cottage cheese from a neighboring kindergarten.

Comrade Z., under pressure from his wife, sent a doctor from the Kremlin hospital and the latter held a consultation with Dr. Zeldovich. Yury Filippovich ran to the chemist. Alarming the pharmacists with his uniform and the inscription *cito!*, he got the medicines without having to stand in line.

Lev Ustinovich shaved the patient gratis, and his children made no noise in the entrance, on the contrary, they tried to amuse Popenkov, reading him verses and singing him oriental songs.

Maria and Agrippina draped the elevator with clean and artistic canvases.

"What will we do about the elevator?" asked Nikolai Nikolayevich at a general meeting of the tenants.

"What about the elevator? What is a elevator, when there's a sick man in it? Damn the elevator!" replied the tenants as one man.

"So that's settled—the elevator is out of action!" Nikolai Nikolayevich summed up, and his usually stern eyes softened.

And so in No. 14 Fonarny Lane the elevator was put out of action. On that we can end the second chapter.

Recollections of Mikhail Fuchinyan, a Diver

Everybody knows me, I'm Fuchinyan, and anybody who doesn't, soon will, and anybody who doesn't want to know me can leave, and if they don't leave, they'll get to know me, and these here are my friends, they're first-rate young men and lads. Bottoms up! Away, lads!

Well, O.K., if anybody's interested, I can tell you about this guy. Only mind you don't interrupt, those who are going to interrupt had better leave right away, or they'll run into trouble.

In short, here is my arm, check it out yourselves, if you want. Well, how is my arm, in order? Biceps, triceps, all in place? The left one's the same, see! In short, before you is my whole humeral belt. On the whole, as you see, no weakling!

One evening the lads and I were sitting in the yard playing dominoes. Tolik, he was a driver at the Central Fish Cannery, had that very day scored about six kilo of dried fish, so as it turned out, we sent the boys for some beer. The boys dragged in two cases of beer and it was turning out to be a nice quiet evening. We were sitting normally, having knocked off the same, we're gorging the dried fish, washing it down with beer and swapping experiences from the Second World War.

Then this booby Benjamin Popenkov appears. He squats down, picks away at the fish, someone poured him a beer, he's sitting there saying nothing. Nice and clean, not like in '48, smelling of Flight eau-de-cologne, in a tie, boots, no worries.

I disliked this little rat from the very beginning—if I were a cat, I'd have gobbled him up and that would be that, but I didn't show my feelings, because it's my principle to live and let live, the lads will tell you that.

But here I began to get mad just looking at him. Oh, you unfortunate fellow, I think, you wretched, homeless creature, everybody's feeding you, everybody's sorry for you, they all throw something your way, and meanwhile you're making yourself comfortable, you damned rook. I just thought God grant that everybody set himself up as well as this wretch. True, he hasn't got an apartment, but then he's got the whole vestibule at his disposal, he's put in screens there, the tenants have only got the narrowest passage from the stairs to the door, and I don't even mention the elevator. Next question: our poor unfortunate has taken himself the best stacked woman in the whole lane and has a ball with her behind the screens, and how—the whole house rocks. Next: Here am I, a diver, a highly paid worker, well, for my two-hundred and fifty I squirm around on the bottom of the Moscow River like a crab, while that bastard walks around up top in a suit the like I've never dreamed of, and the smells in the vestibule are so gastronomic, there's never anything like them in my place. If you look at it this way, there's an unfortunate devil walking around looking at everybody as if they all owed him something. It's a sort of hypnotism, like with magicians, such as the Kio brothers or Cleo Dorotti.

Well anyway, I got mad and I took a sharp turn towards trouble. Tolik Proglotilin was just recounting an operation on Tsemissk Bay, and Popenkov kept humoring him, nodding away with his beak. Here I interrupt Tolik and say:

"Why don't you share your war-time experiences, Popenkov? I suppose you were defending Tashkent? No doubt you struck a blow to the dried apricots?" He smiles, the cad, smiles a mysterious, contained, incredible smile.

"Ah, Misha," he says to me, "you know nothing about my war. Your war is over, but mine isn't. My war will be more terrible than yours."

Everybody fell silent, sensing there was going to be trouble, everybody knows I don't like my fighting past being insulted.

"Who could you fight, you sparrow, you chicken feed," I say, with my voice raised. "Women? You wouldn't have the strength for anything else, you tom-tit!"

But he keeps on grinning away, and suddenly he fixes his orbs on me, so that a blast of heat comes my way, like out of a ship's furnace.

"In the first place, Misha, I'm no sparrow or tom-tit, and in the second place, not everybody knows his real strength. Perhaps I am stronger than you, eh Misha?"

So. Like that. That's how it's going to be,

Then I lift my right arm, this very arm you see before you, and put my elbow on the table.

"O.K., strong man, let's put it to the test."

It's a real laugh, but he too places his wasted paw on the table, his pale, moderately hairy paw. The lads are bursting with laughter, because I am the champion at this business, not just in Fonarny Lane, but in the whole of the Arbat district, and for that matter I don't know who in the whole of Moscow could pin my arm to the table, except perhaps Grigory Novak.

So we engaged, and gently, almost without trying I bent his paw down, but about ten centimeters from the table it somehow jammed. I doubled my pressure, to no avail. I trebled it, but it was no go. It was as if my arm were resting on solid metal, practically tank armor. I looked into his eyes, with their yellow fire. On his lips was an amiable smile. I quadrupled my efforts and at this point my arm, as if it didn't belong to me, moved upwards, and then down under the force of a pressure that just couldn't be human, it had to be mechanical, and there it was flattened on the table. Everybody was silent.

"He beat you by sheer nerve, Misha, sheer nerve," whispered Vaska Axiomov. "Have another go. Flex your muscles...."

"Quite right," says Popenkov, "it wasn't my muscle power that beat Misha, it was the superiority of my nervous system. If you like, we could have another go...."

We tried again—the result was the same.

We tried a third time—no go.

Here, to tell you the truth, my temperament got the better of me—as you know, my father is of Armenian origin—and I leapt on Popenkov. I rolled him, I pummelled him, I spun him, I bent him, and suddenly I was pinned down by both shoulder blades, touché, and above me yellow fires, ugh!, his damned eyes.

"Nerves," said Tolik Proglotilin, "he's got nerves of steel. We've all got weak nerves, but they," indicating Popenkov with respect, "they've got nerves of steel."

A gentleman acknowledges defeat, and I did so, I slapped Popenkov on the shoulder (he practically collapsed) and sent for vodka.

Popenkov sat quiet and modest, I must say he didn't brag at all. We drank. To smooth it over the lads began singing songs from the war and prewar years, different marching songs.

> Where the infantry can't pass
> Nor armored train race by
> Nor heavy tank crawl through
> The Steel Bird will fly.

"Here's our steel bird," said Vaska Axiomov, embracing Popenkov, "our very own real steel bird."

"Steel, all metal," continued Tolik Proglotilin affectionately.

And a new version was composed.

> Where Axiomov is not outstripped
> Where Proglotilin can't race by
> Nor Fuchinyan crawl through
> The Steel Bird will fly.

Well, naturally, they all roared laughing. You just have to hold a finger up to our boys and they guffaw.

And here, pals, something very strange took place, just like they describe in novels. Popenkov jumped up, began waving his arms around, just like a bird, his eyes burning feverishly, he became pretty terrifying, and began yelling in some half-intelligible language:

"Kertl für linker, I knew it, at last! Yes, I am a Steel zhiza, chuiza drong! Aha, we've got... fricheki, klocheki kryt, kryt, kryt! In flight—the whistle and claw of a... percator!"

We were all dumbfounded, looking at this freak, then suddenly he was silent, got embarrassed, smiled gently and squatted down.

"Not a bad trick I played on you, eh? A funny one, eh?"

Everybody breathed a sigh of relief and burst out laughing, "What a card! A steel bird, all right, what a nervous system!"

But he called me aside.

"Actually, Misha, I was after your hide," he told me softly.

I began to shake, and resolved to resist to the end, defend to the death.

"You couldn't help me to install some furniture tomorrow, I suppose?" he asked. "I can't manage alone, and my wife, you know, is a weak woman. You see, we have decided to furnish the place, as it is, it's like being on bivouac. It would be nice to have furniture for when our relatives come."

"Sure, Steel Bird," I said, to tell the truth relieved that my hide hadn't been required after all. "Sure, Steel Bird, we'll do whatever we can. I'll be along tomorrow with Vaska and Tolik." So that's how it was, guys! We went on with what we were doing. Bottoms up! Salute. Oh yes, we carried the furniture in for him, and that evening he nailed up the main entrance. Since then the tenants have been using the back entrance.

The Doctor's Recollections

I treated him many times, each time as if I were blindfolded, each time the diagnosis was completely unclear to me. In the end I began to think his getting better had nothing to do with my treatment, the antibiotics or the physiotherapy, it was just his own will, the same way as he got sick.

Each summons to him was agony for me, an exertion of all my spiritual strength, that is, all the strength of my higher nervous system. In the first place, I sometimes began to think that there was something powerful and mysterious about him, in his organism, something of the sort that completely contradicts my outlook as a Soviet doctor. In the second place, I noticed each time that this secret force plunged me into a state of absolute abulia, that is, the absence of any voluntary reactions, into the torpid state of a domestic animal, merely awaiting orders and the lash.

One day he asked me to admit one of his relatives to the hospital for two weeks. This relative was a strapping bull, like a blacksmith. I examined him and naturally refused to hospitalize a perfectly healthy man. What on earth for, I thought, after all even the hospital corridors were crammed with critically ill patients, really in need of treatment.

"Try to understand, Doctor," Popenkov wheedled, "this man has traveled a long distance, he has spent a month in the foundations of the Palace of Soviets, he'll die if you don't save him."

"Not at all, Comrade Popenkov," I objected. "Your relative is in fine working condition. If he is tired from the journey, he can rest at your place. I've noticed that your vestibule has turned into a fairly comfortable apartment." At this point I permitted myself a grin.

That was in a very difficult time for we medicos, the winter of 1953. Just a short while before a group of professors had been arrested and charged with terrible crimes. All my life I had admired these scholars, in point of fact they were my teachers, and I couldn't understand their logic. How could they leave the high road of humanism for the path of crime against humanity? Naturally I kept my thoughts to myself.

It was all aggravated by the fact that the crimes of these scholars ricocheted on all of us honest Soviet doctors. Some folks even developed a distrust of anything in a white coat. In the clinic where I conducted consultations once a week I had occasion to meet such instances of suspicion and also insulting comments, can you imagine, apropos of my nose. I never would have thought that a nose had anything to do with medicine.

One night as I lay in bed I heard the elevator coming up. The elevator in our building hadn't been used for several years, so this unusual and unexpected sound put me on my guard.

"You can't make an omelette without breaking eggs," I thought and quickly got up and put on warm clothes.

There was a soft knock at the door. I calmly opened it, and on the landing stood Popenkov.

"I wanted to have a word with you, Doctor," he said, "I can't understand what's going on. Two days ago you gave me some medicine for my ears, and my liver acted up. Forgive me, but for some time I have been noticing some strange things, fuchi melazi rikatuer, you prescribe something for the heart, and there's a sharp pain in the ureter, kryt, kryt, liska bul chvar, your vitamins cause severe vitamin deficiency. What is it all about? Can you give me an explanation?"

On my word of honor, he said all that to me.

"Yes, I see," I replied, "I am sorry, it won't happen again."

Next morning I took his relative to the hospital.

The Doctors' Consilium, Having Taken Place in the Summer of 1956

"Yes, we must look the facts boldly in the face. There is still much in nature that has not been studied...."

"You will excuse me, Comrades, perhaps you will think me mad, but...."

"Why did you stop? Go on!"

"No, wait a bit."

"Let's compare our data once more with the anthrocometry and the test data and x-rays of a homo sapiens."

"Nonsense, colleague! Perhaps you are assuming that normal anatomy and physiology can have somehow changed recently."

"Comrades, you will think I'm mad, but...."

"You've stopped again? Say it."

"No, I'll wait a bit."

"However our data is so astonishing that one inevitably begins wondering..."

"Doctors, let us remain within the bounds of science. Miracles don't happen."

"No, but that way we will never get out of the impasse."

"Comrades, I must be mad, but...."

"Well, say it!"

"Go on, say it!"

"Have your say!"

"... but could we not surmise that we have an airplane before us?"

"Imagine, the same thing occurred to me, but I couldn't bring myself to say it."

"Colleagues, colleagues, let us stay within the bounds...."

"... and yet I am convinced that before us is no homo sapiens, but an ordinary steel airplane."

"Let's not be too hasty, let's call in a construction engineer. I'll ring an engineer I know."

....

Tupolev arrived and was acquainted with the data.

"No, this is not altogether an airplane," he said, "although it has many features in common with a fighter-interceptor."

....

"Comrades, perhaps my train of thought will seem strange, but...??"

"... but would it be impossible to assume we have a bird before us?"

"I wanted to suggest that myself, but couldn't bring myself to do so."

"Let's not rush to conclusions, Doctor, let's call in an ornithologist."

....

Academician Bukhvostov arrived and was acquainted with the data.

"Although it has some similarities," he said, "it is not a bird. It can't be a bird with such obvious features of a fighter-interceptor."

....

"Might we not, Comrades—of course, this may throw us way off—but might we not, considering all the statements and summing up the opinions of authoritative specialists, and likewise the nature of the subject's behavior, his somewhat frequent use of sound combinations as yet unknown on earth, might we not assume, with all due caution, naturally, could we not tentatively assume that we are dealing with a completely new species with a unique combination of organic and inorganic features, could it not be assumed that in this given instance we are pioneers, might we not be dealing with a Steel Bird?"

"I ask you all to rise, I ask you all to remember that the records of this consilium are absolutely confidential."

Part for Cornet-à-Pistons

Theme: We were born to make fantasy fact, overcome distance and space....

Improvisation: The doors are nailed up with rusty nails, what are we tenants to do about him? It's hard to get through the dirty back way, but still if we must, we will go that way. As long as there's concord, peace, and splendor, and the fire regulations are observed.

End of theme:... Steel arm-wings gave us reason, and in place of a heart a combustion engine.

The Barber's Recollections

Our downstairs neighbor from the vestibule pinned me to the wall. "I beg your pardon," I say, "what's going on?" And he says: "Kryt kryt, fil burore liap," that is, in some foreign language. "And what if I have a go at you with the cutthroat? Snap, and the razor snapped. Let me through," but he doesn't. "And what if I have a go at you with scissors?" Snap, and the scissors snapped. "And what if I give you a blow wave?" "That—by all means!" he says. "And what if I freshen you up with Flight eau-de-cologne?" "By all means," he says. "And what about a face massage with nourishing cream?" "By all means," he says, and lets me through.

Chapter 3

The dreary necessity of plodding along with the plot obliges me to try to reconstruct the chronological sequence of events.

In 1950, or maybe a year before or later, a quarrel of unusual force blew up between the Z.s. It started, of course, on account of old French tapestries and other such objects from the time of Mme. Pompadour. The Deputy Minister was becoming impoverished terrifyingly fast, his wardrobe was wearing out, the food was deteriorating daily, all his salary and extra allowances, and even a certain portion of their rations went on antiques. It reached the point where Z. began hitting on his guard Yury Filippovich for a North cigarette. That's what it had come to—sinking from Herzegovina Flors to Norths, and somebody else's, at that.

"You know, Zinaida," said Z., "it's high time to put a stop to this. Our apartment has turned into a second-hand shop. It's bourgeois decadence and cosmopolitanism."

"You've no sensitivity, you're a ruffian, you're rusty," sobbed Zinaida. "I get no understanding from you, no flicker of interest. All you want to do is to wink at that vulgar Tsvetkova. I'm leaving."

"What has Tsvetkova got to do with it? Where are you going? Who to? God, what's going on?" wailed Z. The thought that Zinochka might deprive him of her embraces seemed incredibly awful, quite hellish. Incidentally he thought of the unpleasantnesses at work, of explanations in the party, of the whole complex of unpleasantnesses associated with a wife's departure.

"I am going to a man who speaks my language. To a man whose esthetic views agree with my own," announced Zinochka.

And she went downstairs, to the vestibule, to Popenkov, who had for ages been jumping in wild anticipation all over the squares of the mosaic.

"Will you have me?" she asked dramatically.

"My love, light of my eyes, kuvyral lekur lekuvirl ki ki!" Popenkov danced in delight.

"How about that! I've toppled the Deputy Minister," he thought, beside himself with joy and exhilarating optimism.

There was an immediate division of property, after which Z. was left in his rooms alone with a cot, a bedside table, a battered wardrobe and a few books in his speciality. He was standing there at a complete loss, almost prostrate, when in walked Popenkov with the aim of delivering the final blow to k.o. the ungrateful Deputy Minister.

"As a man and a knight," he addressed himself to Z., "I am obliged to intervene on behalf of the unfortunate woman you have tormented and in addition to everything else accused of cosmopolitanism. Zinaida is not a cosmopolitan, she is a true Soviet citizen, whereas you, Comrade Z., would do well to remember those peculiar notions and doubts which you shared with your wife after disconnecting the telephone and tucking up in the blankets. Remember, I am in the know. By the way, Zinaida asked me to bring down this little cupboard. A woman can't exist without a wardrobe, and you'll get by without it. Adios."

Effortlessly lifting the huge wardrobe and shaking out Z.'s last few things, he departed.

All night long the vestibule was noisy with the squeak of springs and incomprehensible throaty utterances, while on the first-floor landing Z. and Yury Filippovich suffered bitterly over a half-liter.

"We have been orphaned, you and I, Filippich," wept Z. "We are alone, Filippich.... How shall we bear it?"

"Go into seclusion, Comrade Deputy Minister," advised the sergeant, "withdraw into yourself and think only of work...."

Quite understandably, from that night Z.'s career took a sharp downward turn.

Popenkov and his young consort gradually normalized their surroundings. Relatives frequently arrived to do their bit. Relative Koka helped with his hammer, relative Goga with his paint brush, relative Dmitry turned out to be good at everything.

The vestibule was partitioned, creating rooms, alcoves, boudoirs, and sanitary areas. Peter the Great's boots ended up in Popenkov's study. The Japanese theme adorned Zinochka's boudoir, intimately and yet delicately. The knights, Vikings and Novgorodians ended up in the sitting room, which must have greatly inspired visiting relatives as they frequently sang warlike songs together there.

Their diet steadily improved, Zinochka grew kinder, succulent, with milky-waxy, sugary-creamy ripeness. Her life was complete harmony, her inner world was ruled by subtropical calm, splendor, and magnificent peace.

Popenkov would appear in her boudoir always suddenly, purposefully, throwing from the threshold a daggerlike glance into the blue lagoons of her eyes, fling himself in, drown in delights, boiling furiously.

"You are my geisha!" he would cry out. "My courtesan! My Lorelei!"

In the winter of 1953 an important event took place in Moscow—J.V.

Stalin died. The nation's grief overwhelmed No. 14 Fonarny Lane too. Hollow groans could be heard there for several days. Up on the first floor two lone wolves, Yury Filippovich and the Deputy Minister, wept bitterly at night. The shrill desperate notes of the cornet-à-pistons penetrated every apartment, taking advantage of the tragic freedom of those days.

Nikolai Nikolayevich Nikolayev all but perished in the scuffle on Trubnaya Square. Misha Fuchinyan, Tolik Proglotilin and Vaska Axiomov just managed to drag him out of the sewerage hatch. These men organized a battle unit and somehow or other rescued the tortured inhabitants of Fonarny Lane from the Trubnaya. So, not one of them pushed through into the Hall of Columns.

Nobody, that is, except of course, Popenkov, who without himself knowing how, perhaps by supernatural means and without special effort or bodily harm found himself in the "holy of holies," saw everything in the greatest detail and even brought back as a souvenir a scrap of the mourning crepe from the chandelier.

The whole day after that he was preoccupied, absorbed in himself, he repulsed the relatives and even Zinochka, he stood in Peter's Wellingtons and thought and thought.

Well, he decided towards the end of the day, here is the result of half measures and running in place. The sad result, the consequence of an unnecessary masquerade. Fuchi elazi kompror, and kindly lie in a coffin. No, we will take another route, ru hioplastr, ru!

Then he took his elevator up to the fifth floor and went into Maria Samopalov's flat, thundering in his iron boots.

As he anticipated, Maria and Agrippina were sitting griefstricken by their idle loom. Folding his arms on his breast, Popenkov mourned with them several minutes in complete silence. Then he said his piece.

"Maria Timofeyevna and you, Agrippina! Our grief is boundless, but life goes on. We mustn't forget our nearest, we mustn't forget the thousands who await joy and light from us, who desire to worship art daily. We must work. We must respond with labor!"

At this, Maria and Agrippina roused themselves and set the loom in motion. Popenkov stood for a while watching the next masterpiece emerge, then left quietly so as not to disturb the creative process.

Maria and her daughter had worked all these years, barely sleeping a wink. They understood perfectly the importance of their job, after all Benjamin Fedoseyevich's relatives, those disinterested culture-peddlers, were spreading antique French tapestries throughout the Far East and in Siberia, the Ukraine, the Trans-Caucasian and Central Asian republics.

Popenkov took the barber on himself, had a chat with him, expounding the importance of Maria's work. He had a chat with Zulphia, too, who soon afterwards set on her husband, demanding a small tapestry for their apartment, and forcing Lev Ustinovich to loosen the purse-strings.

After this purchase the Samopalov family's attitude to Maria became very respectful, moreover over the years all the members of the family had grown accustomed to the noise of the loom which they now perceived as something dear and familiar.

House manager Nikolayev marveled: the squabbles in Apt. 31 had stopped and so had the scandals and constant petitions to himself and Stalin. Mind you, the latter addressee, as everybody knows, soon dropped out of the picture, having tasted very little of the quiet life.

Nikolai Nikolayevich lived in constant terror. He was afraid Popenkov might unmask him to the tenants, show him up as a common cornet-à-pistons player, a frivolous musician and not a manager.

When they met he would adopt a superior dourness and show interest in the organization of his quarters.

"Well, how is it? Are you getting organized? Can you cope with the discomfort? Can I send you a metal worker?"

Popenkov would smile understandingly, give him a wink and turn around conspiratorially.

"And how about you, Nikolai Nikolayevich? Are you still improvising? I'm keeping mum."

And Nikolai Nikolayevich would be lost, drop his superior tone and crumple before Popenkov like a delinquent schoolboy before the headmaster.

"I put up with the discomfort, of course, Nikolai Nikolayevich. You know for yourself, the apartment is like a thoroughfare. My wife's nerves are in a bad way."

And Popenkov would adopt his favorite pose, squatting on his haunches and looking up at Nikolai Nikolayevich with his burning gaze.

"But what can be done, Benjamin Fedoseyevich, I can't think of anything, it's an entrance hall, after all," said Nikolayev.

"Hulo marano ri!" Popenkov exclaimed, jumped up and rubbed his hands wildly.

"What did you say?" Nikolai Nikolayevich began to tremble like an aspen leaf.

"I beg your pardon," Popenkov feigned embarrassment, "I meant to say that it will be no great misfortune if we decide to do away with the unnecessary extravagant vulgar so-called main entrance, which was once used by jurors and other servants of the bourgeoisie, and direct the stream of tenants through the so-called back entrance, which is really quite convenient and even a more expedient entrance."

"That of course... is of course reasonable," mumbled Nikolayev, "but the so-called back entrance is terribly narrow. A man of my size can only squeeze through with a great effort, and in the event of somebody buying a piano or somebody's death, how would you carry in a piano or a coffin?"

"What are the windows for?" exclaimed Popenkov, but recollecting, burst out laughing. "But what am I saying—the windows are quite unacceptable to you.... Wait, wait the windows could easily be used for raising a piano or lowering a coffin. A bracket, a pully, a strong rope, that's all! Do you follow me?"

"A bold... a bold..." muttered Nikolayev, "a very bold solution to the problem, but...."

"You needn't worry about the rest, dear Nikolai Nikolayevich, I'll handle the tenants' reaction. Don't you worry yourself over anything, just keep on quietly making music, ha-ha-ha! Yes, I understand, I understand, I won't say a word, not a word!"

And so the main entrance was nailed up and the white marble staircase was walled up. Relative Goga made a really aristocratic candelabra for Zinochka out of the snake door handles. In the beginning the windows were used for getting in and out of the fashionable apartment, but later, when the tenants were used to the new regime, the front entrance was reopened, but only for the Popenkov family's private use.

And so the first stage was completed, and although it had taken quite a number of years, Popenkov was satisfied, went around serene and proud, but his eyes betrayed their former heavy yellow heat, the ancient dream and longing of Tamerlane.

Sometimes at night he would interrupt his delights and put a question to his spouse.

"Are you content with your fate, Zinaida?"

The fabulously magnificent Zinaida would stretch in servile languor.

"I am almost content, 99.9 percent content, and if you were to...."

"I understand your restless soul, I understand the magnitude of that .1 percent, he said and began to boil furiously, and then a little later asked again, "but do you understand me?"

Zinochka, now 99.99 percent content, replied:

"I think I understand you and the beauty of your dream. You, like a mighty spirit, have transformed this foul vestibule into a majestic palace, an esthetic temple to our fatal passion, and you are different from the gray drab men, the deputy ministers, and policemen, doctors, barbers and divers that I knew before you, you are a hurricane of fire and steel, a powerful and proud spirit, but sometimes, Benjamin, I am bewildered, I still cannot understand your mysterious words...."

"Which words...?" Popenkov laughed excitedly.

"Well, for example, the words which you utter in an excess of passion—bu zhiza hoku romuar, tebet felari...."

"... kukubu?" cried Popenkov. The dialogue was temporarily interrupted.

"Yes, those words, what do they mean?" Zinochka asked weakly afterwards.

"Ha-ha," Popenkov was euphoric, "but you know I am no ordinary man, and some of my characteristics are even different from those of a bird. I am the steel bird. That's our language, the language of steel birds."

"Oh, how fascinating! How exciting! A *steel* bird!" breathed Zinochka.

"Kukubu!" cried Popenkov.

Once more there was an interruption in the conversation.

"But are there any others? Are there more in the world like you?" Zinochka renewed the conversation.

"Not many yet, but not so few, either. Earlier attempts unfortunately fell through, in my opinion because of half-measures and running in place. Chivi, chivi zol farar, do you understand me?"

"Almost."

"For the time being we are forced to get around in jackets and shoes and lisp English, French or Spanish. And I have to use the great and wonderful, truthful and free,[15] damn it, chuchumo rogi far! But never mind, the time will come! What strength I feel! What predestination! You know," he whispered, "I am the chief steel bird...."

"You are the chief! The chief! The chief!" breathed Zinochka.

"Kukubu!" cried Popenkov.

"Let me in on your plans, my steel bird," Zinochka cooed tenderly after a short pause.

Popenkov ran out of the boudoir and returned with the iron boots on his bare legs.

"I can do anything," he said, striding around the bed, "I shall arrange everything as I want it. First I shall complete my little experiment with this puny six-story house. I'll sit them all at looms, all these intellectuals. They'll all be weaving tapestries for me, all these Samopalovs, Zeldoviches, Nikolaevs, Fuchinyans, Proglotilins, Axiomovs, Tsvetkovas...."

"Tsvetkova too?" Zinochka inquired drily. "I think Tsvetkova should be treated differently."

"Ha-ha-ha, you want to deal with Tsvetkova?" Popenkov laughed patronizingly. "By all means, pet."

"Thank you," Zinochka smiled secretively.

"What do you want to do with her? Fuchi elazi kompfor trandiratsiu?" asked Popenkov.

"Fuchi emazi kir madagor," replied Zinochka.

"Kekl fedekl?" Popenkov roared with laughter.

"Chlok buritano," giggled Zinochka.

"Mugi halogi ku?"

"Lachi artugo holeonon."

"Burtl?"

"Holo oloh, ha-ha-ha!" shrieked Zinochka madly, like a mare.

"Kukubu!" cried Popenkov.

A pause and silence, desire and lust, scuffling and profanation, loathing, rotting, rebirth and self-generation, quivering, swallowing, absorption, expulsion, smothering, annihilation of a live, light, good person with the gait of a calf, the eyes of a young deer, with apple breasts, with emerald eyes, with a little orange of a heart and a mysterious soul, annihilation.

And meanwhile the chapter comes to an end, and the years pass, certain individuals are growing old, some are growing up and see love and college, records, fame and earthly goods on soft pillows and sweaty fists, and nobody sees death, on the contrary, everybody sees scenes from life, and nobody hears in his sleep the soft rumble of the apparently nonfunctioning elevator going up and down, even Dr. Zeldovich sleeps soundly now, his warm things hidden in a trunk with naphthalene till winter.

The Night Flight of the Steel Bird

a)   *Address to the Bronze Horseman.*
      Whence did you think to threaten the Swedes?
      Tut-tut. And this city you founded to spite
      an arrogant neighbor? Tut-tut. Were all your deeds
      the fleet, Poltava, a window on Europe?
      Well, do you know who stands before you? I am
      the Steel Zhiza Chuiza Drong! I

need no monuments, I myself am
a flying monument. If I want,
I devour, if I want, I pardon. I shan't
pardon you, don't expect it. I will gobble you up,
Peter Alexeyevich.

b)   *Address to the monument to Yury Dolgoruky.*
I shall devour your horse, make shashliks
of your horse. To the Aragvi with your
horse, to the kitchens! You I have already devoured.

c)   *Address to the monument commemorating a
       thousand years of Russia.*
What a date—a miserable thousand!
What sort of creatures are these in cassocks, in
cloaks, in armor, in jerkins, in
frock coats? I'll smelt you all and make
a porridge of bronze, and here will be a monument
to bronze porridge! and I will eat it.

d)   *Address to the monument to Abraham Lincoln.*
"Don't look down your nose, Abe! You freed
the Negroes? Nothing to be proud of.
No protests! to the rubbish heap!

e)   *Address to the monument to the Warsaw ghetto.*
Well, no need for discussion here! Everyone
into the oven, and I've already eaten Mordechai Anilewicz.

f)   *Conversion to Earth Satellite and address to all mankind.*
This is Earth Satellite the Steel Bird
speaking. All your artificial satellites
I have already devoured. Honored comrades, a great
surprise is being made ready,
a big purge, a purge of the planet from
the monuments of the past. There will be no past,
there will be no future, and I have devoured the present
already. Honored comrades, eat up monuments
disciplinedly! Now you have one monument—the charming satellite, the Steel Bird. Make ready
perches, a perch from each city, or I
shall eat you up.

The Doctor's Recollections

He came to see me and complained about his appetite. His stomach actually was swollen and covered with blue lines. My appetite has disappeared, he said. Then take the matter to the police, I advised boldly. What about the digestive tract, he asked. Some rivets in the gut really had worked loose, there were bolts rattling around, and some welded seams had come apart. When all's said and done I'm no engineer and we're not living in some science fiction novel, but in ordinary Soviet reality, I announced to him and washed my hands of it. Very well, Zeldovich, you'll end up in here, he said and slapped his swollen belly. I opened the window and suggested he vacate the flat. He flew out of the window. His flight was heavy, sometimes he would fall, like a plane in air pockets, but then he would suddenly soar and disappear. Of course, I realize I'll have to pay for my boldness, but the prospect of ending up in his stomach, in that steel bag, I tell you straight, I don't relish in the least.

The Building Inspector's Report

In the course of the years, due to the rebuilding of the ground floor, and likewise due to the almost incessant rhythmic shaking in the right-hand corner of the former vestibule, the foundations of No. 14 are collapsing and the right-hand corner sinking after the fashion of an Italian tower in Pisa (Consultation with U.S.S.R.-Italian Friendship Society). Sewage from the new autonomous sewage system is vigorously washing away the soil.

The situation is catastrophic, one could say, Help, good people! A representative for the foundation, the corner stone, declared in a private conversation that they can't hold out more than two months.

I hereby give warning and take this opportunity to state, on the basis of the above, that in the continuing absence of measures to organize a reprieve for No. 14, which I love and adore, I relinquish my commission as building inspector and in a state of spiritual disharmony will put an end to myself by means of a hemp rope.

Part for Cornet-à-Pistons

Theme: A smell of crisp crusts floats out the windows, and a flutter of hands behind the curtain....

Improvisation: The foundations are collapsing, clouds are gathering, it leans like a willow, our dear home, It has inclined like the tower in Pisa, it leaks, sewage at that. Young tenants, old heroes go on living in it, unsuspecting. There will be a disaster, my heart is thumping, my arms hang loose, there is grief in my gut....

End of theme: Help, good people!

Chapter 4

Returning once again to a strictly chronological narrative, I must inform you that exactly eighteen years have passed since the beginning of this story. Every reader is aware of the changes that have taken place during that period in the life of society, so there's no need to elaborate on them. I shall continue my dreary task and weave the web of the plot, the web in which my heroes have been trapped without realizing it, and in which for the time being they are basking, their emerald tummies turned upwards to the caressing May sun.

One wonderful May evening the barber Samopalov's eldest son Ahmed, by now a very famous, almost fantastically famous young writer, one of those idols of the young that drive around in small Zaporozhets[16] cars and have the habit of turning up exactly where they are least expected, well, this same Ahmed Lvovich Samopalov was going to his home in Fonarny Lane. Ahmed had recently smashed his Zaporozhets and sold it for scrap, so he was returning home on foot. He was excited by his battles in the Central Writers' club and was still passionately engaged in mental polemics with his opponents.

"It didn't come off, the old man didn't die," he thought. "Well then, all right, you're aligning, you come along, you vipers, sit and snigger, you crawl, and interfere with the game, right? And to finish it off you pit against me one of your well-trained scum, right? You think that he's got a strong attack and a good defense, don't you? You've got Ahmed Samopalov already buried, haven't you? I'll show you, I only need two serves to find his weak points, I see quite clearly that he won't get a twister into the right-hand corner of the table. First I serve him a couple of strong hits from the right, he gets them, I foreshorten, he gets it, then I smash one into the right corner and even if by some miracle he gets it I immediately cut in from the left and he's done for, the point goes my way. Fine activists and geniuses when they can't even hold a racket correctly, poor little pricks!"

And here Ahmed suddenly gasped, shuddered, clutched at his heart, then his pulse, next closed his eyes, opened them again, and then pinched himself on the leg.

In the shadow on the other side of the street, in the blue marine ozone strode along a rare specimen of the human race, a long-legged, blue-eyed, tanned, sexy, fair, provocative girl. Ahmed began drumming to himself a militant literary anthem, because this specimen was the ideal, the idol, the clarion call of 1965 young Moscow prose, the secret dream of all Zaporozhets car owners, starting with Anatoly Gladilin.[17]

I don't know what it will be in the printed text, but I just numbered this page 88 in my manuscript. This was completely fortuitous, but significant, since 88 in the language of radio operators means love, as was proclaimed by the poet Robert Ivanovich Rozhdestvensky.

Ahmed Lvovich drummed the anthem and darted purposefully forward.

"Ninochka! What a surprise! Have you been back long? Did you see anyone from home?" he cried, feigning unprecedented and absolutely platonic delight.

"Hello, Ahmed Lvovich," said the girl awkwardly, slowing her pace, blushing and lowering her eyes.

"Popularity, blasted popularity, monstrous fame," raced wildly through Ahmed's head.

"Well, how are the folks there? How tan you are, how you've grown, you're a grown woman," he burbled affectionately, taking her by the elbow. "Have you been back long, Ninochka?"

"I beg your pardon, Ahmed Lvovich, but I'm not Ninochka, my name is Alya, I'm Alya Tsvetkova from across the landing," lisped the girl, "and I saw your folks this morning, Lev Ustinovich and Aunty Zulphia, and Auntie Maria, and Auntie Agrippina, and Zurab took me for a ride on his motorcycle.... But I haven't seen *you* for about five days, Ahmed Lvovich."

It was quite understandable that she hadn't seen him for so long. Ahmed Lvovich hadn't slept at home for five days, he had been hanging around the literary scene, playing dice, buru, preference, Fool, King, nines,[18] ping-pong.

"Good God, so you're Alya then, Marina's daughter!" cried Ahmed. "What has happened to you in the last five days?"

"I've no idea what's happened," replied Alya. "You can see how I've changed in the last five days. Men won't leave me alone, and your brother Zurab takes me for a ride on his motorcycle every morning. Last week he wouldn't let me near his motorcycle, he wouldn't let me lay a finger on it," she sobbed.

"There, there, there, Alya, Alya, Alyechka, Alyechka," muttered Ahmed thinking: "If Zurab gets in the way I'll wrap his motorcycle around his head!" They were already in Fonarny Lane, and destiny herself skated towards them in the form of a jolly, purposeful old man on roller skates with a perky turned-up goatee, and with a long pole, by means of which he was lighting the luminescent lamps, as if they were the gas lanterns of blessed nineteenth-century memory, and the lanterns lit up in the sun, which, like destiny, was sitting on the chimney of No. 14., dangling its thin legs in striped stockings, smoking and winking away, and the sky was blue, like their bright blue destiny, and without a single cross, a single fighter plane, an antediluvian blissful sky with small orange corners.

"Well, have you read any of my books?" Ahmed suddenly remembered his position in society.

"Of course I have," replied Alya. "We did them in school, Brovner-Dunduchnikov, our literature teacher, analyzed your books and really ran you down, but I told him I loved you."

"What?" exclaimed Ahmed, giving Alya's elbow a tight squeeze.

"I did, that's just what I said to him. I love Ahmed Samopalov's work because it treats the problem of alienation very interestingly. And then we had a joint conference about your work with Soft Toys Factory No. 4, and all the girls at the factory said that you give an interesting treatment of alienation, and Brovner-Dunduchnikov couldn't say anything. You might say it was only because of this common interest that I went to work at Soft Toys Factory No. 4 after I left school."

For the fourth time Zurab Samopalov's motorcycle dashed by, minus its muffler, expressing its indignation with the most dreadful din. Zurab himself ran after it in utter despair, in a state of dreadful oriental jealousy.

"So you love me?" Ahmed asked insinuatingly.

"On the whole, as a writer," said Alya.

With these words, they entered the yard.

In the yard two members of the pensioners' council were sitting in the blazing sun—former Deputy Minister Z. and Lev Ustinovich Samopalov, along with the janitor, Yury Filippovich Isayev. They had for hours been discussing matters of literature and art.

"What I think about these abstract artists," said Yury Filippovich, "is if you can't draw, then don't try, don't muck about. Personally I love painting and understand what's what. I used to draw myself once. I love Levitan's "Eternal Peace," now that's an outstanding watercolor. Have you ever noticed, comrades, how well it portrays vast expanse? And now we are conquering that expanse, that's why the painting is so good. Now your Ivan, Lev Ustinovich, is a real abstractionist, a formalist, an unreliable element. I don't know which way Nikolayev is looking, what he's thinking about in the House Office, when there are abstractionists under his nose spreading their rotten influence on spiritually ripe young people."

"That's not true, Filippich, my Ivan is a figuratist!" objected Lev Ustinovich heatedly. "Of course, he does distort, he filters, so to speak, nature through his imagination, through his fantasy, but that's not formalism, Filippich, that's a search for new forms."

"A figuratist, you say?" Yury Filippovich was indignant. "Just recently I posed for him, and how do you suppose he depicted me? A tiny forehead, a face like a fat blister, and a blue knife drawn on from the side, now what was that supposed to represent?"

"You shouldn't take offense, Filippich, he was portraying your inner self, not printing a photograph."

"Then my inner self is a fat blister?"

"That's right," concurred Samopalov.

"They should be pulled out by the roots, your figuratists!" bawled Isayev. "In other times they would have been dug out at the root and that would be that. Isn't that right, Comrade Zinolyubov?"[19]

"You must have Belinsky's times in mind, Yury Filippovich? The times of the violent Visarrion?" Z. smiled gently.

"That's right, Comrade Zinolyubov! Precisely those times!" yelled the janitor.

"Not so loud," said Z., "a bit more gently, delicately. Don't forget, Yury Filippovich, you have to tread carefully with talent, not all at once."

"What are you ranting about, Filippich," said Samopalov. "What are you cursing for? Why should you be losing sleep over my sons? We're all going to die soon, we'll be grains of sand in the stream of the universe."

"Philosophically correct," remarked Z.

"What did I say? You think I don't agree? Of course, we'll soon be grains of sand in the philosophical whirlwind of the universe," said the janitor, "That's why we should let a few of them have what for before it's too late, strike at the roots of this whole fraternity."

"Easy, easy, Yury Filippovich, gently, gently, be more cultivated," Z. admonished his former bodyguard.

And so the pensioners sat for hours on end, discussing issues of literature and art. Every week these issues were put on the agenda of the Pensioners' committee meeting, where opinions were recorded for posterity.

Meanwhile in the middle of the yard, the dominoes had been cast aside, and Fuchinyan, Proglotilin and Axiomov were discussing questions of literature and art.

"Today I started up the machine, got a book, and I'm reading away," Vasily Axiomov was telling the others. "Well, I'm reading this little book. Up comes the chief engineer. 'What are you reading, Axiomov?' I turned the book over and read the title. It turns out this book was written by our Ahmed Samopalov. *Look Back in Delight*, it was called. 'Do you like it?' asks the chief engineer. 'Pretty powerfully put together,' I say, 'the way he rips through the full stops and commas.' 'Crap!' yells Mitya Kosholkis from his machine. 'I know the book inside out,' he yells, 'it's pure crap.' Well, then all the boys begin talking at once. Some of them are shouting: 'he's out of touch with the people!' Others that: 'he *is* in touch with the people!' You can't make head or tail of it. The chief engineer says: 'Opinions are divided. Let's have a discussion. Stop the machines.' We stopped the machines and began discussing Ahmed's book. Our foreman Shcherbakov spoke from notes. The director came and joined in. We've got a fiery director, he's easy to get going. We argued till lunch-time."

"I've read that book," said Tolik Proglotilin. "Yesterday the supervisor gave it to me together with my assignment. Something funny happened. I'm driving down Sadovy Street, reading. I nearly went through a red light. I look around and the sergeant is sitting in his box reading. What are you reading, Sarge? I ask. He holds it up—it's *Look Back in Delight*. Pretty, good, isn't it? I yell. Not bad, he says with a sour smile, you can see Bunin's influence, Robbe-Grillet's too. Just then a semitrailer ran into the back of me. The driver got carried away with the book too. So we had an instant book discussion."

"I've read that book too," said Fuchinyan. "Yesterday we were repairing a cable under Crimea Bridge, so I put it in my diving-suit. I put it inside my mask, in front of my eyes, I'm repairing the cable and reading away. To tell you the truth, guys, I was engrossed. I didn't notice that the air tube broke. Ahmed really deals well with alienation of the individual."

"That's true. What's true is true," agreed Axiomov and Proglotilin. In short it was a peaceful warm spring evening. In three windows people were playing violins, in five more—the piano. One window was transmitting a number for cornet-à-pistons via the radio. Furniture movers were unhurriedly hoisting up another two pianos on pulleys, one of them dangled for the moment at third-floor level and the other was crawling up to the sixth. From Maria Samopalov's window the incessant tap of a loom floated down. Agrippina had hung several new Old French tapestries in the yard and was beating the dust of labor out of them. The artist-figuratist Ivan Samopalov displayed his latest portrait in his window, the likeness of a man-bird shot with burnished steel, product of the figuratist imagination. A still captivating Marina Tsvetkova was training a mirror on ex-Deputy Minister Zinolyubov through the wild ivy shading her window.

Well, what else? Yes, the junior footballers were neatly hitting the ground floor windows. And a furious motorcycle burst into the yard. Zurab had finally got it saddled and begun circling the yard, from time to time shooting up onto the fireproof wall. And then the youngest Samopalov, Valentin, entered the yard in Texan jeans, flippers, and a mask, with an aqualung on his back, a transistor on his chest, a movie camera in his pocket, a guitar in his hands, playing big beat,[20] whirling a hula hoop and shooting an amateur movie through his pocket. And last of all, to everyone's surprise, Ahmed was kissing young Alya Tsvetkova under the arch, punctuating the kisses with vows of eternal love.

Dr. Zeldovich appeared under the arch. Catching sight of Ahmed kissing, he addressed him:

"Good evening, Ahmed. Good evening, Alenka. Here's a candy for you. You know, Ahmed, during an operation today we got to arguing about literature. We opened up an abdominal cavity and somehow got talking. Well, naturally we remembered your *Look Back in Delight.* The surgical nurse was reading it in the operating room and said she was mad about it. I gave you your due too, Ahmed, although I confess I did criticize certain shortcomings. Our anesthetist was completely on your side, but the patient we were operating on said that the book might well be interesting, but that it was harmful...."

"He should have been given an anesthetic," said Ahmed disapprovingly.

"Just imagine, the strange thing was that he was talking under anesthetic," said Zeldovich. "Anyway, we got into a discussion and decided to conduct the operation in two stages. The patient said he would marshall his arguments together with quotes for the second stage. But I beg your pardon, I am disturbing you. All the best. Every success."

Zeldovich was about to whisk through the back entry, but he bolted straight back out because Benjamin Fedoseyevich and his wife Zinaida were coming out towards him.

Popenkov had changed little over the years, he had merely acquired stability, a slight heaviness and a distinct imperiousness in his gaze. Zinaida reminded one of a festive cake. The instant they appeared the radio went off on the fifth floor and into the yard ran a breathless Nikolai Nikolayevich, pulling on his suspenders as he ran. Apologizing for being late, he joined the Popenkovs and walked after them, just a little behind.

A tense silence immediately settled on the yard, if you ignore the kisses and intermittent whispering under the arch, the clatter of the motorcycle, the cries of big beat and the lowing of the frivolous artist.

"Cut off the Samopalov's water and power for the disrespectful formalist caricature," Popenkov threw over his shoulder.

Nikolai Nikolayevich made a note of it.

"How will we manage without water and power?" gasped Lev Ustinovich. "I've got a large family, Benjamin Fedoseyevich, you know yourself, it won't be possible to have a shave or a haircut...."

"Why kumni tari huchi cha?" shouted an enraged Popenkov.

"What?"

"Why doesn't your son want to put his talent to the service of the people?" translated Zinaida.

"Benjamin Fedoseyevich, what about my application? Have you looked into it?" he was addressed by Zinolyubov.

"The marriage to Tsvetkova?" grinned Popenkov.

"Chichi michi kholeonon," Zinaida whispered into his ear and burst out laughing.

"Quite so, marriage to Marina Nikitichna Tsvetkova," affirmed Zinolyubov. "The realization of an old dream. At one time you used to say that you had saved my life on several occasions, Benjamin Fedoseyevich, and on one occasion you saved it indeed," with a sideways glance at Zinochka. "Now you have yet another opportunity."

"Kukubu with Tsvetkova? Chivilikh! Klocheki, drocheki rykl ekl!"

"Marriage to Tsvetkova? Never! In the event of insubordination we will cut off your power, water and sewage," translated Zinaida, adding on her own account, "The sewage, understand? Do you understand what that smells of, Comrade Zinolyubov?"

"He is forgetting Russian altogether, this steel bird," said Ahmed to Alya.

"Oh, damn *him*," said Alya. "Kiss me again please, Ahmed Lvovich."

The tour of the yard continued. Popenkov stopped in the center and began examining the walls and open windows of the building very carefully.

"Benjamin Fedoseyevich, I meant to tell you yesterday," began Nikolayev carefully. "The fact is, Benjamin Fedoseyevich, they have begun taking an interest in you."

"What? How? Where?" cried Popenkov. "Where have they begun taking an interest in me?"

"Up there," said Nikolayev significantly, indicating the sky with his thumb.

Popenkov dropped onto his belly and began crawling, twisting his head round like a guilty dog and poking out his tongue. Then he jumped up and slid around the yard on tiptoe, to tragic music that only he could hear.

"Assa," he whispered to himself, "assa, a dance to feast the eyes, oom-pa, oom-pa, oom-pa-pa!"

The whole yard followed with interest Popenkov's pirouettes, his jumps, the tragic clapping and convolutions of his hands, his fiery smiles, bows and equivocation towards the spectators, the top-like gyrations quivering to a stop.

Nikolai Nikolayevich, at first bewitched by the dance; almost expired with fright when Popenkov lay down on the asphalt. He ran to him, lay down alongside and whispered:

"Benjamin Fedoseyevich, get up, my dear man! Don't torment me. They want to put you on the commission for decent living. They acknowledge your experience, Benjamin Fedoseyevich, your grasp of the subject, your taste...."

Popenkov quickly jumped to his feet and shook himself.

"Why not, I'm willing!" he exclaimed. "I'll join the commission gladly. It's high time they put me on the commission, shushi marushi formazatron!"

"I'll introduce order into life," translated Zinochka.

"By the way, Nikolayev," Popenkov made a slow tour around the yard and motioned to the Zhek chief to follow him. "By the way, rufir haratari koblo bator...."

"Please, speak Russian," begged Nikolayev.

"It's time you understood," said Popenkov in irritation. "Very well. Well, it's like this. Tomorrow my relatives want to remodel the roof, make a hatch so I can get straight out of the elevator onto the roof."

"What for?" asked Nikolayev in panic.

"What do you mean, what for? You know I occasionally use the elevator to... to go for a ride. Sometimes I feel like having a sit on the roof."

"Of course, I understand that," said Nikolayev, "I understand your desire, but the fact is, Benjamin Fedoseyevich, that our building is in a very precarious state, almost a state of collapse. The building inspector gave me a report on it today, and I am afraid that an opening in the roof may finally shatter the foundations."

"Rubbish. Panic-mongering. It's high time the building inspector passed on to the next world," said Popenkov. "In short, the discussion is closed. Tomorrow my relatives make the hatch."

Suddenly a cry resounded over the yard.

"Citizens!"

And everybody looked up to see the building inspector standing on the fifth-floor ledge. He was waving his hands to balance himself, like a large butterfly beating against an invisible window.

"Citizens!" he cried. "This is the third night I am unable to sleep, I can't eat, my teeth have worked loose, my strength is ebbing away... Citizens, our building is in a state of collapse! Take a look, can't you see it has become like the Italian tower in the city of Pisa? The foundations can't hold for more than a week. They themselves told me that! Citizens, urgent measures are called for! Citizens, all my reports just get shelved!"

To stop himself falling the building inspector was making circular movements with his arms, but he didn't look like a bird, rather like an unfortunate butterfly, because he was wearing his wife's vast floral dressing gown, from under which his bare legs poked out.

Nobody noticed how Popenkov appeared on the ledge, they only saw him quickly sliding towards the building inspector.

"Citizens!" called the building inspector for the last time and was just then seized in the steel grasp of Popenkov, quick as a wink crushing the bold fabric of the dressing gown.

"Did you see the madman?" barked Popenkov to those below, scattering bolts of lightning from his burning eyes, dragging the limp body of the building inspector. "Citizens, he is mad! Nikulu chikulu gram, ous, suo!"

"There is no place in civilized life for madmen and panic mongers!" cried Zinaida.

Popenkov clambered up the water pipe with the speed of light with the building inspector's body, clattered across the roof and disappeared through the dormer window.

The tenants, stunned and aroused, crowded round Nikolai Nikolaye-vich. What was it all about? What had happened? Was there any reason to evacuate? What had set the building inspector off?

"Citizens, remain calm, remain in your places," Nikolayev admonished them. "Of course, there are certain grounds for concern, the foundations are in a pretty stressed position, I talked to them, too, but disaster is projected only in the long range, somewhere at the end of the quarter, no sooner. Citizens, tomorrow I will go to the regional housing office[21] to do battle, I shall return either defeated, or victorious. I would like your thoughts and hearts to be with me at that moment."

"What was that we heard, Nikolai Nikolayevich?" shouted Proglotilin. "Is Popenkov intending to smash the roof?"

"That way we won't make it to the end of the quarter, the shack will collapse!" screamed Axiomov.

Fuchinyan, his muscles flexed, jumped into the center of the circle.

"Fuchinyan is here!" he shouted. "Everybody knows me—I am here! I will not permit it. The roof shall be whole! And we shall break the Steel Bird's wings. Vaska, Tolik, am I talking sense?"

"We'll carve the Steel Bird up into hair combs!" cried Vaska.

The tenants were in an uproar.

"Nikulu chikulu gram, ous, suo!" cried Zinaida Popenkova in a panic. "Nikolai Nikolayevich, what is going on? Crowd hysteria?"

"Citizens, quiet! Citizens, order," admonished Nikolayev. "The removal of part of the roof does not threaten instant disaster. Citizens, you must understand Benjamin Fedoseyevich, see his point of view. Citizens, quiet. Citizens, let's talk it over."

But the crowd grew even noisier, aroused by the belligerent and assertive appearance of Fuchinyan.

"It's all Popenkov's fault!" people shouted.

"He shakes the building in the most incredible fashion all night!"

"Evict him!"

"Open up the front entrance!"

"We're sick of it!"

"Away with the Steel Bird!"

"Citizens, I'll try to see Benjamin Fedoseyevich on this matter," entreated Nikolayev. Nobody recognized the stern administrator, "I'll try to beat him down. Citizens, I practically promise that the roof will remain whole."

The sun set, the shadows thickened, but the tenants still did not disperse and in the buzzing crowd there was the flash of matches, the flicker of cigarette-lighter flames, cigarettes and eyes, the whole dark yard was an uneasy volatile flicker. Fuchinyan, Proglotilin and Axiomov climbed up onto the roof via the fire escape. They had resolved to save it by means of their vigilant watch and readiness for any kind of battle, even to the death. The young Samopalovs, Zurab and Valentin, blockaded the back entrance, Ahmed and Alya Tsvetkova were called on to keep watch in the garden. Comrade Zinolyubov took up an observation post in Tsvetkova's apartment. Maria Samopalov and Agrippina declared a strike and went to bed for the first time in eighteen years. Lev Ustinovich got his cutthroat ready and armed Zulphia with the scissors. In a word, all the tenants did what they could in the collective protest against Popenkov's arbitrariness.

The night passed uneasily, people slept in fits, kissed feverishly, smoked, and smoked, some of them drank, others made ready to evacuate, nobody knew what morning would bring.

Fuchinyan, Proglotilin and Axiomov sat on the ridge of the roof, knocking off a bottle, they were elated, remembering bygone battles on the vast expanse between the Volga and the Spree. Several times it seemed to them that a dark body passed over them with a quiet reactive whistle, blocking out the stars, and then they regretted not having anti-aircraft artillery at their disposal.

The sun rose high, dragged itself out of the city's ravines, and hung over Moscow. The roof immediately got scorching hot.

At eight o'clock in the morning the self-defense brigade got the feeling there was someone below them in the attic. They quickly assumed their battle positions, and were ready. Out of the dormer windows crawled Popenkov's relatives—relative Koka, relative Goga and relative Dmitry. They were armed with axes, hand saws and hammers.

"Hello, lads! Sunbathing?" said relative Dmitry to the self-defense brigade. "We are getting an early start to work."

"Now then, boys, back down without any fuss!" commanded Fuchinyan and advanced.

"Look Mitya," said relative Goga, looking down at the pavement, "it's a big drop. If anyone should accidentally get pushed, he'd be squashed flat as a pancake! What do you think?"

"He'd be like jelly," suggested relative Koka sadly.

"Liquid," relative Dmitry summed up and began sawing the roof.

"Now we'll test out what would happen," said the self-defense brigade and rolled up its sleeves. The roof swelled and cracked under their first heavy step.

The relatives, abandoning their jests, also flexed their muscles and advanced. Their tattooed muscles swelled up to such an extent it seemed as though this was not three men moving, but a series of terrifying balloons; in a flick the narrow strings of pocket knives leaped out of their fists; bared gold teeth reflected the sun; so did signet rings, bracelets, pendants, earrings and rings. In the blazing light of the morning sunlight, joyous death advanced on the self-defense brigade in foreign waist-coats and jack boots.

"Vaska, you get the one on the right! Tolik, the one on the left! And I'll get Goga the Bad!" yelled Fuchinyan and dashed forward.

A self-defense without arms began. The relatives' Argentinian pocket knives swished through the air, but collected nothing. Fuchinyan, Proglotilin and Axiomov, remembering their street fighting days, pulled at the relatives' legs and punched them on the noses. The relatives' tears and snot rose like fountains to the blue sky, but nevertheless knives are knives, and blood flowed, and they drove our lads to the edge of the roof.

Suddenly there was a crash to the rear of the relatives. The four Samopalov brothers were crawling along the roof, the writer, the artist, the motorcyclist and big beat.

"Retreat!" ordered relative Dmitry and he jumped off first. Relative Koka and relative Goga flung themselves off after him.

The self-defense brigade leaned over in horror, imagining the conversion of these powerful organisms into a pancake, jelly and liquid respectively. However, the relatives landed unharmed and took to their heels in different directions.

At eight hours thirty minutes the first crack appeared on the northern side of the building. Maria Samopalova leaned out through the crack and shouted to the whole of Fonarny Lane:

"Fight, good people!"

At eight hours forty-five minutes all the inhabitants of No. 14 had gathered by the front entrance, as had the sympathetic occupants of neighboring buildings. Domestic animals, cats, Pomeranians, fox terriers, Great Danes jumped out the windows onto the pavement. Siskins, canaries and parrots, that had been released from their cages, soared above the crowd. The emerald water of aquariums ran out of the water pipes, carrying veiltails, redfins and loaches. Shutters flapped, draughts blew through empty apartments, overturning pots of everlastings. There were groaning sounds. The tenants sighed over abandoned possessions, over everyday articles and expensive and cherished knick-knacks.

The building inspector bustled about in the crowd in his wife's billowing dressing-gown.

"Citizens!" he cried. "I have done some calculations. The building can hold another twenty-seven minutes. It's still possible to save a few things! We only need to open up the front entrance! Clean out the vestibule!"

"Open the front entrance!"

"Break down the doors!"

"To hell with them!"

"But the set, my good fellows, we've just bought it! We saved seven years for it, we hardly ate or drank!"

"Break it down!"

The doors were already bending under the force of the crowd, but inside Popenkov was calmly tying his tie, pinning a diamond into it, polishing his nails and getting into his iron boots.

"You'll think of something, won't you?" Zinaida was dashing about, bouncing like a push-ball. "You'll find a way out, my darling, my love, mankind's genius, my gigantic steel bird?? Zhuzho zhirnava zhuko zhuro?"

"Noki murloki kvakl chitazu!" replied Popenkov calmly. "Are you afraid of this crowd, my Lorelei? This pitiful crowd, these lice. Ten minutes work for a cyclone. Filio drong chiriolan!"

And wrenching out all the nails in one go, he flung open the door and stood in front of the tenants.

Silence fell. The building inspector, remembering yesterday's treatment, hid in the crowd.

"What are you all here for? What do you want?" asked Popenkov, his arms folded on his breast.

"We want to throw you out, Steel Bird," replied the bandaged and altogether heroic Fuchinyan.

"Throw me out?" grinned Popenkov. "Now hear my conditions." And his eyes kindled with a distant secret and terrifying fire, sounds like a jet's exhaust issued from his throat. "Drong haleoti fyng, syng! Zhofrys hi lasr furi talot...."

"We don't understand your language!" cried voices from the crowd. "Leave, Comrade, while you still can!"

Popenkov switched to Russian with a visible effort.

"These are my conditions. Everybody returns to his apartment, is to get a loom, the looms will be here by evening and... to work! Is that understood? Naturally some sacrifices will have to be made. Some of you will be subjected to chiziolastrofitation. Chuchukhu, klocheki, drocheki?"

"If you want to take us on a 'get it-got it' basis," said Fuchinyan "then we want to take you on a 'get it-got it' basis. Got it?"

He stepped forward again, and they all stepped forward, and Popen-

kov suddenly actually realized that he was going to come off the worst:
the circle tightened, and the damned tin awning hung directly over
him. Of course, it would be possible to break through it, but in that instant somebody would grab him by his iron legs. There was practically
no way out, and he almost burst into tragic laughter inside at such a ludicrous end to his great cause.

At one point there was suddenly complete silence, and in this instant the staccato clatter of approaching hooves reached them. The
sound of hooves in Moscow is an out-of-the-ordinary occurrence, so
they all turned round and saw a galloping white horse at the end of
Fonarny lane, and on it Nikolai Nikolayevich Nikolayev, head of ZhEK.
It was nine hours fifteen minutes, Nikolayev was returning from the regional housing commission with his shield, and to boot on a white
horse with a wide chest, round powerful croup, cunning pink eyes, a
fringe fluttering like a holiday flag. Galloping unhurriedly, the horse
brought to mind an old-time caravel, merrily sailing across a fresh sea
beneath billowing white sails.

Drawing near and seeing the crowd at the entrance, the wide-open
windows and branched cracks in the walls, Nikolai Nikolayevich pulled
out from under his shirt a cornet-à-pistons which glittered in the sun,
and raised it to his lips.

"Dear citizens, sisters and brothers!" sang the cornet triumphantly.
"The regional housing commission has allotted us a building! It's eight
stories high, practically all glass, practically all plastic, I assure you! In a
fabulous experimental area, a palace being erected for all to admire!
Blue bathrooms, adjacent lavatories and waste disposal units await you!
A solarium each, a dendrarium each, a dining room each, a swimming
pool each! Make ready, citizens, sisters and brothers, we are going to
trot off towards happiness in a piebald caravan!"

"Hoorah!" the tenants all shouted, and, forgetting Popenkov, they
dashed into their disintegrating dwelling for their belongings. Popenkov managed to dive into the elevator.

At nine hours thirty minutes a wagon train, sent by the regional
housing commission, drew up at the entrance. There were shaggy lively
ponies, perkily chewing on their figured bits, pounding the asphalt
with their strong little hooves. They were harnessed into small, but ca-
pacious carts, decorated with carved folk motifs.

At nine hours thirty nine minutes the loading of goods and chattel
was completed and the wagon train trotted cheerfully off down
Fonarny Lane. The hooves clattered, the little bells rang, colored ribbons and flags fluttered, harmonicas, guitars, transistors were playing,

and at the head rode Nikolai Nikolayevich on a white horse with his cornet-à-pistons. The long caravan wound through Moscow streets, headed for a new life, to New Cheryomukhy.[22]

At nine hours forty four minutes No. 14 collapsed. When the brick dust had cleared the few who had stayed behind in Fonarny Lane saw that only the elevator shaft rose above the ruins. Soon after, the elevator began ascending out of its depths. In it stood a completely withdrawn Benjamin Fedoseyevich Popenkov. When the elevator stopped at the top of its shaft, Popenkov opened the door, squatted on his haunches and froze, fixing his lifeless gaze on the boundless expanse. Nobody knows what he was thinking or what he saw in the distance. Nor is it certain whether he saw Zinaida bouncing like a push-ball along Fonarny Lane.

For long months he sat on the carcass of the elevator shaft quite motionless, like one of the chimera of Paris' Notre Dame cathedral.

One day bulldozers appeared in Fonarny Lane. Hearing the officious rumbling of their engines, Popenkov roused himself, jumped and flew off over Moscow, over the lanes of the Arbat, the blue saucer of Moscow's swimming pool, the big Kamenny bridge.... Two dark trails stretched out behind him. Then the wind dispersed them.

The End

The Steel Bird's Farewell Monologue

Rurrro kalitto Zhiza Chuiza Drong! Chivilikh zhifafa koblo urazzo! Rykl, ekl, filimocha absterchurare? Fylo sylo ylar urar!

Shur yramtura y, y, y! Zhastry chastry gastry nefol! Nefol foliadavr logi zhu-zhu? Uzh zhu ruzh zhur oruzh zhuro oleozhar! Razha!

Faga!

Lirri-otul!

Chivilokh zuzamaza azam ula lu? Luzi urozi klockek tupak! Z fftshch! Zhmin percator sapala! Sa! Pa! La! Al! Spi! Vspyl sevel fuk zhuraru! Refo yarom filioram, otskiuda siplstvo any yna! Any, yna, any, yna, any yna, any! Pshpyl, pshpyl, pshpyl-vzhif, vzhif karakatal!

Chorus

and notwithstanding the flowers bloom and childhood lives on in every
head and old age asks for a hand some depart thereto with a kiss and
merge in passion in order to meet in heaven and butter on a fresh bun
and berries in the morning dew in a jumble of shining dotted lines
where can one find a cunning little face with berries on its lips in the
streets the sentries evoke love with a guitar frost on the pavement
morning voices promise us milk in the latest newspaper the usual reports of the doings of dolphins younger brothers in the light surface
layers of the ocean tend for us shoals of tasty and delicate fish and each
dreams of a ticket on an ordinary thousand-seater airplane to fly over
the ocean with a greeting for the marine shepherds and later return to
their old folk to their cunning little kids falls asleep so as to gallop on
his creaky wooden horse through the forest across the clearings in the
gleam of the spring morning of the spring summer and the autumnal
winter of the summer spring and the wintry autumn of the wintry summer and the summery winter of the wintery spring and the summery
autumn of the spring winter and the autumnal summer.

July 1965
Kalda Farm

                                        Translated by Rae Slonek

NOTES

Destruction of Pompeii [Joel Wilkinson & Slava Yastremski]

1. Before the Revolution, the name Oreanda was associated with the imperial estate located about 4 miles southwest of the Crimean port of Yalta. Known for its picturesque ruins of a Roman castelleum and a chateau (burnt down in 1882) and the beautiful Oreanda church in the Byzantine style, this estate played a prominent role in A. P. Chekhov's story "A Lady with a Dog."

2. "Historic Titan" is an allusion to V. I. Lenin or, perhaps, a fictional titan who represents a loose amalgamation of both Lenin and Stalin. Countless statues of Lenin are erected all over the Soviet Union; some of them are made of bronze (especially in the large cities), but the majority of them are replicas cast from the most famous sculptures. Certain types of poses are prescribed for these statues: Lenin as leader of the Soviet people, with his hand outstretched to symbolize the way to the bright future ahead; Lenin as pillar of the Soviet state, with his hands clutched behind his back and his eyes set in an intent appraisal of the distance ahead; Lenin as thinker, sitting in a chair with a look of deep thought expressed on his face, etc.

3. In the original the worker uses a corrupted form of the Russian verb "to lay." To render his colorful speech, we chose to make use of the confusion on the part of many speakers of English between the verbs "to lie" and "to lay."

4. The opera alluded to here is Georges Bizet's *Carmen* (Paris, 1875).

5. The Russian word *kaif* was probably derived from the American slang "kef," which means a drowsy, dreamy condition that is produced by smoking narcotics. "Kef," in turn, derived from the Arabic word "kaif," which denotes "well-being." As the Russian word *kaif* was used by young people in the Soviet Union during the 1960s it came to have several basic connotations: from a verb meaning "to get high" to exclamations such as "swell," "great," etc.

6. The special relationship between the Dutch and the People's Voluntary Militia of Pompeii is, of course, an anachronism, but it does find a modern parallel in the way Soviet police treat and use some foreigners from such neutral countries as Finland.

7. The inference here is that the poppy is an opium-producing species. In the original the plant is called a "mountain poppy"; we substituted the adjective "wild" because we were not able to substantiate the existence of any opium-producing plant called a "mountain poppy."

8. The surname Karandashkin derives from the Russian for "pencil" (karandash).

9. *Furnace of Health* has a more euphonious sound in English as the name for a newspaper than *Forge of Health* or *The Smithy of Health*, which is what is found in the original (Kuznitsa zdorovia). This is not the name of an actual Soviet newspaper, but the phrase "forge of health" is used in colloquial Russian to refer to sports camps or resorts oriented

towards sports and bodybuilding.

10. Matvei Tryapkin is a name with a Gogolian sound to it. Translated the name means "Matthew Milksop." Phonetically, the surname recalls that of the judge in Nikolai Gogol's play *The Inspector General*: Lyapkin-Tyapkin.

11. *Repercussions at the Quasi-Discrete Level* is a title that suggests the author is a "physicist" turned "lyricist," to use terms hotly debated in the Soviet Union during the 1960s.

12. The allusion here is to Lenin's origin, specifically to the mixture of German (Volga) and Tartar blood in his ancestral lineage.

13. Mont Blanc is a very expensive and elegant fountain pen of Swiss make. Since mention of this type of fountain pen is attributed in a roundabout way to the Historic Titan, it is worthwhile noting that Lenin spent a number of years in Switzerland during his exile abroad. The narrator alludes to this fact, too, in the reference just above in the text to a Swiss clerk.

14. There is no allusion to a historical circumstance in the mentioning here of the American publishing firm Knopf. A plausible reason for referring to this particular publisher is that the firm has an international reputation and the surname Knopf is Germanic so it blends well with the fictionalized Swiss and Austrian setting in this part of the story.

15. In the original Gruber is called a dentist (*dantist*), but the more professional term struck us as being too mild an English equivalent for this neighbor (surely, Austrian) of the Historic Titan whose surname calls to mind Adolf Hitler's other name, Schicklgruber.

16. The variables L and S may well be thinly disguised allusions to Lenin and Stalin. In view of the leader-disciple relationship which develops throughout this story between Arabella and the people who come into contact with her, it is possible that the variable J may be symbolic of Christianity (i.e., alludes to Jesus). In keeping with the way scientists write mathematical formulae in Russian, these variables all appear in Roman letters in the original.

17. The term "Polovtsian aristocrats" is an allusion to the Tartar origin which Bella and HT have in common. Bella, in turn, is an allusion to the contemporary poet Bella Akhmadulina, the prototype for Aksyonov's heroine in this story. In the introduction to her long poem "My Genealogy," Akhmadulina wrote, "My father's grandfather, who endured a bitter orphanage in Kazan living in hellishly difficult poverty, explains—by his surname alone—the simple secret of my Tartar surname." This work was published in Moscow in 1977 with the title *Svecha*.

18. There is a playfully metaphysical idea behind the Russian term for "to prop up [their] existence": *obodriat' k dal'neishemu sushchestvovaniiu* (literally, "to encourage [them] to a further, or future, existence"). In practical everyday life, Arabella is striving to help people realize that a certain amount of *kaif* is accessible to and needed by them. On a higher plane, she uses her artistic talents as a means to "charge people up" rather than the lavish gifts and money which Vladislav Ivanovich Vetryakov employs in the story "Super Deluxe."

19. In the Soviet Union barbershops or, as they are often called, "salons of public beauty" serve many purposes other than the styling or cutting of hair. They may function as centers of information where everything which has not made its way into the official media can be disseminated. Also, one might set up a date here with a local prostitute, especially if the barbershop is located in one of the sea resorts in the South. Finally, for men these places may serve as a kind of clubhouse, where males discuss various domestic and world problems as they wait in line for a haircut.

20. "Great chronicler of the twilight era when public consciousness began to fade" is a

phrase which has the sound of Communist jargon meant to allude to V. I. Lenin.

21. The term for this beverage (Mumbo Jumbo) in Russian is *bormotukha*. Bormotukha is a cheap port wine which is often drunk by alcoholics as a vodka chaser. The origin of the wine's name is the verb *bormotat'*, "to mumble." Chasing vodka with bormotukha has but one purpose: to get so drunk that you cannot say two words straight.

22. Russians often speak of two kinds of emigrants: those who actually leave the homeland to settle abroad and those who remain in the Soviet Union but disassociate themselves with the government in meaningful ways. Both these options are disregarded by the narrator here when he refers to the possibility of emigration as being "just smoldering embers, both inside and out."

23. The mention of Dutch tile at this point in the story may well be an allusion to the mosaic tile floors in Pompeii which have been uncovered by archaeologists. In a Russian context, Dutch tiles are usually associated with stoves, not floors, and with the reign of Peter the Great.

24. Marshal Tarakankin's surname derives from the Russian word for cockroach *(tarakan)*.

25. The detention and, evidently, subsequent demise of seaman Pushinkin in this story has an allegorical quality to it that suggests a veiled allusion to the imprisonment and resultant death of someone in a prison camp. Perhaps, on the other hand, Pushinkin's fate is only to be understood in a broad sense as that suffered by many under the whimsically cruel orders of Marshal Stalin.

26. Agave was the daughter of Cadmus and mother of Pentheus; according to classical mythology, she tore her own son to pieces while he was spying on a Bacchic orgy at Dionysus' instigation (with the aim of stopping these celebrations).

27. "Shipr" is a men's cologne with a heavily alcoholic base.

28. The Russian word for this dance is *triasuchka* (shake, shimmy) and suggests in a way that no name for an analogous dance can in English the earthquakes and volcanic eruptions which took place when Pompeii was destroyed in August 79 A. D. by the violent upheavals of Mount Vesuvius.

29. The Soviet equivalent for the black Tiber automobile is the car called Volga, usually used by Party officials.

30. Ananaskin's surname derives from the Russian word for pineapple *(ananas)*.

31. These two exclamations in the original mean literally "What *kaif!*" Our translation into more idiomatic English is based on the information provided in note 5.

32. These verses are lines 17-20 (fifth stanza) of Bella Akhmadulina's poem "Volcanoes." For the Russian text see Bella Akhmadulina, "Vulkany," in *Sny o Gruzii* (Tbilisi: Merani, 1977), pp. 18-19, where the lines lack the punctuation marks of triple dots.

33. The Historic Titan's remark about Arabella's singing finds an analogue in V. I. Lenin's assessment of Ludwig von Beethoven's music. Russian readers would recognize the source of the Historic Titan's remarks, so the author expanded this paragraph slightly from the original in order to ascribe to HT a multi-volume collected works.

34. The almanac *Metropole* was published and circulated privately in the Soviet Union in 1979. Vassily Aksyonov, Andrei Bitov, Viktor Erofeyev, Fazil Iskander, and Yevgeny Popov were the editors of this almanac which was subsequently published by Ardis (1979) and, in an English translation by W. W. Norton in 1983. Bella Akhmadulina was one of the major contributors to the almanac and it is to her that this note refers.

Super-Deluxe [Joel Wilkinson & Slava Yastremski]

1. Carlsberg is a foreign beer not easily purchased in the Soviet Union. The fact that Vetryakov and his friends drink this Danish beer illustrates that they have access to goods in the restricted food stores where people can make purchases only by means of hard (i.e., foreign) currency or special "ruble certificates" available to foreign diplomats and certain privileged Russians.

2. Duc de Richelieu gained prominence for his furthering of the growth of the town of Odessa. In 1826 a bronze statue of the duke was erected which depicts the Russian provincial governor in Roman costume: the statue stands on the square which is situated at the top of the famous granite steps that descend to the city's harbor.

3. Lyudmila Parkhomenko is a Soviet singer who was a very popular performer in the 1960s.

4. It is common practice in the Soviet Union to name ships for one of the fifteen republics, e.g., Azerbaidzhan or Kazakhstan. The designation *Caravan* has nothing to do with this practice but the correlation seems plausible to Lyuda since all three words end in "-an." Vladislav Ivanovich's somewhat more romantic view of the ship's name calls to mind the nostalgic longing for "nomadic" wandering which was expressed in many of the city romances sung by bards popular in the 1960s. Novella Matveyeva, for example, popularized a song entitled "My Caravan."

5. The Russian term for "to go prospecting" *(idti v razvedku)* can mean both foraging or looking for something in an adventurous way and scouting out or spying on someone. In this instance, there is an ambiguity in the Russian which finds no exact parallel in English.

6. There are state lotteries in the USSR and it is legal to place bets on horseraces, but one does not find Las Vegas type casinos or slot machines in the Soviet Union because they are outlawed. Video games operated by coins have made an inroad into the USSR in the very recent past, but on a limited basis and in small numbers. This does not mean that gambling is no longer a Russian vice (as it was for many during the nineteenth century), but rather that it is not legal in most instances.

7. Odessa-Batumi-Odessa is a holiday cruise across the Black Sea. Odessa is located to the northwest of the Crimean peninsula and Batumi is on the southeastern shore of the Black Sea not too far from the Turkish-USSR border. Batumi is the capital of the Adzhar Autonomous Soviet Socialist Republic.

8. The series of James Bond movies produced largely in the 1960s were an integral part of pop-culture in the West. This phenomenon found a curious echo in the Soviet Union, where Aksyonov and two other writers (O. Gorchakov and G. Pozhenyan) published a novel entitled *Gene Green the Untouchable. The Career of CIA Agent No. 014* under the pseudonym-acronym "Grivady li Gorpozhaks."

9. In A. S. Pushkin's little tragedy entitled *The Covetous Knight* (1830) the main character is a miserly baron. In Russian culture "Covetous Knight" is an epithet analogous in meaning to the names Midas or Scrooge.

10. Prince Myshkin is the hero of Dostoevsky's novel *The Idiot;* he is a person noted for his humility and gentleness as well as for his eccentricity. The first two of these qualities are suggested by the prince's surname, Myshkin, which derives from the Russian word for mouse.

11. "Elemental redistribution" serves a very vital need in the life of all Soviet citizens. Distribution of goods by the state is cumbersome, wasteful, and inefficient; it is one of the worst failings of the economy and centralized planning. "Elemental redistribution" is

sometimes a risky affair since it is quasi-legal at best and illegal if it becomes large-scale blackmarketeering. Aksyonov's term is more precise and neutral than the rather misleading phrase "unofficial economy" and speaks of a phenomenon which is both more comprehensive and organized than the more individualistic way of coping with shortages and deficits known as *blat.*

12. The "White Nights" is a concert program performed in Leningrad during the period from the end of May to the end of June. This period when the sun shines long into the "night" is also referred to in Russian as "white nights." The festival program consists of ballet performances, concerts of classical music and performances by famous vocalists.

13. Hard currency stores stock high quality merchandise produced in the Soviet Union and goods imported from abroad. These stores are closed to ordinary Soviet citizens. (See note 1.)

14. The Russian word for "baroque" *(barokko),* which has a stress on the second syllable, is used by Valentina as a euphemism for "rock" music since the word itself suggests that association.

15. "Memphis" was a popular rock-n-roll tune composed by Chuck Berry in 1959; it became a hit record in 1963. Soviet rock groups, such as the fictional "Seven Wheels" mentioned here, often imitate, perform and even re-record Western music.

16. VTO is an abbreviation for Vsesoiuznoe Teatral'noe Obshchestvo (All-Union Theater Association). The VTO headquarters are located on Moscow's Gorky St. There is a very fine restaurant in the VTO building; it has a western-type bar to which only the members of the VTO ("the people of art") are admitted.

17. Lucius Licinius Lucullus (circa 117-56 B.C.) was a Roman general and statesman. He achieved spectacular success in the war against Mithrodates VI and, as a politician, was noted for his actions against Pompeii. After 59 B.C. Lucullus found his sole pleasure in living luxuriously and this gave rise to the saying "the feast of Lucullus."

18. "Let the days of our life flow like the waves, we know that happiness awaits us ahead" are lyrics from a popular Soviet song.

19. Arkhangelskoe is an old estate of the Yusupov family. It is located near Moscow and has been converted into a museum. A restaurant was built near the museum which became very popular because of its traditional Russian cuisine. The Seventh Heaven is a restaurant located in the Ostankino Television Tower in Moscow. The restaurant attracts Muscovites chiefly because of its architectural novelties (for example, it has a rotating floor) and because it offers a marvelous panoramic view of the city.

20. Dikson is a northeastern Siberian port located on the Karsky Sea and just to the east of the gulf between this sea and the mouth of the Enisei River. Dikson is located at 80 degrees longitude, 75 degrees latitude and Batumi is at approximately 42 degrees longitude, 41 degrees latitude. An imaginary line drawn from Dikson to Batumi would set off "European" Russia from all that east of the Urals.

21. By the phrase "half-breed males from the Caucasus" one should understand Georgian or Armenian men who have Turkish or Mongol blood in their ancestral lineage and/or who have been raised culturally as Russians. There is an apparent allusion here to Georgians who emulate Stalin. The original speaks of "half-Caucasians" or "semi-Caucasians"—terms which have the sound of ethnic slurs when rendered literally into English because of the association of "Caucasian" with "WASP."

22. Mao Tse-Tung was former Chairman of the Chinese Communist Party; Yemelyan Pugachev led a peasant uprising in eighteenth-century Russia; Denis Davydov was a hussar soldier who became a hero in the 1812 war against Napoleon, especially because he organized a partisan movement against the French. Davydov also wrote poetry in which he glorified hussar life, drinking and love.

23. A Sochi tie is a narrow black tie with silver or red streaks. This kind of tie was very fashionable in the 1960s. The trend was set by Georgians who traveled to the cities in the North to sell oranges or flowers at the markets and for whom the tie was a sort of trade mark.

24. The source for Aristotle's ideas presented in this story is the philosopher's treatise known best by its Latin title *De Anima*.

25. The term is taken from palmistry, where the Mount of Venus designates the part of the palm below the thumb.

26. The association of Vladislav Ivanovich's outlook on life with a kaleidoscope identifies him as a kind of fictional cousin to Volodya Teleskopov of *Surplussed Barrelware*. The surname Vetryakov (*veter*=wind) speaks to this character's involvement in the system of "elemental redistribution" and to his chameleon-like adaptability in appropriating the ideas of his friends and in adjusting to a variety of social occasions. However, at heart, Vladislav Ivanovich is an optimist and, what's more, one who genuinely loves life.

27. The expression "physicists and lyricists" was coined by the poet Boris Slutsky and used as the title for a poem he wrote in 1959. Subsequent to the publication of this poem Slutsky's expression became a euphemism for "the sciences and the humanities"; his ideas spurred an extensive and sometimes acerbic debate about the merits and accomplishments of technologists and humanists, and found widespread reverberation as a literary theme in the decade of the sixties.

28. In suggesting that Vladislav Ivanovich go to the Baltic Seashore or to Tashkent the bogdykhan is being genuinely lenient in dealing with the likable physicist. Within the Soviet Union the three Baltic republics of Latvia, Lithuania and Estonia are noted for their relatively high standard of living and for their tolerance towards individuals who are living on the fringe of Soviet society. Tashkent, the capital of the Uzbek Republic and the fourth largest city in the USSR, does not share this reputation, but it is in the heart of Central Asia and therefore a place where "elemental redistribution" is a more time-honored and accepted *modus vivendi* than in the large Russian cities.

29. Sukhumi is a port and a sea resort on the Black Sea in Soviet Georgia.

30. The Macedonian king Phillip II invited Aristotle in 343/342 B.C. to educate his son Alexander. Literature and politics were probably the main subjects of instruction. Aristotle's tutorship ended in 340, when Alexander became a regent for his father. Thus, there is a certain discrepancy here between fact and fiction. Aristotle lived in Athens, not Colchis, from 335 B.C. He left Athens for Colchis only in 323 B.C., after being accused of impiety; he died the following year.

31. Orenburg is a town in Eastern Siberia which is famous for its products made of wool; the village of Palekh is located 200 miles northeast of Moscow—it is a center for the folkcraft of making black lacquer boxes that are hand painted, decorated with gold and feature subjects from Russian folklore; Dagestan is a region in the Caucasus mountains— the necklace referred to here is probably made of embossed metal (in Russian the word *chekanka* is used to speak both of a method of embossing metal and of the artifacts which an artisan produces).

32. The word "design" was one of the catchwords widely used in the 1960s by speakers of Russian. The art of design was believed to be a new mode of expression, a sign of new times. Soon, "design" came to be used not only in connection with a form of art or a theory of communication, but also in place of such words as "picture," "construction," "combination," "outline," etc.

33. OBKhSS is the abbreviation of Otdel bor'by s khishcheniiami sotsialisticheskoi sobstvennosti (Sector to Combat against Theft of Socialist Property). It is a government bureau which exerts control over the bookkeeping, financing, expenditures, etc. of vari-

ous factories, stores, etc. owned by the state.

34. The contents of the attaché case are a clue that Vladislav has prepared himself for going to prison or to a forced labor camp.

35. "Life is Everywhere" is a famous painting by Nikolai Alexandrovich Yaroshenko (1846-98) an artist who belonged to the school called the Wanderers (Peredvizhniki). Yaroshenko's canvas, finished in 1888, depicts a car of a prison train that is hauling prisoners to Siberia. The train car has a window with bars on it and prisoners are looking outside at the free world, where a child is feeding bread to some pigeons.

36. "March to the beat of your own drummer" in the original is the Russian saying "one's hand is the master," which means "one does what and how he/she feels like doing."

37. The Lyceum School (or, simply, the Lyceum) was founded by Aristotle in 335/334 B.C. at a sacred grove of Apollo Lyceus and the Muses in Athens. The school took its name from the epithet of the god; it later became known as the Peripatetic School. In Aristotle's time and under his immediate successor, Theophrastus, scholarly activities at this school flourished, especially in the fields of mathematics, music, botany, politics, medicine, history, metaphysics and ethics.

Rendezvous [Joel Wilkinson & Slava Yastremski]

This story was translated from the text published by the emigre firm Silver Age in 1981, which differs in several places from the original publication in the Soviet literary journal *Avrora* in May 1971. The *Avrora* version is shorter, thanks to the cuts made by the censors.

1. Plants producing military equipment in the Soviet Union are commonly called PO Boxes. It is a state crime to reveal where such plants are located.

2. GAI (pronounced "guy-ee") is the acronym for the Traffic Control Department. The abbreviation is used so often that it has replaced the official name of this administrative department in colloquial speech.

3. Salieri was an Italian composer and friend of Wolfgang Amadeus Mozart. According to legend, Salieri poisoned Mozart out of envy for the latter's talent. In Russian culture this legend became well known thanks to Alexander Pushkin's "little tragedy" *Mozart and Salieri*, written in 1830.

4. Gorky Street is one of the main roads in downtown Moscow; it runs north from Manezh and Red Squares and has many shops which attract local residents and tourists.

5. Maurice Richard, nicknamed Rocket, was one of the most famous Canadian hockey players of the 1950s. He spent 18 years with the Montreal Canadiens and had 544 regular season goals. According to his contemporaries and peers, Richard's accomplishments came largely as a result of his sharp instincts and brute strength.

6. The Kelowna Packers are a hockey team from Kelowna, British Columbia, which has traveled to the USSR to play exhibition games with Soviet teams.

7. Konstantin Loktyev, Alexander Almyetov, Veniamin Alexandrov, Boris and Yevgeny Mayorov, and Vyacheslav Starshinov were the most popular Soviet hockey players in the 1960s. The first three played for the team of the Central Sports Committee of the Red Army (TsSKA), the second threesome for the Moscow team Spartak. These two teams were the main contenders for the Soviet national championship in the decade of the sixties. During the specially organized tournament in the late 1960s between Canadian and Soviet national hockey teams, the six players mentioned above made up the first and second line units at the position of forwards.

8. The *Jen min jih* is the newspaper of the Chinese Communist Party. The rubric "Their Morals" is a heading under which Soviet newspapers report all kinds of oddities and curiosities in Western bourgeois life.

9 Mikhail Tal and Tigran Petrosian are famous Soviet chess grandmasters. Each of them was a World Champion: Tal in 1960-61 and Petrosian in 1963-69. Bobby is Bobby Fischer.

10. "Stavrogin's Confession" is a chapter (sometimes titled "At Tikhon's") in Dostoevsky's novel *The Possessed*. Censors objected to inclusion of this chapter in the novel on the grounds that the subject matter (the atheist Stavrogin's complicity in the sordid death of a young girl named Matryosha) was unsuitable for the general public and Dostoevsky acquiesced. Thus, this section of the novel was not included in editions of *The Possessed* published during Dostoevsky's lifetime. Subsequently, some critics have considered this chapter central to the novel as a whole and essential for understanding the complexities and sordid aspects of Stavrogin's personality.

11. Lyova uses the word *filin* (eagle owl) as an endearment for his wife Nina and this term implies that she wears glasses. *Bubo bubo* is the Latin term for this bird and we have used it since it sounds more like a nickname in English than does eagle owl.

12. Viktor Shklovsky (1893-84) is a Soviet Russian writer, philologist and literary critic. In the 1920s he was one of the leading figures of the Society for Studies of Poetic Language (known by its acronym OPOYAZ) and one of the founders of the Formalist school of literary criticism. In the 1930s both Shklovsky and the Formalists fell into disrepute in the Soviet Union and were heavily criticized for their approach to the study of literature. In the 1960s, however, Shklovsky became a father figure for young writers, like Aksyonov, and critics; his new-found popularity was one of the phenomena associated with the cultural and political "thaws" of this decade and, likewise, with the worldwide interest in the ideas of the French Structuralists, who advanced theories similar to and somewhat derivative of those advanced earlier by Russian Formalists.

13. Izmailovo is a district in the southwestern part of Moscow.

14. There is something peculiar about Lyova's purchase of a Soviet car in Italy. Perhaps, the reader is to understand that he bought it for hard currency in order to avoid the usual three- to four-year waiting period if one purchases a car in the USSR in rubles. Or Lyova might have bought one of the Italian Fiats which are produced in the Soviet Union under the brand name Zhiguli.

15. Marfa Posadnitsa was a fifteenth-century patriot and *posadnitsa* (governor) of the city-state of Novgorod who led her people in the unsuccessful resistance to efforts by the princes of Muscovy to bring Novgorod under their control. Modest Mussorgsky wrote an opera called *Marfa Posadnitsa* which is based on this historical figure.

16. This paragraph reconstructs Lyova's trek through the center of Moscow. The Central Telegraph Office is located on the corner of Gorky and Ogaryov Streets, four blocks from Red Square. There is no sentry box there. Manezh Square is situated just to the north of and adjacent to Red Square: it takes its name from the building on it which housed a show ring for horseriding before the Revolution and now functions as the Central Exhibition Hall. Bronnivitsky Gate is the fictional form for Borovitsky Gate, the public entrance to the Kremlin: it is situated right behind the Manezh building.

17. The quote is from Alexander Blok's play *The Rose and the Cross*, written in 1912 and published in 1918. Specifically, the lines translated here are the first five lines of the song sung by Gaetan in Act IV, Scene III. The translation of Blok's play is from Michael Green's *The Russian Symbolist Theater* (Ann Arbor: Ardis, 1986).

18. The Central Children's Theater is located near the Bolshoi Theater on Moscow's Theater Square. This theater specializes in productions for young audiences; its perfor-

mances for the youngest children include adaptations of fairy tales in which various animals are played by special actresses *(travesti)* who act professionally in children's theater.

19. These words are from Act I, Scene I of Blok's *The Rose and the Cross.*

20. Line 4 of Act I, Scene I of *The Rose and the Cross.*

21. The quotation is from Sergei Esenin's poem "I neither pity, nor call, nor cry...."

22. The word "voluntarism" is used incorrectly in Russian by the manager. In modern colloquial Russian this word is often mistakenly employed to mean "an act of independent will which goes beyond that which is necessary or expected" and is therefore considered to be "voluntary" action.

23. *The Tale of Tsar Saltan* is a poetic fairy tale by Alexander Pushkin. In this tale the prince Gvidon shoots a buzzard which tries to kill the swan princess. Baba Yaga is the traditional witch and, often, a villain in Russian fairy tales.

24. Pollitrovich and Zakusonsky are telling surnames. The first derives from the word for a "half-liter bottle" (i.e., of vodka) and the second from the noun for "snacks." Thus, Baba Yaga is saying that he works in order to get enough money for something to drink and a bite to eat.

25. The phrase "the best of our generation, take me for your trumpeter" is taken from Yevgeny Yevtushenko's poem of 1957 called "The Best of Our Generation." "Fellows with upturned collars" is the title of a poem in Robert Rozhdestvensky's collection of verse *The Radius of Action* (1965).

26. Nikolai Ghiaurov is a famous Bulgarian opera singer with a deep bass voice. In 1960 he became a member of Milan's La Scala. Yehudi Menuhin is a world-famous violin player. Viktor Konovalenko is a popular Soviet hockey goalie who played on national and Olympic teams in the 1960s. Yevgeny Yevtushenko is one of the popular Soviet poets of the 1960s who has taken to writing prose and acting in recent years. Valery V. Popenchenko (1937-75) was a famous Soviet boxer; he won European titles in 1963 and 1965, and an Olympic medal in 1964.

27. In the phrase "a trifle internally he gnashed his internal teeth," there is a suggestion that the Buzzard in some way is affiliated with the police agents of the Ministry of the Interior (MVD).

28. "Wild melody of the clarinet" is a line of verse from Nikolai Gumilyov's poem "You and I," which is one of the works in his collection *Campfire* (1918).

29. Thor Heyerdahl is the Swedish scientist and explorer famous for his Kon-Tiki and Ra voyages. He was one of the few foreign scientists who became a well-known figure in the Soviet Union during the 1960s. A Soviet doctor named Yury Senkevich took part in Heyerdahl's second Ra expedition from Peru to the Pacific islands.

30. Jean-Luc Godard is a French film director who, during the 1960s, was a leading representative of *cinéma vérité.* Marina Vlady is a French movie actress of Russian descent who married the Soviet bard Vladimir Vysotsky, who died during the time of the 1980 Olympic Games in Moscow.

31. There is a Russian saying that a person with two crow's tails on the back of his head (or with two "crowns") will be very lucky in life. Malakhitov must be extraordinarily lucky since he has three such crowns.

32. Ortega y Gasset (1883-1955). The idea of reality mentioned here was developed by Ortega in the book *Neither Vitalism nor Rationalism* (1924). For this Spanish thinker the true nature of human life is a "radical reality" *(realidad radical)* which is different from philosophical realism ("natural organic" reality) and philosophical idealism ("natural inorganic" reality). Ortega considered that cultural and physical environments give an individual's "I" its existence: he expressed this thought most cogently in the formulaic and famous expression "I am myself plus my circumstances" *(Yo soy yo i mia circumstancia).*

33. The quotation is from Friedrich Engels' *Herr Eugen Duehring's Revolution in Science* (1878, also known as *Anti-Duehring*), which was directed against vulgar materialsim.

34. These lines of verse by Vyacheslav Ivanov make up the third stanza of his frequently anthologized poem "Voices." Ivanov (1866-1949) was one of the leading Russian Symbolists: his philosophical, aesthetic and critical works expounded the idea that the poet's highest mission is to uncover the symbol at the heart of religious myths.

35. Yu. F. Smelldishchev sounds very much like an anglicized form of the surname Smerdishchev (which would mean, roughly, "stinker") and suggests that Aksyonov's character is a fictional cousin to Dostoevsky's Smerdyakov of *The Brothers Karamazov*.

36. "Spearchucker" is our translation of the Russian word *ostroga*, which designates a kind of spear used in Siberia to catch fish and, by extension, the soup made from the fish which are caught. It is noteworthy that the word for this type of spear is phonetically similar to the old Russian word for a prison *(ostrog)*.

37. Tiksi is a port in northern Siberia. There are a lot of secret plants in the area near Tiksi.

38. In Dostoevsky's *The Possessed*, Tikhon is the monk to whom Stavrogin shows his confessicn. Not all of Tikhon's advice to Stavrogin can be characterized as "humble words," but in general the monk answers Stavrogin's impudence and bravado with controlled and thoughtful responses. Tikhon is able to penetrate to the depths of Stavrogin's soul and discern his ulterior motives.

39. The quotation is from the poem "Three Sisters" by Velemir Khlebnikov (1885-1922), a leading poet in the first decade of this century and a major figure among the Russian futurists.

40. Rkatsiteli is a Georgian dry, white wine.

41. Alexander Blok is famous for his poems dedicated to "The Beautiful Lady." Konstantin Tsyolkovsky (1857-1935), in addition to being a famous inventor and scientist in the field of space exploration, was a writer of science-fiction fantasies. His preoccupation with the ideal interplanetary flight coincided with the activity of the Symbolists and Futurists. Blok and Tsyolkovsky shared a penchant for utopian ideas, whether the application was to romantic love or flights in space.

42. "The morals of a yellow devil" is an expression which means the power of the dollar. After Maxim Gorky returned from his trip to America in 1906, he wrote "The City of the Yellow Devil," castigating the evils of capitalism.

43. Klukhorsky pass (el. 2781 meters) is a divide in the Caucasus Mountains through which the Sukhumi Road passes.

44. The fact that there is a rumor that Lyova Malakhitov has exchanged 4,000 rubles for hard currency is a hint that the exchange took place illegally.

45. Ostankino is the area of Moscow which gave its name to the famous television and radio communications tower of the city.

46. This foundation pit may be an allusion to the project to build the Palace of Congresses in Moscow on the Kropotkinskaya Embankment on the site of the destroyed Church of the Redeemer. The project was abandoned and in the 1960s a swimming pool was built on the site. There may likewise be an allusion to Andrei Platonov and his work *The Foundation Pit.*

47. The quotation is from Pushkin's poem "A Winter Evening."

48. Lev Yashin (b. 1929) may have the distinction of being the most famous Soviet soccer player ever. Chislenko is also a popular soccer player. Andrei Voznesensky and Robert Rozhdestvensky are Soviet poets who came to fame in the 1960s as representatives of "youth literature." Boris Spassky (b. 1937) is a Soviet chess grandmaster and World Champion; he lost his title to Bobby Fischer. John Updike's *The Centaur* was one

of the most popular works translated into Russian; his popularity was particularly evident among members of the younger generation. Arthur Miller's plays *A View from the Bridge* and *The Price* were produced in the Soviet Union and enjoyed great critical success. Dmitry Shostakovich (1906-75) was one of the Soviet Union's greatest composers. Academician (Mikhail A.) Lavrentyev is a Russian-Soviet mathematician and, since 1946, member of the USSR Academy of Sciences; he was the individual who assumed most of the responsibility for creating the scientific research community of Akademgorodok (a "think tank" community located near Novosibirsk). Leonid Leonov is a Soviet cosmonaut, the first man to walk in space. Neil Armstrong was the first man on the moon and, with James Aldrin, one of the American astronauts to fly in the Apollo missions. Jean-Paul Sartre (1905-80), the French philosopher and existentialist, was a popular figure among younger members of the Soviet intelligentsia in the 1960s. Vladimir Vysotsky, who died in 1980, was the most popular bard of the 1960s. S. T. Konenkov (1874-1971) was a prominent Soviet sculptor. Vitsin, Yu. V. Nikulin, and Morgunov are popular Soviet movie comedians; Nikulin began his career as a circus clown.

The Steel Bird [Rae Slonek]

1. In Russian *fonar* means a lamp.
2. (Small) fish.
3. Manager of ZhEK, the local housing office, which is responsible for the maintenance and overseeing of a number of blocks of flats, perhaps a whole street or square.
4. A central district of Moscow.
5. From one of the songs of the Civil War.
6. Raikom: the Regional Party Office.
7. Each Soviet citizen is entitled to a minimum amount of living space.
8. Based on *popa*, euphemism for "arse."
9. International Organization to aid fighters for the Revolution, founded in 1922 at the 21st Communist International Congress.
10. Voroshilov gunner. Voroshilov, a cavalry commander during the Revolution, was People's Commissar for Defense 1925-34. With the militarization of sport in the thirties senior school students, tertiary students and young workers learned to shoot in Voroshilov Shooting Clubs. The Voroshilov Gunner badge was awarded to those who attained a certain score in shooting competitions.
11. The K.G.B.
12. The Russian word for "prick."
13. Each citizen must obtain a residence permit and have the address stamped in his passport before taking up residence in an apartment.
14. Famous war-time poem by Konstantin Simonov.
15. Reference to Turgenev's well-known poem in prose on the Russian language.
16. The smallest Soviet-made sedan (a four-seater).
17. One of the fashionable young writers of the sixties, depicting positive Soviet youth. Also notable for innovative style (collage), using colloquial language and drawing on newspaper cuttings, excerpts from radio broadcasts, etc.
18. Card games.
19. Means "Zina-Lover."
20. In English in the original.
21. The office responsible for issuing accommodations, and to which the ZhEK office is subordinate.
22. New area of Moscow with intensive housing development.